# EMBRACING THE EARL

### The St. Clairs
### Book 3

## Alexa Aston

# Books from Dragonblade Publishing

*Queen of Thieves Series* by Andy Peloquin
Child of the Night Guild
Thief of the Night Guild
Queen of the Night Guild

*The Book of Love Series* by Meara Platt
The Look of Love
The Touch of Love

*Dark Gardens Series* by Meara Platt
Garden of Shadows
Garden of Light
Garden of Dragons
Garden of Destiny

*Rulers of the Sky Series* by Paula Quinn
Scorched
Ember
White Hot

*Hearts of the Highlands Series* by Paula Quinn
Heart of Ashes
Heart of Shadows
Heart of Stone

*Highlands Forever Series* by Violetta Rand
Unbreakable
Undeniable
Unyielding

*Viking's Fury Series* by Violetta Rand
Love's Fury
Desire's Fury
Passion's Fury

*Also from Violetta Rand*
Viking Hearts

# PROLOGUE

*London—February, 1812*

L ADY CAROLINE ANDREWS helped her mother into their London
townhome. Though she'd recently turned forty, the Countess of
Templeton moved as if she were eighty. Ill health and losing her
younger daughter had aged her overnight.

"Mama, let's go upstairs. I'll have tea brought up to warm us."

The blustery winter day had chilled Caroline to the point her teeth
chattered during the entire graveside service for her sister.

"No. Nothing for me," her mother said wearily. "I just want my
bed." She leaned heavily into her only child.

"Of course."

By now, the countess was on the verge of collapse. Caroline motioned to their butler to join them since her father had already passed
them by without a backward glance and gone into his study. The Earl
of Templeton had a marked disdain for any kind of weakness or illness
and obviously couldn't be bothered to aid his grieving wife.

"Stinch will help get you up the stairs, Mama."

The butler took the countess in hand and between the two of
them, they were able to get her upstairs, where her lady's maid
anxiously awaited. The countess slumped in a chair, sobbing.

"Have tea sent up, Stinch," Caroline said quietly and watched the
butler slip from the room.

She took out a night rail for her mother as the maid undressed her mistress. It took both women to dress the countess and get her into bed. By then, the tea had arrived and Caroline insisted her mother drink some. After only a few sips, she pushed it away.

"Give me some laudanum."

Reluctantly, Caroline nodded and the maid slipped from the room. She thought her mother took too much of it, which was why it was now kept under lock and key.

"It will be here soon," she said soothingly, stroking her mother's hair, noticing the gray was starting to dominate the fading, blond locks.

"What will I do without Cynthia?" her mother wailed, dissolving into fresh tears.

She had no reply.

Her sister had always been delicate in health, favoring her mother in that respect. Caroline had the hardier constitution of their father, along with his caramel-colored hair that was streaked with blond highlights throughout the brown. She did resemble her mother some, with the same warm, brown eyes and porcelain skin, as well as having her ample bosom.

"Please, Mama. Try not to weep. It won't bring Cynthia back and it upsets you so."

She took a handkerchief and wiped away her mother's tears. Caroline had already cried ones of her own when her sister passed two days ago—on Caroline's birthday. She doubted she could ever celebrate the day of her birth again with any joy, knowing she was alive while Cynthia lay cold in her grave.

The last year had been emotionally draining, especially because the two sisters had been so close. They were eleven months apart in age and had always been the best of friends. Caroline even delayed her come-out, choosing to make her debut with Cynthia when she turned eighteen. Instead of the two girls dancing at balls and attending the opera and garden parties last spring and summer, Caroline had been nursing her sick sister. Always frail, Cynthia had begun having trouble breathing and could only walk a few paces without tiring. Their physician had diagnosed a faulty heart and told them it was only a matter of time before Cynthia succumbed.

Her sister encouraged Caroline to go ahead with the come-out since she was already nineteen and a year older than most girls who made their debut, but she'd resisted, staying home to care for Cynthia and spend as much time with her as she could. Papa refused to be around her, claiming it ate at him to see his younger daughter wasting away. Caroline supposed that was also his excuse for ignoring Mama all these years since she, too, was frail. It had fallen to Caroline to nurse Cynthia.

And now she was gone.

The maid returned with the laudanum and Caroline gave her mother the dose that would put her to sleep for the rest of the afternoon and most likely until tomorrow morning. She sat holding her mother's hand until the countess closed her eyes and her breathing evened out.

"Stay with her," she instructed the maid.

She poured herself a cup from the teapot and took it with her. The tea took some of the chill from her body but nothing could comfort her soul at the loss she'd suffered. For the last month, a piece of her had died every time she looked at her sister and saw how she slipped further and further away each day. She believed now that Cynthia was gone, the same would happen with her mother. Mama was already so weak in body and spirit. It wouldn't surprise her if Mama simply lost the will to live.

As she reached her bedchamber, she heard a voice call her name and saw Stinch coming toward her.

"The earl wishes to speak with you, Lady Caroline. He's in his study."

A confrontation with her father was the last thing she wanted. She knew exactly why he wanted to see her—and would resist what he had to say.

"Thank you, Stinch."

The butler's eyes misted over. "We are all sorry for your loss, my lady. Lady Cynthia was always kind to the staff. She will be missed."

"Thank you." She stiffened her spine and handed him the half-drunk cup of tea. "Would you see this back to the kitchen?"

Caroline walked resolutely to her father's study. She knocked and was bidden to enter.

He sat in his favorite chair, a crystal tumbler of brandy in his hand. She remembered in her youth thinking him handsome but not anymore. Drink and too many late nights at the gaming tables and with his various mistresses had etched deep lines into his face.

"Sit," he commanded.

She did and decided he would need to make the first move in their verbal chess game. When she remained mute, he finally spoke.

"You are now twenty, Caroline."

"I am aware of my age, Papa. Cynthia passed on my birthday two days ago."

He winced slightly and she mentally awarded herself the first point.

"You delayed your come-out so you could do so with your sister. That did not occur last spring because of her infirmity. This year's Season will start in a little over two months' time. I want you to be ready for it. It's time you got yourself a husband, Caroline, though at your advanced age you won't have as great a selection as most women."

Score one for the earl.

"I don't plan to take part in the upcoming Season, Papa. I will be in mourning. It would be inappropriate for me to be seen dancing when I've recently lost my beloved sister."

Two for her.

He frowned. When he saw she wasn't moved by his disapproval, the frown morphed into a glare. "I was afraid you'd say that. I suppose I'll give you another choice."

"My only choice is to mourn, Papa."

"You do love your mother?" he asked.

"Of course." She wanted to ask if he loved his wife but kept quiet. "What has that to do with anything?"

"Your mother is not well. She has always been fragile, even as a girl. When I married her, I'd hoped for sons and only got two daughters off her. After that, the doctors said more children weren't possible."

Caroline had always wondered why no other babies came after her and Cynthia. Knowing her father, he must have hated his wife for not providing an heir.

She remained silent, so he continued. "Losing Cynthia has been hard on her."

Naturally, it had been hard on her mother. It was hard on Caroline, too. The only one who didn't seem to care one whit was her father.

"Because of that, I think she needs a change of scenery."

Would her father send them to the country? They rarely went to their country estate. He adored life in London, with his mistresses and gambling and friends. She looked blankly at him, as if she didn't know what he was about to do. He was going to dump them in the country. Who knew how long they would be there before he would remember he had a wife and a daughter? Her anger stirred and she tamped it down, unwilling for him to see he'd gotten under her skin.

"Knowing you would reject the Season, I've already made arrangements for you to go to America."

"What?" she cried. "Why on earth would you send Mama and me there?"

"Your aunt lives there. My sister."

Caroline was baffled. "I've never heard you mention a sister. Why?"

He shrugged. "Because I disowned her years ago."

"I'm sure she displeased you," she snapped.

His eyes narrowed at her words. "Evangeline disgraced the Andrews' family name. Instead of wedding the viscount she was engaged to, she eloped with an American sea captain."

She'd never heard any of this—and she'd listened to servants gossiping her entire life, learning early that eavesdropping had its benefits.

"Evangeline presented him to me. I told her how she'd embarrassed herself and humiliated me. The *ton* is an unforgiving lot. She would never be accepted in Polite Society again. I told her I never wanted to see her again. She abruptly left for America after that."

Caroline already liked this aunt a great deal.

"She wrote to me recently, however. Her husband is now dead. Though I would never accept her back into my household, she did know of you and Cynthia. Evangeline left with her husband just after Cynthia's birth. I told her you—and your mother—might come to visit her in Boston."

Excitement filled her. She'd barely been outside of London, much less beyond England's borders. The chance to go to America and meet this blood relative who'd stood up to her father appealed to Caroline greatly. Still, she kept her features composed, not wanting the father whom she once did everything to impress to know her true feelings.

"Those are your choices," he said firmly. "Either take part in the upcoming Season when April arrives or journey to America with your mother and spend a few months getting to know your aunt."

She wouldn't dishonor Cynthia's memory by refusing to mourn her sister.

"It looks as if Mama and I will be visiting Boston," Caroline proclaimed.

# CHAPTER ONE

*Boston—February, 1815*

C AROLINE FINISHED DRESSING and went downstairs where her
usual tea and toast awaited her.

"Good morning, Mrs. Johnson. How is today's weather?"

"Frigid," the housekeeper replied tersely. "Tippet did his business
and raced back in."

She seated herself and the dog left his spot next to the fire to come
close in order for Caroline to pet him. She stroked his shiny, black fur
and the dog sighed in contentment before curling up partly atop her
feet.

Pouring herself a cup of tea, she added one lump of sugar and a
splash of cream before stirring. Mrs. Johnson sat opposite her and did
the same. Both women spread jam on their toast.

Sometimes, Caroline still marveled at how different America was.
The thought of one of their servants in London sitting down and
eating breakfast with her would have been laughable, yet here in
Boston it was not only accepted but encouraged. She wasn't called
Lady Caroline by anyone. Friends of all ages referred to her as
Caroline, while she introduced herself to strangers as Miss Andrews.
Being a loyal subject of England's king was frowned upon, especially
since the United States was at war again with its former Mother
Country.

At first, she'd resented being in Boston. Though she'd taken to

Aunt Evie immediately, Caroline's mother hadn't fared well on the eight-week transatlantic crossing and she'd died at the end of April, only two weeks after they'd arrived from England. Already grieving her sister's passing, Caroline had to deal with losing her mother, as well. Aunt Evie had been her saving grace, instantly becoming family and close friend in the following weeks. Evie was kind, comforting, and yet no-nonsense all rolled into one. Caroline supposed her aunt had learned to be self-sufficient in the four years since her husband's death. They'd had no children and Evie had to look after herself.

The two women decided Caroline would stay for a few months so they could get to know one another better. Then news of war came that June, effectively trapping her in Boston for the duration of the war.

It looked as if the war might be coming to an end soon. General Jackson had soundly trounced the British in New Orleans only last month and hopes ran high in Boston. New England had never been in favor for what was harshly termed Mr. Madison's War since shipbuilding and ship trading provided the lifeblood of the region. Only the western and southern states had voted to go to war against England, seriously dividing the young nation to the breaking point.

Caroline finished her breakfast and took the dishes back to the kitchen. Mrs. Johnson told her to leave them so Caroline could get to the bookshop. She placed her heavy, plain cloak about her and called Tippet, who came bounding toward her, and they set out for her bookstore. She was finally thinking of the place as hers. It had been exactly a year to the date—and once again, Caroline's birthday—when Aunt Evie had been struck by a runaway team of horses and died of her injuries. Much to her surprise, Caroline found herself the sole heir of Evie's estate. Her aunt had sold Captain Morton's ship after his death and used the proceeds to open a bookstore.

She'd worked in the bookstore alongside her aunt during the first two years in Boston, learning all aspects of the book trade from ordering books to balancing the ledgers. When Aunt Evie died, Caroline grieved but found herself well prepared to run the shop on her own, though she'd hired Josiah Long to help her. In the last year, the shop had its best year of profit, a source of great pride for her.

Tippet kept close as she walked through the narrow streets of Boston, a light snow falling. Once again, she marveled at how she was able to walk the streets of the city alone, with only her dog for company. In London, she would have had to take her maid everywhere. It would be totally unacceptable for her to be unchaperoned. Coming to America had granted her freedoms she never would have experienced if she'd remained in England after Cynthia's death.

By the time she reached the bookshop, the snow had stopped. As she arrived, she saw Jordy, Mr. Frain's apprentice, carrying a bundle of newspapers and headed her way. She unlocked the shop and opened the door for him. Jordy breezed through and set the newspapers on the counter, taking out a pocketknife to cut through the string that bound them together.

"Good morning, Caroline," he said, his usual smile in place. "Do you think today we'll get good news?"

For Jordy, good news meant hearing if the Americans had won another battle.

"It's possible," she said.

"With Jackson's victory in New Orleans, surely the British will give up now."

"They're a tough lot, Jordy. Just look at me," she teased.

He cocked his head. "I forget you're British sometimes, Caroline. It seems as if you've been in Boston forever."

Josiah entered the shop and greeted them.

"I'll be off," Jordy said. "See you tomorrow."

After the door closed, Josiah asked, "Was he talking of the war again?"

"Yes. You know he lost his older brother in battle last year. If Mr.

ALEXA ASTON

Frain didn't need him so badly at the print shop, I believe Jordy would have run off and joined Harrison's or Jackson's army by now."

He shook his head. "It was a foolish war to fight. Even if we win, it's crippled our economy."

She smiled at his New England logic. "At least people still like buying books—and newspapers."

It had been her idea to carry the local newspaper in the shop. Once upon a time, Caroline had been interested in nothing more than fripperies. Matching ribbons to bonnets. What size and color of reticule to carry. Being in Boston made her more aware of politics and economics. She'd become a voracious reader of the news and found she was in similar company. Both men and women in the city were drawn to the topics.

Because of that, she'd encouraged Aunt Evie to buy large bundles of the newspaper each day to entice people to come to the bookshop. Evie had been reluctant at first but let Caroline try her idea out. Within a fortnight, they had regular customers appearing every day. She'd cleared out space for them to sit and read the news sheets. Sometimes, they stayed to browse—and buy. Her best idea had been to stock licorice and toffee in glass jars near the newspapers. When customers purchased a paper, they inevitably saw the nearby sweets. At times, it was hard keeping the candies in stock because they sold out so frequently.

They opened the shop and the usual group filed in. Over the next several hours, she and Josiah sold all of the newspapers and seven books.

Jordy suddenly flew through the door, his cheeks flushed not from the cold but from the excitement that bubbled up and out of him.

"Caroline! Josiah! The war is over!" He waved a handful of half-sheets of news. "Mr. Frain had me bring these over, knowing customers would flock to your store. They are the first off his press."

Happiness filled her. She'd hated that her birth country and the

10

one she'd grown so fond of were at war with one another. It was bad enough that Englishmen had to fight Bonaparte, much less their American cousins.

"Quick, let me see."

Jordy handed her a news sheet and she skimmed it quickly before starting at the beginning and reading every word. What struck her most were the dates mentioned in the article—and the ones she'd read about previously. Diplomats in Belgium had signed a peace treaty at Christmastime, about six weeks ago, but this news was only filtering across the Atlantic. In the meantime, General Jackson and his men had fought the British army under Pakenham at New Orleans on January eight. Both Pakenham and his second-in-command, Gibbs, had been fatally wounded in the battle. The British had lost twenty-six hundred men to injury, death, or capture as prisoners of war, while the Americans only had six wounded and seven killed in action.

That meant that Jackson's resounding victory came after the peace accords had been signed. Since Americans were only hearing about the Treaty of Ghent now, they would assume it was Andy Jackson's win in Louisiana that forced the British hand for both sides to lay down their arms. The British would know better but the Americans would cling to their own point of view.

Caroline looked to Jordy. "Go back to Mr. Frain. Bring me double what you brought now. Tell him I'll be good for it and will settle up with him tomorrow."

The young man ran out without a backward glance and, soon, the bookshop was filled with patriotic Americans, buying both news sheets and licorice. Somewhere outside the shop a barrel appeared, and customers came in with mugs of ale as they gossiped about the end of the war.

Amidst all the noise, Josiah turned to her and asked, "Will you go home now?"

Caroline finally understood that she had a choice for the first time in three years. Though she loved her newfound freedom, she longed for London.

Slowly, she nodded. "As soon as I can make the arrangements."

CAROLINE DISEMBARKED FROM the packet boat, Tippet's leash in one hand and Davy Redmond's hand in the other. The ship had made good time and crossed the Atlantic in six weeks. She'd been one of a dozen passengers aboard and would now travel from Bristol to London by coach.

It surprised her how quickly things came together once she decided to leave Boston. Aunt Evie's will had left everything to Caroline. She'd found a buyer for the bookshop and made keeping Josiah on a part of the sale agreement. The house sold even more quickly and Mrs. Johnson had decided to stay on and work for the couple who purchased it. They had seven children and the childless housekeeper was looking forward to having young people in the house.

She waited near where they disembarked for her two trunks to arrive. Once they did, she left Davy with Tippet to guard them while she went in search of transportation. She had quite a bit of money from the sale of the shop and house but had grown frugal during her stay in Boston, aware of money for the first time. Instead of hiring a post-chaise, which would cost her approximately a pound for each mile they traveled, she looked for a mail coach instead. After asking, she was directed to a mail coach office only a stone's throw away.

A mail coach was loading as she arrived. Already, the interior of the coach had filled up with four passengers and bags of mail and she watched as seven people climbed atop the vehicle, one sitting next to the coach driver. She had two trunks, Davy, Tippet, and herself. They would need a mail coach all to themselves if that was how she chose to journey to London.

The vehicle took off and Caroline marched inside the office. After haggling with the clerk on duty, she purchased every ticket on the mail coach that would depart in two hours. It meant not only buying every ticket available but paying double to three passengers that had already bought their tickets. They seemed delighted to accept twice what they'd paid for their tickets and would be able to take a different coach in the morning. The cost still came out to be reasonable and affordable. It would also be much more comfortable for their journey to London.

She hired one of the pleased ticket holders to bring her trunks to the loading area and accompanied him to where Davy and Tippet patiently waited. The boy, only seven, had been orphaned and worked on the packet ship she'd taken from Boston. When he wasn't on duty working as a cabin boy, he'd spent every waking minute with Caroline while she taught him to read. Davy was a quick study and she knew she could find a place for him in her father's household. It would have been criminal to leave him aboard the ship, especially since he'd taken so to her. She'd speak to Stinch about Davy being trained as a footman or stable boy and never bother her father with the details.

Tippet, on the other hand, would be something that required a deft hand. Her father despised dogs and cats equally. Though she and Cynthia had begged for a pet, he'd always refused. The old Lady Caroline would have hidden Tippet in the stables and only visited him each day. The independent Caroline Andrews of Boston would boldly march in with Tippet and dare her father to say anything. Of course, that would mean he would actually have to be home when she arrived. Knowing the Earl of Templeton, he would be at one of his clubs with his cronies, playing cards and drinking the day—or night— away. Or with one of his many mistresses, which he never bothered to hide from his family. She hoped her future husband would use more discretion when it came to having a mistress.

If she even bothered with a husband.

Caroline had thought about that long and hard during the endless days at sea. She would be arriving in London the last week in March. The Season would begin in about two and a half weeks. She had no clothes appropriate to wear to any *ton* event. She would have received no invitations to said events since she'd been gone for over three years and had never made her come-out. Moreover, she was now twenty-three years old, which would be considered on the shelf by most bachelors sampling the Marriage Mart. Those three strikes against her were enough to dissuade her from attempting to participate in her first Season.

The largest factor, though, was the fact that she didn't think she wanted a husband. Her time in Boston had radically changed her. She wasn't the meek, sweet-tempered girl she'd been when she left London. She'd returned informed, opinionated, and with some wealth. If she married, the profits she'd made from the bookshop and selling Aunt Evie's home would belong to her husband the moment she spoke her vows.

Caroline wasn't sure if she wanted to give up her independence and money for some man.

Finally, she had both trunks in hand, along with Davy and Tippet. She sent Davy to buy something for them to eat and he returned with meat pies. Tippet, in particular, enjoyed the treat. They boarded their mail coach when the time came. Her trunks were placed on top, along with several bags of mail, while she and her companions shared the interior with more sacks of correspondence. They changed horses about every two hours and arrived in London early the next afternoon.

Caroline flagged down a hackney driver and had him load her trunks while she hustled Davy and Tippet inside. She gave the driver the address to her father's townhome and then settled in for the ride. Davy had never seen a city as large as London and kept shouting about the sights they passed. It delighted her to see him happy. Tippet barked occasionally, as if chiming in with his own opinion.

As they pulled into the square where the townhouse was located, she saw three riders exiting from the property that sat directly in front of them. It thrilled her that they might finally have neighbors. The place had stood vacant for periods of time and then was leased on occasion for a few months at a time. She'd heard rumors about a boy who was a marquess owning it but never living there since he was at school during the year and at his country estate in the summers. She hoped the boy had grown up and finally taken ownership of it. Perhaps, he'd even wed and had children. Caroline hoped so and that she could befriend his wife.

The cab turned and came to rest in front of her own residence. She lowered Davy to the ground and Tippet jumped out, barking. The driver helped her disembark and then removed her trunks as she watched the three on horseback turn from the square and head toward Hyde Park. The driver finished toting the trunks to the doorstep and Caroline paid him. Taking Davy's hand and Tippet's leash, she started toward the door as the cab pulled away.

Immediately, she halted in her tracks.

A black wreath adorned the front door. It could only mean one thing.

The Earl of Templeton was no more.

# CHAPTER TWO

L UKE ST. CLAIR, Earl of Mayfield, lay propped upon pillows, bare to
his waist. And bored.

Definitely, bored.

His current mistress, Catarina, pretended to be Scheherazade,
dancing in some filmy costume that she'd concocted. He hadn't the
heart to tell her that Scheherazade was a storyteller, not a dancer, as
Catarina tossed off another layer of the gauzy material she wore and it
floated to the ground. Catarina often confused things. Even her own
origins. At one point, she'd claimed to be from Florence. Another time
she led him to believe she was born in Barcelona. Or perhaps Madrid.
Luke couldn't remember. And didn't care.

He had definitely tired of Catarina.

His morning had already included parting ways with his current
*ton* lover. A pretty widow who was almost thirty, the baroness had
actually taught him a thing or two in the bedroom during their torrid
affair of the last few months. When he'd broken the news to her
earlier that he was ending things between them, she'd cried and clung
to him—until he produced a pair of ruby earrings. After that, she
couldn't get him out of her rooms fast enough.

Luke had stopped for lunch at his club and then come straight
here, ready to do the same with Catarina. He was in no mood for the
games she wished to play. Often, she had them pretend to be great
lovers, such as Caesar and Cleopatra or Romeo and Juliet. She knew

the names of these famous pairs but not the fact that their love ended in tragedy and death. Catarina was beautiful and fun to be with. He had no doubt she would find someone new before he returned to his London townhome tonight.

In the meantime, he needed her to stop what she was doing and listen to reason. At times, she had a volatile temper. He was in no mood to deal with it. Tears, possibly, but not shouting and objects being tossed about, particular ones aimed at his head. He glanced up and saw that the last layer of cloth danced through the air. His mistress climbed onto the bed on all fours and made her way up the mattress to him, a ravenous look in her eyes. She was an incredibly beautiful woman.

And Luke felt absolutely nothing for her.

Catalina reached him, her fingers dancing lightly up his bare chest as she straddled him. She pushed them into his hair and bent to kiss him. He allowed it. She broke the kiss almost immediately. He smiled up at her.

"Your mouth is smiling at me, my earl, but it does not reach your eyes," she said sadly. "Is this our end?"

"Yes."

Her palms flattened against his chest and she ran them up and down it, as if committing his body to memory.

"I'll help you find a new protector," he offered.

She laughed. "I have turned down many in the year we have been together, my earl. That won't be a problem. Besides, you leave me in fine shape." She placed a kiss upon his chest. "This wonderful house is paid for. You also found me the best cook in London."

"I may actually want her back," Luke teased.

Catarina playfully swatted at him. "You may not have her. She is mine. Loyal to me alone." She studied him a moment. "It was always going to end this way, wasn't it, my earl?"

She'd never called him by his name, a fact that he appreciated.

Only a handful of people called him Luke. The next woman that called him by his Christian name would become his wife.

He was ready for one.

He'd had three mistresses and several lovers over the past few years. They'd all pleased him in one way or another. There was a time when he thought he would be happy in this kind of life for years to come, only settling down once he passed thirty. The trouble was, his siblings' happiness had affected him more than he'd care to admit.

Jeremy, his older brother and Duke of Everton, had wed Catherine Crawford after his first wife died. They now had four children and were more passionately in love than before they wed and had little ones running around. Rachel, his younger sister, had married Evan Drake, Marquess of Merrick, last summer. She'd given birth to his nephew, Seth, just over three weeks ago. They, too, were madly in love. Both couples were the talk of the *ton* because they didn't bother to hide their deep affection for their spouses.

Luke wanted what they had. Desperately.

Some of his happiest times had been playing with his nieces and nephews. The pull of having children of his own had caused him to part ways today with the two women he was currently involved with. He would go into the upcoming Season unencumbered by any liaison. Hopefully, he would discover his soulmate among the women paraded about on the Marriage Mart.

He looked deeply into Catarina's eyes. "You have given me many happy moments over this past year. I will always look upon you fondly."

Luke kissed her lightly in goodbye and then leaned down and reached for his coat. He withdrew a diamond bracelet and held it up to her.

"A parting gift. I hope you'll think of me sometimes when you wear it."

Her eyes lit up. He could see her calculating the bracelet's worth.

"Will you put it on me?"

"Of course."

He unfastened the clasp and brought it about her slender wrist. Once he secured it, she held her arm out, admiring her new bauble.

"It's quite beautiful," she said, looking at it from different angles.

"Not as beautiful as you."

Her eyes misted over. "I will miss you, my earl." She pushed away from him and left the bed. "I don't think you need my help to dress. Please, see yourself out. Goodbye."

She reached for a dressing gown lying across a nearby chair and shrugged into it before opening the door and exiting the room. Luke quickly dressed, a sense of relief overwhelming him. Catarina had been demanding, both physically and emotionally. He was looking forward to not being drained as he had after every visit to her. Slipping on his Hessians, he glanced about the room a final time and then left the bedchamber and house without seeing anyone.

Outside, his horse awaited him and Luke mounted it. He would ride to see Rachel and Evan and visit with his new nephew. They'd only arrived in London two days ago and this would be his first time to see the newest addition to the St. Clair family. Luke knew Seth was only a St. Clair through his mother but he hoped the boy would have the St. Clair emerald eyes and black hair.

Arriving at the Merrick townhouse, he glanced across the square and saw the mourning wreath adorning the door of the late Earl of Templeton. The *ton* had been scandalized to learn the earl had been set upon by footpads, robbed and stabbed, and his body thrown into the Thames. Rumor had it that Templeton was destitute at his death and that everything would have to be sold in order to pay his debts. Luke felt sorry for his widow and any children left behind. He couldn't remember hearing of any. He hadn't gone to school with any Templeton boys or danced with any Templeton girls at balls since he'd graduated from university. It would be for the best if the earl had died with no wife and no children left behind to bear the shame of his behavior.

Luke handed his horse off to a groomsman who hurried to greet him and then knocked upon the front door. Kent, the Merricks' butler, opened the door.

"Good afternoon, Lord Mayfield."

"Hello, Kent," Luke replied as he stepped inside the residence.

Taking Luke's hat and cloak, the butler said, "Follow me and I will announce you to the marquess and marchioness."

"I really didn't come to see them," he confided. "I'm strictly here for my new nephew."

Kent's lips twitched in amusement. "Lord Seth is already a favorite of everyone's, my lord."

The butler led him upstairs to the drawing room. Luke saw Rachel on a settee with her son in her arms and her husband sitting next to her. She gave her brother a joyful smile as Evan stood and greeted him with a handshake.

Leaning down, Luke held out his arms. "I've got to hold him."

Rachel handed the baby over and Luke gazed down, instantly falling in love with his latest nephew.

"He's absolutely perfect. Of course, I would expect nothing less from you and Evan."

"He is, isn't he?" Rachel agreed.

Luke took the baby and sat opposite the couple in a large wingchair. Seth slept on, oblivious to the world.

"How was the trip from Edgemere to London?" he asked.

"Uneventful," Rachel said. "Seth slept most of the way."

"Unlike Everton's brood," Evan said with a wicked smile. "From what Catherine told us yesterday, Philip exercised his lungs most of the way, while Timothy and Delia bounced from cushion to cushion. Only Jenny seemed to be at rest, quietly reading her latest book from Merrifield while her siblings drove her parents close to madness."

Luke chuckled. A friendly competition had sprung up between Jeremy and Evan, first centered on how much each one loved his wife. Luke could see it had extended to their children.

"How is Merrifield?" he asked, referring to the earl who'd courted Rachel last Season, only to lose her to Evan.

Surprisingly enough, Merrifield remained good friends with both Rachel and Evan and Luke had grown close to him, as well. Along with Leah, Catherine's sister, and her husband, Alex, the group comprised Luke's best friends.

"You just missed him. He left not half an hour ago. He brought Seth his first book." Rachel picked it up from the table and Luke laughed. "I see it's one Catherine authored."

Their sister-in-law had begun writing children's books during the years she'd cared for her invalid father. Jeremy had encouraged her to continue since it was something she enjoyed doing. Now, every book the Duchess of Everton's wrote became a bestseller.

"Are you ready for the Season?" he asked, deciding to bring up the purpose of his visit.

"My brother is actually mentioning the Season?" Rachel asked, studying him. "Have you changed your mind? Do you want me to look for a bride for you when I do the same for Merrifield?"

His sister, feeling guilty that she'd let down Merrifield, had determined she would make it up to her former beau by finding him a wife. She'd offered to do the same for Luke, who'd put her off, claiming Merrifield was older and needed her help before he did.

"Yes," he said simply.

A satisfied smile lit up her face. "You're ready to wed." Then she frowned. "What about Catarina?"

"What? You know about her?" Luke glared accusingly at his brother-in-law.

Evan held up his hands. "It wasn't from me. You know how the *ton* gossips. Rachel could have heard about your mistress from any number of people."

"I pride myself on being discreet," he said testily.

"I've known about all three," his sister proclaimed. "And a few of your lovers, as well. Lady Morton, for instance."

Surprise rushed through him. "How could you know about her?"

"I overheard her gossiping about you in the ladies' retiring room last summer," Rachel said. "You'd be amazed at what you can overhear while you're adjusting your hair."

"What did she say?" he asked guardedly, knowing their relationship hadn't ended well.

"She claimed you were the best lover she'd ever had and that when you decided to end your affair, she threatened to tell her husband. Lady Morton admitted she hadn't slept with Lord Morton since she gave birth to his spare." Rachel grinned. "And then she said her husband would challenge you to a duel."

Luke certainly remembered that conversation. He'd told the woman that she didn't want to do that because he was a crack shot and would shoot to kill. He convinced his lover that she needed her husband around for the sake of their two sons. She'd considered his words and then screamed for him to get out. He hadn't spoken to her since. They'd coolly nodded at one another at social events. Luke had heard she'd taken on a new lover—as had Lord Morton.

"Have you gotten rid of them—*all* of them?" Rachel demanded.

Luke pressed a kiss to his nephew's forehead. "As a matter of fact, that's what has occupied my time today. I parted ways with a lovely widow this morning. I think she cared more about the earrings I gifted her with than our time together. As for the fiery Catarina? I just came from her house. That, too, has ended."

"You *are* serious," Rachel said, approval in her voice. "What changed your mind? The last you told me, you were going to sow your wild oats and worry about a wife and children years down the road."

22

He glanced at his nephew. "Seth, for one. And my other nieces and nephews. I can't seem to get enough of them." He sighed. "And seeing how batty my brother and sister are for their spouses."

He rose and handed Seth back to her. "I can't help but feel there's something missing in my life. I enjoy being around my family and friends but I want more. Someone to share what happened during my day. Someone that understands me better than anyone else I know. Someone to care for—and love. If I can find her. If she even exists."

Evan met his eye. "You won't have to find love, Luke. It will find you." He put his arm around Rachel and tenderly kissed her brow. "I was the last man who wanted a wife—and I found the perfect one for me."

Rachel turned and kissed her husband. Luke was used to it by now. Both she and Jeremy never shied away from expressing their feelings for their spouses, despite the *ton's* mixed reactions to their behavior. Luke knew that when Evan had come home from war, he'd suffered not only physical wounds but emotional ones, as well. He'd been prickly, holding everyone at arm's distance, but he had been irresistibly drawn to Rachel. Seeing their happiness—along with Jeremy and Catherine and Leah and Alex—was what now led Luke to admit how much he wanted to find his soulmate.

"Let's go riding in the park," Rachel declared.

"Are you ready for that?" Evan asked, concern crossing his brow.

"The doctor said I could whenever I felt so. Besides, I've missed being on Calypso. Let me take Seth to the nursery for his nap and change into my riding habit."

After she left, Luke teased, "You know my sister only married you for Calypso." The dapple gray had been a wedding present from Evan to Rachel.

"She is mad for that horse," Evan agreed. "She spends almost as much time atop it as she does me."

Luke roared with laughter. "Wouldn't the *ton* like to hear you admit that in public?"

"They already think I'm scandalous enough. I don't care. I love my wife and adore making love to her."

Evan rang for Kent and asked for their horses to be saddled. By the time Rachel returned and they went outside, their mounts awaited them. They swung into the saddle as a carriage passed, pulling around and stopping in front of Templeton's place. Curious, they all turned and glanced over their shoulders before riding from the square and turning toward the park.

"Who could she be?" Rachel asked, referring to the woman they'd all seen leave the carriage. "She had a boy with her. And a dog. I wonder if she's Templeton's daughter. She looked a little older than me." She turned to her husband. "What do you think?"

"I haven't the foggiest idea. You know we haven't lived here but two years though the property was mine for years before that."

"You and Rachel weren't friendly with your neighbor?" Luke asked.

Evan laughed. "Not in the least bit. Templeton was years older than us. His drinking and gambling were legendary."

"Well, I thought her quite pretty," Rachel said. "If she is his daughter, I wouldn't mind getting to know her. She could certainly use a friend in town, especially after what happened to her father. If he's her father."

Luke thought of the glimpse he'd gotten of the woman, whose trim figure looked very fine to him. The sun had struck her hair, burnishing its caramel color. He only wished he could have seen her face. He wouldn't mind getting to know her, now that he was of a mind to open his heart to the possibility of love.

Wouldn't it be an odd twist of fate if he'd just seen the woman that might actually be his soulmate?

# CHAPTER THREE

C AROLINE PAUSED A moment to steady herself and then led Davy and Tippet to the door. She sat the boy atop one of her trunks and then handed him the dog's leash.

"Davy, I'm going to ask that you sit here and guard my trunks for me."

"And watch Tippet?" he asked eagerly.

"That, too. My father has . . . an allergy to dogs . . . and I'll have to see where Tippet is to stay."

"In the stables would be good. I could sleep with him," the boy offered.

"That might work. Let me go inside and find out. You wait right here. I'll be back as soon as I can."

She tried to open the door and it didn't budge. She'd never carried a key to the place. When she'd left to go somewhere with her mother and sister, they'd always returned and were greeted by a servant so she had no need of a key. She supposed she should knock. There was always a footman about near the foyer. He could let her in.

Raising her hand to do so, the door opened before she had a chance to summon anyone.

"Stinch!" she cried, recognizing their butler, who looked dressed to go out.

"Lady Caroline," he said, shaking his head in wonder. "Is it really you?"

"It is. May I come in?"

An odd look crossed his face. Still, he stepped aside and she gained admittance to the place that had been home for her first twenty years. As Stinch closed the door, she frowned.

"Where is the settee that used to rest there? And the painting that hung above it?" Glancing around, Caroline saw the suit of armor that had stood in the hall for as long as she remembered was also missing.

"Gone, Lady Caroline," Stinch said sadly. "I suppose you saw the mourning wreath on the door?"

"It's for Papa, isn't it?"

The butler nodded solemnly. "He . . . passed. Three days ago. There were . . . debts which needed to be paid. No servant received any wages for months before the earl went."

"Stinch! Are you still here, man?" a voice called out, sounding none too pleased.

Caroline heard approaching heels clicking on the floor and looked at the butler in confusion. Then a man appeared in the foyer, a scowl on his face. His bald pate gleamed. His waistcoat was a poor fit.

"Who are *you*?" he demanded. Before she could answer, he said, "You're too early. The sale doesn't start until tomorrow."

"Sale? What sale? I live here," she said.

"Oh." He nervously shifted from one foot to the other several times.

"This is Lady Caroline Andrews," Stinch said with dignity. "Lord Templeton's daughter."

"I see." The man looked her up and down. "Well, you don't live here anymore," he said abruptly. Turning to the butler, he said, "You've done your job, Stinch. I'll speak privately with Lady Caroline."

She looked from the stranger back to Stinch. "What's going on?"

"Go with Mr. Morrow, my lady. He'll explain everything to you."

"Where will you be?" she asked anxiously.

Standing tall, he replied, "Looking for another position." He pulled a slip of paper from his pocket and pressed it into her hand. "I've taken a room at this address. I would be greatly honored if you might write me a reference."

Understanding dawned on her. Caroline had vaguely known that since her father had no sons and no relatives to speak of, his title would revert to the crown. What she hadn't thought about was that this house, being part of the Templeton estate, might also be returned to the king. And their country estate.

*Where would she live?*

"Goodbye, Lady Caroline," the butler said and departed the residence.

She turned back to the man Stinch had referred to as Morrow. "Mr. Morrow, I would like to be informed of what is happening. We can go into my father's study. It's just off the foyer."

Without waiting for him to protest, she walked quickly to the room—and found all kinds of tags on the furniture.

"What is all of this?" she demanded.

"*This* is an estate sale, my lady," Morrow said succinctly. "It will begin tomorrow. Stinch helped me place labels identifying various pieces of furniture and objects. Each one describes the piece and suggests a price for the buyers that will descend in the morning."

Caroline sank into a chair. "Will everything be sold?"

"Absolutely. Lord Templeton's debts are massive."

His words were like a physical blow, rendering her speechless.

"What kind of debts?" she asked quietly.

"The usual kind gentlemen amass. His tailor. His bootmaker. His wine merchant. Far more, however, is owed to gambling houses and gentlemen from his various clubs. I am your father's solicitor. It has fallen to me to sell everything Lord Templeton had not already parted with to cover as many of his debts as I can."

"That's where the suit of armor went," she said, wishing she could have seen it one last time. As a child, she'd made up stories about it and the man who wore it. To never see it again brought her deep sadness.

"Yes. In the last three years, during your and Lady Templeton's absence, he had begun selling off various items." Morrow cleared his throat. "Is your mother outside in a carriage?"

"My mother died in Boston shortly after we arrived," she said quietly, feeling a fresh flash of pain after the ache had been dulled for so long.

"I am sorry for your loss," the solicitor said, his voice gentling. "I know it must be hard coming home to this."

"I suppose there is nothing left for me."

"From the London townhouse and the country estate, no, nothing at all. You do have your dowry and actually your sister's, as well. That money was set aside long ago. It came from your mother when she married the earl and was designated for any daughters that resulted from the marriage."

"And if I don't wed?" she challenged.

"It would become yours on your birthday when you turn twenty-five. If I recall, that would be a little less than two years from now."

"What am I supposed to live on in the meantime? Am I even allowed to claim my own clothing that I left in the wardrobe when I went to America three years ago?"

Morrow thought a moment. "I suppose it would be all right for you to take that. But no furniture. No knickknacks. Nothing else." He flushed a dull red. "I am sorry, Lady Caroline, but you cannot touch the money now. If you wed, it will go to your husband. If you don't, you may access it in two years' time."

He began shuffling his feet again, much as a small boy would. "I know you have no living relatives in England. I do know of a woman who has an agency. She pairs . . . impoverished gentlewomen . . . with suitable employers. I could put you in touch with her. You could act as a lady's companion. Or governess."

Mustering all the dignity she could, Caroline said, "I have a small inheritance from my American aunt that will suffice. Give me your card, Mr. Morrow. I'll need to know how to reach you so that I can claim my dowry for myself when I am of age."

As he pulled a card from his inner pocket, the solicitor said, "Or if you wed. I'll be happy to draw up the papers. Since you are of legal age, you may sign them, as will your future husband."

Rage poured through her. "A husband is the last thing I'd be interested in acquiring, Mr. Morrow. It did my mother no good. My father squander all of his money, leaving his only child destitute. I plan on keeping my money to myself because, at this point, I'm the only person I trust. Good day, sir."

Caroline stormed from the study. She fought to contain the anger, not wanting any more to spill from her onto Davy. The young orphan had had his share of woes. She would not burden him with new ones. She paced in the foyer, cooling her heels.

She had never depended upon her father before. She'd tried as a young girl to impress him with all she'd learned from her governess. He'd brushed her off, telling her girls didn't interest him. She'd finally given up wanting to please him, though she'd kept to her book learning. They'd never had a relationship before—and now it was too late. Caroline couldn't help but wonder if his gambling and mounting debts were the true reason he'd sent her and Mama to America. Getting or receiving word from England had been impossible during the war. He'd gone to his own grave, not knowing his own wife had been buried in a Boston churchyard.

She would have to decide where to go. A hotel would prove too expensive over a long period of time. It would be better to rent rooms. She would have to depend upon herself now. And she had Davy and Tippet to care for.

A calm descended over her. She would do what she knew how to do.

*Open a bookstore.*

She understood how to buy and sell the right kinds of books. She knew how to keep her own ledgers. The book smart but unworldly Lady Caroline who'd left London in 1812 had given way to a more confident, more knowledgeable Caroline Andrews. She had no doubts that she could make a success of the venture.

First, she would check to see if any bookshops were for sale and what areas they might be located in. Foot traffic was important. Aunt Evie's shop had been on a busy street with many people passing by its doors each day. Caroline didn't want to locate her store along a street where few ventured. If she couldn't find an existing shop in a preferred location for sale, then she would start from scratch. Her inheritance from Aunt Evie would allow it. In fact, it might be wise to invest in a small house, as well, instead of renting rooms. She'd learned to be frugal during her time in America. She could do the same here. Ideally, if she could find living space above the shop, that would be the perfect solution.

Satisfied that she could make a go of things, Caroline left her house for the final time. She didn't need the clothing from her bedchamber. The styles would already be outdated and the gowns probably wouldn't even fit her. She'd left London quite slender. Though still thin, she'd developed curves during her time in Boston. Her bosom definitely was larger. That would keep her from wearing anything she'd left behind. Let Mr. Morrow sell it all.

She closed the door behind her and found Davy still sitting on the trunk, humming a tune. Tippet thumped his tail against the pavement, happy to see her once again. She stroked the dog lovingly and then patted the boy on the head.

"Can Tippet and I stay in the stables?" he asked.

"No, we are going elsewhere," Caroline said, sitting down on her other trunk. Before she could continue, her eyes were drawn to the same three riders that approached the square. They were talking and laughing, two men and a woman.

One of the men caught her eye. He sat quite tall in the saddle and was very handsome. He turned his head in her direction and nodded politely.

They trotted up to the house sitting opposite and two grooms claimed the horses from the trio. The woman waved and smiled brightly, making her way across the square. The two men fell into step behind her.

Caroline stood. "Good day," she called out as the party approached.

"Hello," the woman said. "I'm Lady Merrick." She indicated the man who stepped up on her left. "This is my husband, the Marquess of Merrick. We live just across the way." Lady Merrick gestured toward the second man, the one who'd caught Caroline's attention. "And this is my brother, Lord Mayfield. He lives but a few blocks from here."

"It's very nice to meet you. I'm Lady Caroline Andrews. This is Davy. And Tippet."

Lady Merrick knelt and held out her hand. "Good to meet you, Davy."

The boy's eyes widened. "Pl-pleased to meet you, my lady."

The marchioness petted Tippet. "Hello to you, Tippet. I've been wanting a dog." She rose and shot her husband a pleading look.

"You have a new baby," the marquess said, his arm slipping around her waist. "I would think Seth would keep you more than busy. If he doesn't, I can think of a few ways to occupy your time." He kissed her cheek and looked as if he wished to do much more than that.

Caroline saw the affection between the two as the couple smiled at one another, though she blushed at Lord Merrick's suggestive words. It was obvious what he meant. She wasn't used to hearing something like that voiced aloud, not even in America where people freely spoke their minds.

Lord Mayfield laughed easily and said, "They are disgusting, aren't they? So much in love that they sometimes ignore all those around them. My brother and his wife are the same way."

She was immediately drawn in by his eyes. They glowed as emeralds did and seemed to hold more than a hint of mischief. His jet black hair was a stark contrast to them. Caroline couldn't get over how appealing his face was, only rivaled by his tall, athletic frame. Something stirred within her that puzzled her. Confused her. She pushed it aside, thinking she would address it later.

"Are you Lord Templeton's daughter?" the marquess asked.

"I am. Mama and I went to visit my aunt in Boston three years ago. The war broke out and there was no way to safely return to England. Once word of the peace treaty arrived in Boston, I decided to return home."

"Is your mother with you now or did she remain behind?" Lady Merrick asked.

"Mama passed away shortly after we arrived."

The noblewoman looked at her with pity. "I am so sorry to hear that, Lady Caroline. That must have been difficult. And then to have to remain in America all this time."

"My aunt was loving and kind to me. It was the first time I remembered meeting her. She'd left England with her husband, an American ship captain, when I was barely walking."

Lady Merrick took Caroline's hands in hers. "It's good that you had her then. I suppose you have learned of your father's recent death?"

"Oh, indeed. Mr. Morrow, his solicitor, is inside preparing for an estate sale that begins tomorrow. It appears Papa accumulated tremendous debts and everything is to be sold off, the townhouse and all its contents. You see, he had no relatives, and so the crown will reclaim the title."

"That is distressing news to receive just as you've arrived back in England," Lord Merrick said. He glanced at his wife and Caroline saw something unspoken pass between them. "You'll need a place to stay," the marquess told her. "We'd be delighted if you remained with us for as long as you'd like."

His generosity struck her. "Lord Merrick, I am a stranger to you. Your offer is much too generous."

Lady Merrick squeezed Caroline's hands. "Please. We insist. Unless you have somewhere else you'd rather go."

Tears welled in her eyes. "I have nowhere," she admitted. "No relatives. Even my aunt in Boston is now gone."

"That is what neighbors are for," the marquess said. He bent and lifted the trunk she'd sat upon, easing it onto his shoulder. "Luke, fetch the other if you will."

Luke—Lord Mayfield—leaned over and swung Davy from the trunk. "Hold Tippet's leash, Davy, and come along," he said easily.

He picked the trunk up as if it weighed next to nothing. Placing it on his shoulder, he followed his brother-in-law across the square, Davy and Tippet shadowing his every step.

Lady Merrick released Caroline's hands and slipped her arm through Caroline's. "Call me Rachel," she suggested as she led Caroline toward her home.

In a daze, Caroline went along.

They went inside and Lady Merrick instructed a footman to summon the housekeeper. She told the two men where to take Caroline's trunks and they disappeared up the stairs. The housekeeper quickly appeared and the marchioness told the woman they had a houseguest that would be staying indefinitely.

"Is Davy your ward?"

"No. He was a cabin boy on the ship that brought me here. He's an orphan. I'd thought to place him in my father's stables and have him trained as a footman."

Once again, the marchioness went to her knees so she was on the same level as the boy. "Davy, where would you like to be?"

"In the stables. With Tippet."

She motioned the same footman over. "Take Davy and Tippet to the stables. See that they're settled there." Turning back to Caroline, she said, "They can stay, too, as long as you do."

Davy hugged her tightly and then followed the footman. Tippet pranced happily along beside the boy.

"I can't begin to thank you, Lady Merrick."

"Rachel. We are neighbors. We'll be living in the same house."

"Not for long, I hope." When she saw the marchioness' face fall, she quickly added, "I hope to find lodging of my own soon."

By now, the two men appeared again. Caroline could feel Lord Mayfield's intense gaze upon her and sensed her cheeks heating.

"We need tea after our ride and all that moving," the marquess proclaimed. "Come up to the drawing room, Lady Caroline."

He took his wife's arm and escorted her up the stairs. That left Caroline with Lord Mayfield.

He smiled and offered his arm. She took it and was hit by a jolt of lightning. Her eyes flew to his face and she saw confusion—and then satisfaction.

"It's this way, Lady Caroline," he said smoothly.

She swallowed, her heart racing and her breathing suddenly shallow. She had no experience with whatever was happening with her body. The moment they reached the drawing room, she released his arm.

Caroline would need to stay far away from this man.

# CHAPTER FOUR

L UKE ENJOYED BEING around beautiful women. He was used to sharing their company, especially in his tightknit family. His sister was one of the great acknowledged beauties in London with her St. Clair midnight black hair and bold, green eyes. Both Crawford sisters, Catherine and Leah, were as sisters to him now. Catherine had striking auburn hair and bright blue eyes while Leah had golden tresses and green eyes. Even Cor, his grandmother, was still dazzling at seventy-five, her lovely face bearing but a few wrinkles and her snow white hair setting off crystal blue eyes.

The women Luke had taken as lovers over the years all had beauty in common. He liked looking at them. He never bothered getting to know them, though. They weren't to be a permanent fixture in his life. He took what he wanted but gave amply in return.

His entire world had changed in the last minute, though.

Lady Caroline Andrews was breathtaking—*and* he wished to know her—a first for him. This was a poised woman, not some young miss pushed straight from the schoolroom onto the Marriage Mart as the Season began. He wondered if she'd made her come-out before she'd left for America, for he believed he would have remembered if she had. What a shame she'd been buried in such a desolate place, stuck while the war raged on. Not only had she suffered the loss of her mother and aunt during her years away from home, she'd arrived in England and learned her father was also dead and buried.

Yet she appeared composed and serene, even having learned that her family homes were being sold and she was displaced, with nowhere to go. Any other woman of the *ton* would have fallen apart, hysterical, crying for her smelling salts. Lady Caroline calmly accepted what she'd learned.

This was a woman worth knowing.

It didn't hurt that she had rich, caramel hair, streaked with as much blond as brown. Or that her brown eyes reflected warmth and a hint of humor. Her ample bosom and tiny waist also appealed to him. Her attractiveness was merely a nice addition, a bow on the mysterious package that he wished to unwrap.

What really captured Luke's attention was when they'd touched. The electricity between them was palpable. He'd never experienced anything so raw and real. They owed it to themselves to get to know one another. Conveniently, Lady Caroline staying with Rachel would help throw them together more often than if they merely saw one another at events during the Season.

Luke determined by Season's end that Caroline Andrews would be his, body and soul.

They entered the drawing room and Evan rang for tea. It arrived almost immediately. As Rachel poured cups for all of them, Lady Caroline assisted by passing around slices of the cake that accompanied it.

"May I ask about your horse, Rachel?" the newcomer asked in her gentle, cultured voice.

Ah, his sister had already endeared herself and prompted her guest to use first names. That pleased Luke tremendously. It would also give him an advantage over other bachelors who would swarm Lady Caroline at the first event of the Season.

Rachel smiled dreamily. "Calypso was a wedding gift from Evan."

She reached for his hand and squeezed it, love for her husband shining brightly from her eyes. Something else good, in Luke's opinion. Lady Caroline would see what a loving couple Rachel and Evan were and what a loving family Luke came from. Another advantage for him.

"Did you ride much in America?" he asked, wanting to claim some of her attention himself.

"Not much. We walked everywhere. To shops. Church. My aunt's bookstore."

"Oh, she had a bookstore?" Luke's interest grew.

"Do you like books?" she asked, eyeing him, her intrigue obvious.

"Very much so. I was a terrible student at Eton and university but I've always enjoyed reading. I don't care what the topic. I buy books by the dozens," he admitted, something he usually kept a secret from others.

"Then you are the type of customer I will seek," Lady Caroline said.

"Customer?" he asked.

"Yes. I plan to open a bookstore in London."

"How interesting," Rachel said. "Will it be like your aunt's in Boston?"

"I hope so. I plan to call it Evie's, after her. She was Evangeline but everyone called her Evie. I think that sounds warm and friendly, just the kind of atmosphere I want to create."

"Opening a business requires a great deal of knowledge," Evan said.

"Oh, I have it," their guest said confidently. "I don't mean to sound like a braggart. Aunt Evie taught me all about her business. She sold her husband's ship when he passed away and used the proceeds to open her own shop. She expanded it twice. During my time in Boston, I worked alongside her. I learned not only about how to sell a book to a customer but all about inventory and keeping ledgers. I even negotiated a lower rent for her building."

Luke's admiration for her grew. "Do you have an idea where

you'll locate Evie's?"

"Not yet. We literally arrived in London only today. I'm hoping
that I can purchase an existing bookstore. If not, I can lease or buy a
building and then build my inventory from the ground up." She
looked at him. "Perhaps you can give me some pointers on the type of
books London gentlemen read, Lord Mayfield."

"I'd be happy to do so, Lady Caroline," he replied.

Rachel caught his eye and he realized he'd sounded a bit too flirta-
tious. He'd need to tone it down in order not to scare off Lady
Caroline.

"I'm interested in a busy thoroughfare," she continued. "One
where a large number of customers would pass. I'd pressed Aunt Evie
to carry newspapers and created a reading circle where people stopped
by each day and not only purchased their news sheet but remained to
read it."

"That's a lovely idea," said Rachel.

"I did more. I started carrying candies—licorice, toffee, sometimes
chocolates. I think here in London, with everyone's great love of tea, I
will combine my bookshop with a tearoom, as well. People can shop
for their books and then stay for a spot of tea or even a baked scone. If
I can find the right property, I can rearrange the shelving to suit my
purpose and have both inside one establishment. If not, I will look into
buying an adjacent building and knocking out a few walls in order to
create the tearoom addition."

"That an ambitious enterprise," Evan noted. "You will need a
business manager. And a solicitor to handle the contracts."

Lady Caroline sniffed. "Well, I won't be using Mr. Morrow. Before
he'd even shared his name, he was already telling me that I had no
roof over my head and that I wasn't allowed to take even one small
item of remembrance since everything was going to pay off my
father's enormous debts." Her cheeks flushed with anger, only making
her look all the more appealing to him.

"Forgive me for getting so worked up," she apologized.

"That's unnecessary. The man should be tarred and feathered for treating you so abominably, Caroline," Rachel said.

"I have a few names I can recommend to you," Evan said.

"I'd be interested in getting those from you, my lord. I'd like to get moving on this project as soon as possible. With the Season about to begin, London will be full of extra people. I want to appeal to them and become *the* place to shop for their books."

"I have an idea," Luke declared, trying to find a way to ingratiate himself with her. "What would say to a book signing?"

Lady Caroline frowned. "What do you mean?"

"Our sister-in-law, Catherine, is an author. A quite famous one. She's the Duchess of Everton and writes children's books. I know if we asked her, she would happily help you out and appear at your new store to autograph copies of her books. Possibly at your opening."

The radiant smile she gave him sent Luke to the heavens and beyond.

"What a wonderful idea," she said brightly and then bit her lip. "I don't know her, though."

He waved away her comment. "Catherine would love to help you out. Don't worry, I know her. She cannot refuse a request from her brother-in-law." He caught Rachel grinning shamelessly at him.

"I must ask, Lady Caroline, if you have the capital to see your plans through," Evan said. "If not, I'd be happy to become an investor in your venture."

Luke wanted to pinch himself, wishing he'd thought of that first.

"Aunt Evie had no children so I received her entire inheritance. From my experience, I know I have the funds to see this through."

"It might be difficult for you to do this and partake in the Season," Rachel said.

"Oh, I have no plans to be a part of the Season," Lady Caroline said airily. "I never even made my come-out."

"Why not?" Rachel asked, curiosity written on her face.

"I was very close to my sister, Cynthia. We were less than a year apart and decided we'd do our come-outs together. Unfortunately, Cynthia's health was never good. When we would have made our debut, I was nursing her instead. She passed away and Papa suggested that Mama and I travel to visit Aunt Evie." She shrugged. "You know the rest. Mr. Madison declared war upon the kingdom and I was stuck in Boston for the duration of the war."

"So you've never been introduced to society," Rachel said.

"No. And I don't plan to ever do so. My clothes are too American and out of date. I'm not going to waste good money that could go toward my bookstore on something as frivolous as clothes. Besides, I can assume the *ton* thought little of my father, amassing the kind of debts he did. No one knows I'm back in the city, much less will they issue invitations to their social events."

Caroline looked around the room. "And why would I want to take part in the Season? I don't ever plan to marry."

"You can't be serious," Luke sputtered.

"Oh, I'm quite serious, Lord Mayfield," she said with utter certainty. "Everyone around me has died. My sister. Mama. Aunt Evie. My father. I fear I am somehow cursed. What man would wish to take a wife under those circumstances? I believe I've done well without a husband for my first twenty-three years. The *ton* would consider me already on the shelf as it is. No man of quality would wish to be saddled with a woman whose father had such a dubious reputation, much less one who is homeless. I'm better off making my own way in the world. I can care for myself, Davy, and Tippet quite nicely."

Luke was flabbergasted by her words. How could she think she was cursed? Or too old to wed?

Rachel stood. "We need to check on Seth in the nursery. Luke, could you entertain Caroline for a few minutes?"

Rachel grabbed Evan's hand and led him from the drawing room, leaving the two of them alone.

"Do you think I shocked your sister?" Caroline asked hesitantly. "She's already been so welcoming to me. Perhaps my outspokenness offended her."

"Far from it," Luke assured her. "If anything, Rachel's admiration for you has only grown during our conversation."

*As has mine.*

Luke couldn't tell her that his sister vacated the room so that he could have time alone with Caroline, hoping to change her mind. How was he supposed to do that? She seemed confident and opinionated, more than any woman of his acquaintance.

Bloody hell. He actually *liked* that about her. He liked everything about Caroline Andrews. How could he convince her to take part in the Season—and become a part of his life?

Then it came to him. Something scathingly brilliant. Lady Caroline would not be able to turn his proposal down.

"Might I accompany you on your search for a place for your bookstore? We could start tomorrow since you're eager to locate somewhere and get it set up if at all possible before the Season begins."

"Would you, Lord Mayfield?" She gave him a brilliant smile, one that would have brought Luke to his knees if he'd been standing.

"I'd be delighted to. One can never be too careful about the location for a business." He lifted his saucer. "Might I have more tea?"

"Of course." She took the cup and saucer from him and poured a full cup.

"Two lumps of sugar, please." He smiled. "I've a sweet tooth."

"So do I," she confided and returned the saucer to him.

They talked pleasantly for a few minutes about her time in America and her return across the Atlantic and then he paused, mid-sentence.

"What is it?" she asked, concern in her voice.

"I've just had an idea," he said, speaking slowly. "May I share it with you?"

"Of course. Is it where my bookstore should be located?"

Oh, this woman would be the death of him.

"No," he said. "But it does involve it. I know you said you weren't interested in participating in the Season."

"I'm not. I have no time for frivolity and, as I mentioned, no need of a husband. If I married, I'd have to turn over all of Evie's inheritance to him—and my bookstore, as well."

"I know you're against it but . . ." He let his voice trail off.

"But?" she asked, sitting up, her interest piqued.

"I merely thought that if the *ton* is who you wish to patronize your bookstore, then it might be wise to get to know some of them. Go to their events. Through conversation, see what their tastes are."

Luke saw the seed he'd planted begin to bloom in her mind's eye.

"I hadn't thought of it quite like that," she said thoughtfully.

"It's just an idea," he said modestly, hoping his words would slowly reel her in.

"It's a good one," she said with enthusiasm. "To get to know my clientele in a social situation. To subtly recommend they shop at Evie's." She brightened. "It's a very worthwhile idea, Lord Mayfield. Very much, indeed."

"What idea?" Evan said as he and Rachel reentered the drawing room.

Briefly, Lady Caroline explained what Luke had come up with. Rachel nodded with approval, a smile tugging at the corner of her mouth.

"I think it's a brilliant idea," his sister proclaimed.

"Of course, I don't have any invitations," Lady Caroline said glumly.

"Oh, Evan and I can remedy that," Rachel promised. "You are our houseguest. Of course, you'll be invited to the same events we are. We would refuse to leave you at home. Our attendance depends upon your attendance," she said loftily.

"I think you're both quite clever," Lady Caroline proclaimed. "I am fortunate to have made such good friends on my first day back in London."

"Would you like to meet Seth?" Rachel asked out of nowhere. "I gave birth to him less than a month ago but he's already my entire life."

"Seth is your priority—but don't forget about me," Evan called out as the women stood and left the room. Turning to Luke, his brother-in-law said, "That was a close one."

"You mean the fact that the woman I'm dying to kiss proclaimed she wasn't interested in ever marrying? And that I was able to turn the situation around so that she'll attend most every event of the upcoming Season, where I will be able to woo her? As well as take her around London, scouting for places to locate her bookstore?"

Evan roared with laughter. "Yes. Exactly that. Well played, Luke. Well played. But you'll have your work cut out with that one."

"Just as you did with Rachel?"

"Touché." His brother-in-law grinned. "I can't wait to watch this unique romance unfold."

"Neither can I, Evan. I'm already half in love with the woman—and haven't even kissed her yet."

Luke snagged another scone and settled back in his chair, a smile playing about his lips.

# CHAPTER FIVE

L UKE FINISHED HIS scone and told Evan to make his excuses to the
women. Rachel was used to him dropping in and out so it
wouldn't surprise her that her brother was gone. He had a most
important errand to run and then research to conduct. He retrieved his
horse and only had to ride a few blocks to the St. Clair townhouse. It
was fortunate the three siblings lived so close to one another in
London and that Leah and Alex were also located nearby. He'd enlist
their help in his endeavor to win Caroline Andrews' hand—after he
spoke with Jeremy and Catherine.

He arrived and handed his horse off to a groom and then knocked
on the front door. Barton, the Everton butler, invited him in.

"It's good to see you again, Lord Mayfield." Barton cleared his
throat. "The Duke and Duchess are . . . indisposed at the moment."

Barton's words were code that let him know his brother and sister-
in-law were upstairs frolicking in their bedchamber.

"I'm here to see the children first," he said. "Hopefully, they will
see fit to come out before I leave."

Knowing that Catherine must have been recently cleared by her
doctor to resume marital relations since Philip had been born just over
eight weeks ago, Luke knew his brother was making up for lost time.
If the couple didn't appear within an hour, he would make a nuisance
of himself and pound upon their door until they answered.

He climbed to the top floor of the house, where the nursery and schoolroom were located. Opening the door, he saw Sara, the nursemaid, rocking young Philip. Jenny played with two dolls while the twins were building something with blocks. They'd both gone block mad after Merrifield had brought new blocks to Timothy. His nephew was kind enough to share with his sister, though Luke knew the headstrong Delia would have barreled her way in and demanded to play if her brother hadn't been so accommodating. Sometimes, Luke thought Delia would be the most stubborn St. Clair of them all.

She was the first to see him. "Uncle Luke!"

Both twins ran to him, wrapping their arms around each of his legs. Jenny glanced up and smiled sweetly before returning to her dolls.

"Play with us," Timothy insisted.

"I will," he promised. "As soon as I spend a few minutes with your little brother."

They released him and returned to the floor, where he supposed two hundred blocks had been spread out. Delia began stacking them while Timothy started counting some.

He went to Sara and held out his arms. "May I?"

"Of course, my lord."

She rose and carefully handed the baby to him. Luke took her place in the chair and gazed down at the boy. Though he supposed all babies looked somewhat alike, he thought Philip and Seth favored each other. He envied them, being so close in age. They would be sent to school together after forming a close bond in their early years. Jeremy had been years older than Luke, having been the result from the duke's first marriage, and so they hadn't spent much time together in childhood. Luke had been closer to Rachel, who was four years his junior and came from their father's third wife. All three women had died in childbirth, giving birth to the three St. Clair children. Thank goodness Catherine, Rachel, and Leah were made of hardier stock.

Philip opened his eyes and yawned sleepily. Luke proceeded to tell his nephew a story, one which he borrowed from a book Catherine had authored just last year. The other three children gathered at his feet as he did so, entranced at his use of different voices for the various characters. When he finished, Delia demanded it was her time with Uncle Luke and so he reluctantly returned Philip to Sara. Jenny went back to her dolls and Luke sprawled on the floor.

"What are we building?" he asked.

"The Tower of London," Delia proclaimed.

"We better start with Tower Bridge then so people can get to it," he said.

For half an hour they worked on the structure. Both twins declared the bridge sound. While Timothy was content to go on building, Delia, who was the more active of the two, demanded a horsey ride. Luke said only if everyone shared in a turn, which his niece agreed to—as long as she went first. As he got down on all fours and she climbed onto his back, he knew this St. Clair would be one who always got her way.

Delia was on her third ride when Luke noticed Jeremy and Catherine standing in the nursery's doorway. Timothy and Jenny went to greet them but not Delia. She had her hands fisted in his hair and was determined to make the most of her ride.

"Enough, Delia," Catherine said. "It's time for your supper. Let poor Uncle Luke up."

She released her hold on him and slid from his back. "Thank you, Uncle. Will you come back and help finish the Tower?"

"I certainly will. And I might bring a friend," he added.

"Merrifield?" Timothy asked, his face lighting up.

"Maybe," Luke said mysteriously. "Enjoy your meal."

He pushed himself to his feet and ran his fingers through his hair before joining Jeremy and Catherine in the corridor.

"I notice you're also combing your fingers through your hair," he told his brother. "I suppose you've also been giving rides this afternoon." Luke winked at Catherine, who blushed to her auburn roots.

"Duchess, should I throw out this rude bastard?" Jeremy asked, capturing her hand and bringing it to his lips for a kiss.

"I don't know, Duke. He does entertain the children quite well. I'd hate to lose him."

Jeremy kissed his wife's hand again. "Then I suppose I'll allow him to remain." He released Catherine's hand and turned to Luke. "Would you like to stay for an early dinner? We're used to keeping country hours and only arrived in town yesterday."

"I'd like that."

They went downstairs to a small parlor and Luke got right to it.

"I've met someone," he announced. "Someone I'm very interested in."

Catherine clapped her hands in glee. "It's about time you got rid of Catarina and thought about finding lasting happiness."

Luke sighed. "Did all of London know about Catarina? I thought I'd been careful. Almost secretive."

She snorted. "You bought the woman a house. The entire *ton* knew you as her protector. Is it over?"

"It is."

"Good," his brother said. "It's about time you followed the shining example of your brother and sister and found love. Who is this someone you're interested in?"

"Lady Caroline Andrews. The Earl of Templeton's daughter."

Fortunately, Luke didn't have to hesitate in naming Caroline. Though her father was still the subject of gossip days after his death, Luke knew Jeremy and Catherine were the last people to judge anyone. They were fair and open-minded and would never look down upon the daughter for the sins of her father.

"I don't know her," Catherine said. "Tell us about her. How you met. What she's like?"

Briefly, Luke described how they'd met Caroline soon after her return to London and how she'd been in America visiting her aunt when war broke out and what occurred during her stay in Boston.

"How awful to be so far from home and unable to return," Catherine said. "And the fact that her mother and aunt died while she was there. Poor, lonely girl."

"She made good use of her time. Worked in her aunt's bookshop and then ran it upon Lady Evangeline's death. When news arrived about the Treaty of Ghent, she sold the shop and home that were bequeathed to her and returned to London."

"I don't remember her from before. I'm usually good recalling girls who make their come-out," Catherine said.

"Lady Caroline never did." He explained why she'd delayed it and saw sympathy in Catherine's eyes. Knowing how close she and Leah were, he couldn't imagine one of them dying, leaving the other behind.

"I suppose it's never too late to make a come-out," Jeremy said. "At least being in social situations, you'll get to be around her. I'm assuming you wish to court this woman?"

"That's the problem—she isn't interested in that kind of thing. In fact, she doesn't want to get married at all."

"What?" the happily married couple both cried.

Luke explained how mature Lady Caroline was and that her focus was on opening her own bookstore and tearoom so she could provide for herself, an orphan, and her dog.

"She's learned quite a bit about business from having run one in America. She's bright and articulate. I think she would be reluctant to turn the reins over to a husband, who would, by law, immediately own her property and claim all monies that belonged to her."

"And this is the woman you're so taken with?" Jeremy asked, his lips twitching in amusement.

"I know," Luke lamented. "It seems hopeless, doesn't it? But I've made up some ground there. I've told her she must attend *ton* events to get to know her customers and their tastes."

Catherine chuckled. "You are a sly one, Luke St. Clair. What can we do to help?"

He grinned. "I'm glad you asked. Since you are holding the first ball of the Season, I'm asking that you invite Lady Caroline to it. No one knows she's back in London after being exiled in America. If the Duchess of Everton invites the lady, everyone else will, too. She's staying with Rachel and Evan since Templeton's solicitor practically threw her out of the house. It and its contents all go up for auction tomorrow and Lady Caroline had nowhere to stay."

"How convenient that she'll be staying with your sister so you can visit frequently," Jeremy noted.

"We can certainly invite her to our ball. I can also mention her to others. The invitations will pour in."

"That's what I was counting on, Catherine. And something else."

"What?" she asked eagerly.

"I'm to help her find an existing bookstore to purchase or property where she can establish one. I told her my dear sister-in-law was a famous author and said I would ask if you would attend the opening day of the shop—and if you would sign copies of your books that were for sale."

Catherine beamed. "I'd be delighted to. I've never done that before. Oh, how wonderful to see the people who buy my book. Why, I could possibly give a reading while at the store."

"That would be marvelous," Luke said. "Caroline would like that very much."

"So it's already Caroline?" Jeremy asked.

He shrugged. "I think of her that way. I'm not addressing her as such, though she and Rachel are on a first name basis. With the time I hope to spend with her, I believe that she could be Caroline to me very soon."

"You *are* taken with her," his brother said in wonder. "I didn't know if I would ever see you this way."

"I don't know for sure that she's the one but I want to get to know her and give our relationship a chance to grow. She's beautiful, intelligent, and mature. The most confident woman I've met, excluding present company, of course. I already want to spend time with her and have her meet the rest of my family—and I haven't even kissed her!" Luke declared.

Jeremy and Catherine exchanged one of their looks.

"Then I think before the Season begins, Duke, we need to invite Lady Caroline to an intimate dinner. Only family in attendance."

His hand cupped the back of her neck. "A wonderful idea, Duchess." He leaned in to kiss her.

"Forgot dinner," Luke said. "You two may eat alone. I have much to do before I go hunting for a bookstore tomorrow with Lady Caroline."

He rose and kissed Catherine's cheek. "Thank you."

"I am always happy to help. Especially in matters of the heart," she replied. "Bring Lady Caroline for tea tomorrow afternoon. I'll be sure Rachel and Evan come, as well. Leah and Alex, too. We ladies can speak about the Season and I'll extend an invitation for everyone to stay for dinner." Her eyes lit with mischief. "Of course, I'll let the others know now. I'll pen notes to them after dinner."

"Be sure those notes get written because I see the hungry look in my brother's eyes," Luke warned. "I'd tell him no bedroom games until after that gets done."

"Get out," Jeremy said pleasantly. "The sooner you're gone and these notes are written, the sooner my appetite can be appeased."

Luke left, laughing. He was now on a mission—to learn everything about bookstores before he met up with Lady Caroline Andrews in the morning.

# CHAPTER SIX

CAROLINE DRESSED CAREFULLY, knowing she would be seeing Lord Mayfield today. Seeing what Rachel had worn yesterday made her realize just how informal her wardrobe had become while living in America. Boston claimed to be the cradle of freedom and boasted of its classless society. Caroline had quickly adapted to her temporary home and enjoyed wearing less fussy clothing.

Being back in London, though, and wanting to become not only a businesswoman but one who could effortlessly blend into *ton* events meant a total revamping of her wardrobe. Though she hated to part with the coin, she would have to do so and have several outfits made up for everyday wear, as well as social occasions. Hopefully, Rachel could recommend a modiste to her. Caroline would need to see one soon in order for there to be enough time for new clothing to be made up.

She ventured downstairs and found Rachel and the marquess at breakfast, though their roles seemed reversed. Rachel had the newspaper open and was reading aloud from it, while Merrick bounced Seth in his arms, cooing softly to his son.

"Good morning," she said.

"Plenty to eat on the sideboard," the marquess said. "Help yourself. Mornings are casual."

As Caroline fixed her plate, Rachel said, "I cannot believe Bonaparte. This is outrageous!"

"What of him? We had very little news about him and the war in Europe."

"That's right," Merrick said. "You've been isolated and then traveling at sea. Tell her, Rachel."

His wife's nose crinkled in disgust. "Boney was captured last year and exiled to Elba, an island in the Mediterranean. The fools in charge allowed him to keep a personal guard of over six hundred men. He remained three hundred days and escaped to France less than a month ago."

Caroline placed her plate on the table and took a seat opposite Rachel. "Oh, no."

Rachel snapped the newspaper in her hands. "This says he entered Paris five days ago. The little idiot will start the bloody war all over again." She closed the paper and thrust it aside. "Let's talk of more pleasant things."

The marquess handed his son over to his wife. "Let Seth soothe that hot St. Clair temper of yours."

Immediately, Rachel's features softened as she smoothed the baby's hair.

Caroline decided to broach the subject. "Could we speak of clothes? I'm going to be in need of a modiste. Very little of what I brought back from Boston is appropriate for *ton* events. I also need some day dresses to go about town, ones I can wear when I open my shop."

"I have just the modiste for you," her new friend said. "She's quite busy at other times of the year but in the weeks leading up to the Season, she works exclusively for Catherine. By extension, Catherine allows Leah and me to use Madame Toufours, as well."

"You think she will take me on?"

"Of course. Madame Toufours is always eager to please the Duchess of Everton and her two sisters, though I'm merely one by marriage. Catherine releases her from obligation usually two weeks after the Season has begun and then ladies beat a path to Madame Toufours' door, wanting to be dressed in a similar fashion to the Duchess of Everton."

"I'm almost afraid to meet her. She sounds so grand."

"Not at all. Catherine is unpretentious and quite kind." Rachel indicated a pile of correspondence sitting next to her. "In fact, she's invited us for tea today."

"Oh, I'm supposed to be out with Lord Mayfield all day, looking for a place to locate my bookstore."

"Even if you're on the hunt all day, you'll be ready for some tea and cakes by late afternoon. Have Luke bring you there. It will be an ideal way to meet Jeremy and Catherine."

"I've never met a duke or duchess before."

Merrick snorted. "They're just the same as you, Lady Caroline."

"Evan, please call her Caroline. Caroline, you do the same to Evan."

She frowned. "I'm not sure that's appropriate."

"I'm already Rachel to you. We are going to be close friends. I insist."

Caroline looked to the marquess and he nodded. "Very well," she said.

"And that means calling Luke by his Christian name," Rachel added.

She felt her face flame. "Oh, I couldn't do that."

"Of course, you can. He's family, too." Rachel frowned. "Although I'll need to have one of the maids accompany you today."

"Why?" Caroline asked, puzzled.

"You must be chaperoned."

"No. That's not necessary. I went all over Boston on my own without needing a chaperone. Besides, I have no plans to marry Lord Mayfield or any other gentleman. We'll be out together today strictly on business."

Rachel gave her a dubious glance but didn't protest further. Instead, she said, "Spend your day finding a proper location. Then at tea this afternoon, we'll talk about your wardrobe. I'll check with Catherine and see if Madame Toufours can see you tomorrow. She'll need your measurements so she can start on a few pieces for you."

"Is she very expensive? I mean, if she's creating gowns for a duchess, I'm sure she must charge quite a bit."

Rachel waved away her concerns. "Don't worry about that."

Caroline remained silent. She would have to pull aside Madame Toufours and obtain prices from the woman and then limit the number of garments to be created.

"I think I will go visit Davy and Tippet in the stables. I want to see how Davy's getting along and I missed Tippet's company last night. He usually sleeps with me."

"Then he should continue to do so," Rachel said as Evan grunted.

"No, I think Davy needs the company more than I do. He's been uprooted several times in his young life. Tippet will be a good companion to him until I find a place of my own and become settled."

"There's no rush," Evan said. "You are welcome to remain for the entire Season and beyond."

"Thank you," she said. "Both you and Rachel have been so kind to me. Opening your house and offering me your friendship." Caroline rose. "I'll be back soon."

She left the house by the nearby front door and circled around to the back, quickly spying the stables. Entering them, she saw a man in his mid-forties with merry eyes and graying hair.

"You must be Lady Caroline," he said jovially. "I'm Brimley. Let me take you to young Davy. He's quite a boy. Eager to learn and fast at it. A bit small for his age but already a hard worker."

They found Davy mucking out a stall. He turned as Brimley called his name and grinned.

"Lady Caroline! I'm already working for the marquess. Mr. Brimley says he's glad I came to London because he needed someone like me."

"You may visit with Lady Caroline, Davy, then it's back to work for you." The groom tipped his cap to her and left them to speak in private.

"How is everything?" she asked.

Davy talked without coming up for air, excited to share with her everything he'd been doing. He showed her his new clothes and where he and Tippet were sleeping. The dog lay curled up on the boy's bed and Caroline went and loved on him briefly. She let Davy show her around the stables as he told her everything he would be learning about in the coming days and weeks. She wondered if this might be a better place for him than if she took him to work at her bookstore. It would require some thought on her part and she would definitely ask the boy's opinion about what he'd rather do.

Davy led her back to the front of the stables and told her he needed to get back to work. She stepped out into the cold morning and ran smack into Lord Mayfield.

He caught her elbows to steady her. Caroline experienced a wonderful rush of excitement whirling inside her. The earl smiled down at her and then released her.

"I heard you'd come to check on Davy and Tippet. How are they managing?"

"Quite well," she said, surprised to hear her voice sounded normal. "Davy already seems to be an expert on horses."

"Did you plan for him to remain with Merrick or take him with you?" Mayfield asked.

"I've some time to make that decision," she said, trying to calm the butterflies beating about her belly.

"I've brought my carriage today. We've a lot of ground to cover and I've learned things that I must share with you before we start viewing properties." He offered her his arm. "Are you ready?"

"I don't have my reticule with me but I doubt I'll need it today. I don't plan on buying any property without sleeping on the decision." She placed her hand gingerly on his forearm. "Lead the way, Lord Mayfield."

He took her to the square, where a magnificent carriage awaited them. She deliberately averted her eyes from gazing at her former home, knowing today was the day the property and its entire contents would go on sale. She listened as Mayfield gave instructions to his driver and then assisted her inside. She thought he would seat himself opposite her. Instead he sat directly beside her. His thigh brushed against her skirts, sending a frisson of pleasure rippling through her.

"I want to discuss with you what I've discovered since we spoke yesterday afternoon and compare it to how things are done in America. Or Boston, in particular, since that is what you are familiar with."

"Go on," she encouraged, curious as to what research he'd done.

"Being a member of the upper class, I purchase all of my books from a bookseller," he began. "My library is extensive because of my broad taste in literature and nonfiction. All of my copies are bound in leather, though I know some books are bound in cloth."

"Aunt Evie carried a handful of books bound by leather for her most prosperous customers. Most of the rest of the inventory was in cloth or a cheaper material."

"Ah, so you're aware of that."

Caroline sniffed. "I told you I am familiar with all aspects of the book business."

"Did Boston have circulating libraries?"

"I knew of one. I was interested and would have investigated it further had I not had the opportunity to return to England. Please, tell me what you have found."

"Though I don't patronize them, circulating libraries have grown in popularity in London in recent years. Several are owned and operated by booksellers. They charge a guinea for establishing an initial subscription and then a small fee for each book lent to a patron. Minerva Library is one we will visit today, one of the largest of these circulating libraries. It's important for you to see it in operation if you want to become one of its competitors."

"So you feel I'll need to not only sell books but lend them, as well."

"Yes."

"What are you looking for in setting up your operation?" he asked.

Caroline reminded him again of how location was very important to her. She also described wanting a large expanse of plate glass windows in order to display her books and possibly other wares.

"Are you still interested in combining your store with a tearoom?"

"Yes, of course."

"The reason I ask is that I have learned some of these circulating libraries have become like a club for women of the upper and middle classes."

"Really? How so?"

"Gentleman have their clubs in which to gather. Women do not. Though circulating libraries require that a subscription be purchased in order to rent books, a lady can visit these libraries whenever she wishes. No fee is due beyond the subscription. Because of that, women are flocking to them, not for merely books, but for the social aspect. Some offer games and raffles. Some even stock merchandise for sale. Others have reading areas, as you did in Boston, where women are afforded an opportunity to read anything they choose. Poetry. Biographies. Histories. Whatever is available."

"That is terribly exciting. It gives me hope that I do have a place in the city and can help others."

The carriage slowed and then came to a halt. Caroline looked out the window and murmured, "Temple of Muses," as she stared up at the multi-storied building.

"The Temple of Muses is our first stop of many," Lord Mayfield confirmed.

He opened the carriage door and leaped out. She stood and before the footman riding on the back was able to bring the stairs around, the earl had clasped her waist in his hands and swung her to the ground. Her mouth grew dry as his fingers lingered and then he released her.

"Shall we?" he asked, offering her his arm.

She took it—and entered a world of wonder.

The shop was light and airy, with a large front desk staffed with clerks who both sold and lent books. Areas affording seating were scattered throughout the bottom floor and several ladies sat engrossed in both reading and conversing about books. A secret thrill shot through Caroline. This was what she wanted to do with her life.

She stopped a clerk and peppered him with questions, learning that publishers had first been wary of circulating libraries, preferring to sell books rather than lend them out. Since the circulating libraries used a unique, marble patterned paper binding to distinguish library books from others, it was easy to see the difference in the stock. The marbled binding was cheaper, meaning the books didn't hold up as well, and had to be ordered again from the publishing houses, allaying the fears of publishers. The clerk said these days more than half of a print run of a book was designated for circulating libraries, putting them on almost equal footing as those purchased.

Lord Mayfield took her to several other stops. She thoroughly enjoyed her visit to Minerva Press Circulating Library, simply for its scope and size. A handful of the libraries and stores they visited had close to five thousand titles. Minerva boasted of five times that amount. Minerva Press published both sentimental romance novels and Gothic horrors. Those genres had proven to be the most popular forms of literature, which Caroline learned from speaking to another clerk. She would definitely stock many copies of those kinds of books.

What impressed her most about Minerva Press was the colossal circular counter in the middle of the bookshop. She also noted the wide staircase that led upstairs to what the Minerva Press clerk termed lounging rooms, along with row after row of bookshelves. This bookstore also carried printed musical scores, which could also be lent to patrons, as well as magazines and graphic arts. And as Lord Mayfield had informed her, she saw a handful of bookstores carrying items for women, from parasols and reticules to gloves and fichus.

Everywhere she went, she saw scads of women. Only a tenth of the customers were men. Already, ideas danced through her head, knowing her bookstore—and now circulating library—would cater almost exclusively to women. Because of that, she made a note of the most popular books carried. Without a doubt, copies of the six volumes of Maria Edgeworth's *Tales of Fashionable Life* dominated sales, based upon what her eyes noted and the numerous conversations with store clerks revealed.

By the time they left what Lord Mayfield said was their last stop, Caroline was elated—and exhausted.

The earl gave her a rueful smile. "With so many places to visit, I quite forgot about the time. I'm famished and regret I did not stop and feed you during this whirlwind tour."

"That's quite all right, my lord. I wanted to see as much as I could today."

"I know we didn't have a chance to look at properties yet."

"Don't worry," she assured him. "I needed to see all that you showed me today. It's given me a score of ideas and the direction I want to take in my endeavor."

"You can't do that on an empty stomach. I was to take tea at my brother's this afternoon." He consulted his pocket watch. "It's almost that time now."

"Yes, Rachel mentioned that she and Evan were also invited to tea."

He frowned. "They are Rachel and Evan to you, while I'm still Mayfield." The earl shook his head. "That won't do at all. We've spent hours and hours together today. Please. Call me Luke."

A nervous giggle sounded from her and she swallowed, trying to shove it down. "Very well. Then I am to be Caroline."

"Caroline," he said thoughtfully. "That sounds . . . right to my ears."

She closed her eyes. Everything was right to her in regard to this man. He was handsome beyond description, with his mesmerizing green eyes and dark, thick hair that was black as night. His tall frame seemed to dwarf her at times and yet his touch was gentle. Sitting so close to him, she could smell his clean, masculine scent from the soap he'd used with his morning bath. Her lips itched to touch against his, which was the most outlandish idea that had ever occurred to her.

Caroline had never kissed a man. She'd decided she didn't want to marry. And yet the thought of never kissing Luke was causing the most awful heart palpitations.

"Are you unwell?" he asked softly.

She opened her eyes. "No. On the contrary, I'm feeling exhilarated." She smiled. "I must thank you for squiring me about today. I had no idea what awaited me. If you hadn't done your research and showed me what I was up against, I fear my bookshop would have been a massive failure, one which did not cater to the needs of women."

The carriage came to a halt. Caroline looked out and saw an enormous townhouse.

"Is this your brother's residence?" she asked with trepidation.

"Yes, I grew up here. And at Eversleigh, the ducal country estate."

He opened the door and, as before, lifted her from the carriage with ease.

Tucking her hand through the crook of his arm, he said, "I cannot wait for you to meet my family."

# CHAPTER SEVEN

A BUTLER ANSWERED the door and granted them entrance. Caroline tamped down the sudden rush of nerves that ran through her. She had been raised an earl's daughter but stepping inside this townhome immediately showed her the difference between an earl's residence and that of a duke's. The servants seemed to stand taller and possess more dignity. The furnishings were more sumptuous. As the butler led them up the stairs, she noted even the carpet seemed more plush.

"Don't bother announcing us, Barton," Luke said. "We're expected for tea."

"Right you are, Lord Mayfield. I'll see that it's brought at once." He turned and retraced his footsteps as they continued on.

They reached oak doors intricately carved, what many would consider works of art themselves, and Luke opened one, gesturing for her to enter. She did—and froze.

The duke and duchess were engaged in a kiss. Not a simple kiss. One that seemed to Caroline as if the duke inhaled his wife whole.

Luke took her arm and guided her toward the couple. As they reached the pair, he cleared his throat.

The duke broke the kiss and looked up, annoyance clear on his face. "Haven't you ever heard of knocking?" he asked and then glanced to Caroline. Rising, he said more graciously, "Good afternoon, Lady Caroline. I'm Everton." He turned and took his wife's hand and she seemed to float to her feet. "This is my duchess, Catherine."

Caroline curtseyed and the duke swept her hand up for a kiss. She couldn't help but stare at him. He and Luke were very much alike. She'd thought Rachel and Luke favored one another but Luke's resemblance to his brother was startling. She could see what the younger brother would look like in the years to come, thinking the duke must be in his early thirties.

The duchess offered her hand and squeezed Caroline's fingers gently. "It's so good to meet you, Lady Caroline. I'm jealous that Rachel and Evan have already claimed you as their house guest."

"They've been most kind to take me in, Your Grace. Especially since I had nowhere to go."

"Please, come sit. Tea will be here shortly," the duchess said.

The four seated themselves. Luke took a place next to Caroline on a small settee. He seemed to take up even more room than he had in the carriage, causing those pesky butterflies to erupt inside her again.

"We are hosting the first event of the Season. It's to be a ball. Invitations went out today and you will find yours when you return. I do hope you'll be able to attend, Lady Caroline."

Before she could reply, the door opened and Rachel and Evan came in, followed by another handsome couple. They rose and Caroline was introduced to the newcomers, both blond and looking as if they were meant for each other.

Rachel did the honors. "Lady Caroline Andrews, this is the Earl and Countess of Alford. Leah is Catherine's sister and my best friend. The earl and Evan are also best friends from childhood. Our country estates are but a few miles apart so we see each other often."

The earl kissed Caroline's hand. "In fact, Evan and Rachel met at Fairfield when I held a house party. Evan had sold his commission and Rachel helped him put Edgemere to rights again."

"Don't forget that my wife also totally redid our London townhome," Evan added. "Rachel has quite an eye for design. She has fashioned new gardens for us as Edgemere. Perhaps you'd like to see them someday, Caroline."

She smiled. "Gardening is something I'm interested in. I would very much enjoy seeing what Rachel has done at Edgemere."

"I know!" Lady Alford cried. "We should hold another house party, Alex. Once the Season is over. Lady Caroline could stay with us for a while and then go to Edgemere." She slipped her arm through Caroline's. "I'm very happy to make a new friend."

"Have a seat," the duchess suggested. "The tea cart has arrived."

Caroline watched as Barton supervised two footmen in rolling the cart to the group and placing it perfectly. The duchess poured out tea for all of them. Luke began placing items on a plate and then handed it to her.

"You are famished so you get the first plate."

"Did you have a long day?" Rachel asked. She looked to the others. "Luke escorted Caroline about London today. She is searching for a property to open a bookstore."

Murmurs of interest followed and the duke said, "Tell us where you looked."

"Actually, we didn't view any properties today. Luke informed me that many booksellers now operate circulating libraries within their bookstores and so we visited several of them to give me a better idea what is expected and what the layout of my place should consist of."

"I'm a subscribing member at Minerva," Lady Alford said.

"I never knew that," the duchess remarked. "What is it like?"

"We have a substantial library at Fairfield but I have told Alex we need to build up the one in town. I started going to Minerva to purchase books and decided to subscribe. That way I can read a book before making the decision to buy it."

Her husband chuckled. "Leah has recommended many books for me to add. Biographies, in particular, while she's more drawn to romances."

"Romances?" Rachel asked. "Now, I'm interested."

Lord Alford confided, "She reads several a month. I think she's learned a thing or two in her reading." His eyes lit with mischief. "In fact, what you did the other night—"

"Alexander Lock, you would be wise to keep silent," his wife warned, a smile threatening to erupt. "Else I may not try out anything else I've discovered."

He took her hand and laced his fingers through hers, bringing their joined hands up so he could kiss hers. "Yes, dearest."

A pang of jealousy shot through Caroline. She'd quickly noticed how affectionate Rachel and Evan were with one another and had seen firsthand how the duke kissed his duchess. Here was a third couple that seemed bound not simply by wealth and name—but by love. The look the Alfords gave one another tore at her heart.

She would never experience anything like that.

Of course, it was her choice to refrain from marriage. Still, a part of her wished a man would look at her that way. Kiss her fingers and tease her.

*A man like Luke St. Clair.*

Caroline shook her head, trying to clear that thought away.

Luke must have seen her discomfort and steered the conversation back to their day. He spoke of several of the bookstores they visited and how some carried feminine items for purchase. He looked to her and she picked up where he left off.

"Because of that, I believe my bookstore will cater mostly to female customers. I plan to call it Evie's, after my late aunt. It will give women a place to come and socialize, as well as read books. They can buy a new scarf or fichu while they are there. Although I'm going to have to put some of my ideas on hold."

"What would those be?" Luke asked, frowning.

Caroline explained to the others how she'd offered candies at her place in Boston. "I was hoping to extend that further and actually have part of the store be a tearoom. I'd considered buying or renting the space next door to my establishment so that customers could go from one to the other with ease for a bit of refreshment. At the same time, the tearoom would allow outside traffic to stop and enter, as well."

"Why can't you do that?" the duchess inquired. "Are you afraid you won't find the proper location for both?"

"I'm hopeful I can find the right location. I simply don't have the funds to see that part of my dream become reality, after seeing everything I did today. At least not for now. My father, who was recently deceased, had accumulated what I'm led to believe are outrageous debts. In fact, today my childhood home and all of its contents have gone on sale to pay a portion of those debts. I do have my inheritance from my aunt but it is limited. Since I have no other collateral, no bank would be willing to extend me a loan. I merely have to make a go of my bookstore and circulating library and hope I have enough success to add on in the future."

"You have quite a head for business, Caroline," Luke said. "Your ideas are sound and I believe there's a market for what you want to offer both ladies of the *ton* and middle class women. I would be willing to invest in your venture so that you can see all of it brought to life in style."

"I think Caroline will do quite well. I want to invest, as well, as I told you yesterday," Evan proclaimed.

Lady Alford elbowed her husband and he sat up. "I, too, will be interested in giving you some capital. I must warn you that Leah will think that gives her the right to come in and speak her mind."

Overwhelmed, Caroline said, "Lady Alford has frequented this kind of establishment. I would be delighted to hear her opinions."

"Oh, please, we're to be friends—and business partners. You must call us Leah and Alex. I know you're already using the others' first names. I've felt a bit left out," she pouted prettily.

"To have three investors suddenly when there were none before is astonishing," she said. "Are you sure you're not doing so merely to be polite?"

"Not at all," Luke assured her. "I know I speak for us all. What you wish to accomplish will fill a need for women in London. You might as well aim for the stars."

"This will certainly make a difference when we view properties tomorrow," Caroline said. "Now that I have in mind the size of the space I need, I must get busy and see if there's something available for purchase or if I must rent an empty space and create a brand-new inventory from scratch."

"Not tomorrow," Catherine said. "Since you've been gone three years, your wardrobe will be lacking. You must visit Madame Toufours, my modiste, immediately. She will need to start on a few gowns for you for the events you will be invited to attend."

She started to protest and then saw the wisdom in it. If the modiste could take her measurements tomorrow morning, clothing could be started. She must look her best in order to attract her clientele. It still might give her the afternoon to look at spaces in the neighborhoods she had in mind.

"Where would you ladies feel would be a prime location for my bookstore?"

Rachel suggested Oxford Street or the Mayfair area. Catherine thought the Covent Garden area would be a place to search. Leah decided somewhere near Cavendish Square, in the heart of Mayfair, might work since Clark & Debenham was nearby and women of the *ton* had purchased items there for several decades.

That led to the conversation splitting into two, with the women eager to talk fashion with Caroline, while the men gravitated to agriculture.

"You'll need more than gowns," Catherine said. "Not to say that American goods aren't well made, but you'll need to be dressed from the inside out. New corsets and hosiery. Slippers."

"And hats," Rachel added. "I believe that's the most important piece of an ensemble."

They talked so long that Caroline didn't notice when servants came in and lit the lamps. Barton appeared again and spoke quietly to the duchess and left the room.

"Barton has informed me that we've talked so long that dinner is now being served. I hope you'll all decide to join us."

Everyone agreed to do so and Luke gave Caroline his arm, escorting her into what he termed the small dining room. It seated twenty.

"I'd hate to see how many can be seated in the large dining room," she quipped.

"You're leaving out the middle one," he said with a smile. "This is the family dining room. There's another one large enough for dinner parties, fitting both family and friends. The large dining room? It's only slightly smaller than Parliament," he teased.

As they dined, Luke brought up the topic of the bookstore's opening.

"I had a thought regarding a way to bring more customers in," he began. "It involves you, Catherine." Although he had already mentioned this before, Luke thought it would be a good idea to have everyone agree to his idea together.

"How can I help?" she asked graciously.

"Naturally, Caroline will carry books written by the Duchess of Everton," Luke pointed out.

"Of course, she will," said the duke. "No bookstore is a true bookstore without my wife's children's tales on its shelves." His warm gaze told Caroline of the pride and admiration he felt for his duchess.

"Wouldn't it be interesting if not only did the Duchess of Everton attend the opening but that she signed copies of her work for paying customers?" Luke asked.

"Do you think that would help sell books?" the duchess asked.

"Sell books?" Rachel laughed. "You won't be able to keep them in stock. Plus, if the Duchess of Everton is patronizing this bookstore, then others of the *ton* will be sure to follow."

"Would that be acceptable to you, Lady Caroline?" Catherine asked.

"I would be honored to have you do so, Your Grace," she replied.

The radiant smile the duchess gave her caused Caroline to shake her head. She voiced what was in her heart to them. "You all have been so welcoming of me. Offering me a place to stay. Friendship. Funds to help me bring my lofty plans to life. I am humbled by everything."

The duke raised his wine glass. "To Lady Caroline Andrews and Evie's Bookstore and Tearoom."

The others followed suit, echoing Everton's toast. Caroline sensed her cheeks heating at the attention.

Then Luke slipped his hand around hers, under the table and out of sight from those gathered. Its size dwarfed hers. A delicious vibration ran through her with the contact between them and she looked into his eyes.

And saw heat—and desire.

# CHAPTER EIGHT

C AROLINE WOKE IN a fevered state, her body tingling as the dream faded.

Luke St. Clair not only invaded her thoughts while awake but even dominated them while she slept.

What was she going to do?

She'd already decided the direction her life would take. She would be a bookstore owner. One who hovered on the edge of the *ton*, close enough to make vital connections, yet not a woman whose sole purpose in life was to find a husband. She didn't fancy a husband. She didn't require a husband. Not for the life she intended to lead.

But the thought of how Luke had looked at her at dinner last night refused to cooperate with her ambitions. More importantly, Caroline was afraid that her eyes had reflected her own desire as his hand swallowed hers. She'd felt peace. Safety. And need.

Definitely need.

Climbing from the bed, she splashed cold water on her face, trying to cool down. Her dream had involved kissing. That much she remembered. Oh, she wished she had been kissed before so she would understand the yearning deep within her.

Maybe she could ask Luke to kiss her. Just so she would know what it was about. Do it and get it over with. Much as she was researching the kind of bookstore she wished to open. Once she'd been kissed, she would know what it was about and be able to move on.

An image of the Duke and Duchess of Everton filled her mind. The kiss she'd seen them partake in had much more to do than mere lips touching. Their bodies had been locked together in an embrace that still brought a blush to her cheeks as she thought about it.

*Could she ask Luke to kiss her that way?*

No. Definitely not. First, she wasn't that kind of woman. He would be horrified by her request. Second, whatever kind of kiss the duke and duchess had shared had to be meant for married couples. She and Luke would never qualify on that account. Caroline pushed aside her curiosity. She could survive without kissing a man. Especially one as handsome and charming as the Earl of Mayfield.

She dressed, realizing how plain her gown appeared when compared to the ones her new friends wore. Fortunately, they didn't judge her by it. She already knew the three women to care more about her than what she wore. Women of the *ton*, though, were an entirely different matter. She recalled Mama talking about her own come-out Season and how it was impossible to wear the same gown twice, else the *ton* would eviscerate you with their vicious gossip.

How was she to look elegant, though, without spending a fortune? She supposed the key lay with the modiste she would visit today. She would have to pull the woman aside and explain her financial situation and that only a limited amount of gowns would be commissioned.

After breakfast, the Duke of Everton's carriage arrived, drawn by a magnificent team of matched bays. She and Rachel found the duchess and Leah already inside and greeted them.

"Thank you for coming out so early," the duchess told them. "Though most of the *ton* would never consider a visit to a modiste at this time of morning, I know time is of the essence."

"I'd like to thank you again, Your Grace, for allowing me to use your modiste," Caroline said gratefully. "I hope she won't mind that I'll only need a small group of gowns."

"What?" Leah asked. "The Season is about to begin, Caroline. You must look beautiful in order to gain the attention you need in order for Evie's to be successful."

"I understand. But I don't want to frivolously waste my entire inheritance on a wardrobe when I've inventory to buy and a property to lease or purchase."

"That's why you have your three investors," Rachel said. "They will see to that."

The duchess said, "Lady Caroline wants the bulk of her inheritance to go toward setting up her new bookstore. She doesn't want to depend solely on men."

Caroline gave her a grateful smile, realizing the duchess truly understood.

"Because of that, I will be issuing Madame Toufours a challenge." The duchess smiled at Caroline. "We are of a similar size. I have hundreds of gowns in my wardrobe. While you will certainly want to commission some new gowns to be created for you, I think I'll ask Madame Toufours to rework some of my old ones. She designed every one of them. I'd like her to take them and make something new of them for you. That will lessen the cost since she will already have material to work with."

"That's an excellent idea, Your Grace," she said. "Are you sure you don't mind?"

"Not a bit."

"Are you also having new gowns made by Madame Toufours?" Caroline asked Leah.

"I am. I find my hips are a little broader and my bosom slightly fuller after having Rose," she revealed. "What about you, Rachel? Has your figure changed much since Seth arrived?"

"Some," Rachel said. "Enough that I have had to extend my wardrobe." She grinned and told Caroline, "I had the audacity to wear the same gowns during my second Season as I did my first."

"Why?" Caroline asked, filled with curiosity.

"While Leah was fortunate enough to find love and marry Alex after our first Season, no bachelor caught my eye."

"I find that hard to believe," she said. "You are beautiful, Rachel. I'm sure many men offered for you."

"Oh, they did," she said merrily. "And I didn't love a single one of them." Rachel laughed. "I see the disbelief on your face, Caroline. You must remember that I'd seen Jeremy and Catherine's shining example of what marriage should be and was determined that I would only wed if I fell in love. I might have gone five Seasons—ten—without marrying anyone. Fortunately, Evan came along and we realized we were meant for each other."

"I thought what was important was finding a titled, wealthy gentleman," she said carefully.

"I wanted love," Rachel proclaimed. "I didn't care about looks or wealth. So I wore the same gowns. I knew the man who loved me wouldn't care if my gown had been worn before and I was right."

"Of course, certain women gossiped terribly about Rachel," Leah confided. "It didn't matter, though. She found Evan and is most happy. Those same women are envious of her every time Rachel and Evan are on the dance floor. You can tell by the way they look at one another how happy they are together."

"We're here," the duchess said.

As a footman helped the four women from the carriage, Caroline wondered about this family of women who loved their husbands and found their love returned. Her experience regarding marriage was the example set by her parents, who rarely spoke to one another, even if they were in the same room. She'd heard vague gossip about how many women in the nobility took lovers after wedding and producing a suitable number of heirs, while men of the *ton* always seemed to have a mistress tucked away somewhere.

Did true love really exist?

They entered the establishment and Rachel and Leah made their way toward a wall of fabrics. The duchess introduced Caroline to Madame Toufours, who appraised her gown openly, her displeasure obvious. Caroline could see the modiste found her new client lacking in style.

The duchess explained the kind and number of outfits Caroline would need, which she considered was a reasonable amount, and then told the Frenchwoman how she wanted a large number of her own gowns the modiste had designed to be remade for Caroline.

"I know no one else could accept such a challenge and create new from old the way you will," the duchess said, her flattery subtle. "Of course, you would be able to do whatever you wished. The material is already there so the cost to you would be minimal. Whatever you produce will set the new style for this Season and beyond. I have full confidence in your creativity, Madame."

The modiste bowed her head. "You are too kind, Your Grace." Looking up at Caroline, she assessed her, having her turn slowly in a circle.

"Your figure is one that will show my clothes off to their best advantage." She touched Caroline's hair. "Your hair is by far your greatest asset, along with your lovely complexion. I will choose colors that will suit you, warming your skin and hair." Madame wrinkled her nose. "Not what you wear today, of course. I'm sure your undergarments are just as poorly made. We will change everything from your inside to your outside."

Turning, she clapped her hands. "Marie-Therese! Genevieve!"

Two assistants came running. "Take Lady Caroline's measurements while I speak with the duchess."

Caroline was led away and thoroughly poked and prodded. Once her measurements were recorded, Madame Toufours appeared again and took her to another part of the store, holding up swatches of color to her and discussing them with the duchess. Finally, the modiste seemed satisfied and told the duchess she needed to attend to her own fitting for clothes that were ready for her approval. Marie-Therese took the duchess in hand, while Genevieve went to speak with Rachel and Leah.

Caroline was now alone with Madame Toufours and decided to explain to her about the bookstore.

"We are two businesswomen, Madame. I would like to share with you what I am about to open."

Briefly, she explained the type of bookstore and circulating library she would run and how she would offer a unique selection of goods for women of standing to purchase.

"Looking about your shop—and knowing the faith the duchess places in you—I would like to offer you the chance to sell your wares in my bookstore. I believe if I were the only bookseller to exclusively carry goods from Madame Toufours, sales would be brisk. You could even provide your own clerk, who would be knowledgeable about your merchandise."

The Frenchwoman eyed her with admiration. "You are definitely a businesswoman, Lady Caroline. This is an opportunity I cannot refuse. How large an area do you have in mind? I already have an idea of what I would like your store to carry."

The two women discussed items to stock and Caroline offered the percentage she would accept from the modiste in order to sell her goods at Evie's.

"Then we have an understanding," Madame Toufours said.

"We can meet in a week or so, perhaps when I come for my own fittings, and finalize details. I should have decided on a property by then. We can look at it together and discuss the arrangement of the goods."

"I look forward to this venture," the Frenchwoman said with a smile.

Caroline said, "I do, as well, Madame, but as we will be in business together, I must be frank with you. Most of my funds will be directed to my bookstore. Leasing or purchasing a property in a prosperous neighborhood in order to entice my clientele. Buying enough inventory to fill the space. Hiring workers to staff it. That leaves me with little to spend on this new wardrobe."

"Say no more, my lady," the modiste said. "You are giving me a wonderful opportunity to showcase my wares in a different venue. I believe your establishment will be successful—in part because of clever ideas such as including my goods."

Madame Toufours then offered her a generous discount on the new creations she would sew for Caroline, so reasonable that she doubted the woman would make but a small profit.

"Are you certain, Madame?"

The modiste smiled warmly at her. "I am. I think it's the least I can do for the arrangement we've come to. This venture will bring me many new customers." She took Caroline's hand and with a mischievous glint in her eye added, "We businesswomen must stick together, non?"

"Definitely," Caroline said, pleased with the bargain they'd struck.

Once all fittings had been completed, the duchess told Madame Toufours that she would send over the gowns to be remade. She reminded the Frenchwoman that the first event Lady Caroline would attend would be the very ball she and Everton would hold and emphasized the need for Caroline to look her absolute best that night in order to make a lasting impression on the women of the *ton*.

"I can assure you both that Lady Caroline and the gown I design for her will be one of the most spoken about the next day, as will yours, Your Grace," the modiste said.

With that guarantee, they left the shop. Rachel insisted they go next door to her favorite milliner's. Unlike gowns, Caroline was able to buy three hats immediately and she ordered another four that her friends thought would go well with the clothes that had been commissioned this morning.

By now it was noon and the women boarded the ducal coach to return home.

"I'm exhausted," Leah proclaimed. "I think I will go home and nap with Rose."

Rachel laughed. "I plan to do the same with Seth."

"Are you tired, Lady Caroline?" the duchess asked.

"Not a bit," she admitted. "It was stimulating being back in London and shopping for a new wardrobe. I'm still hoping to look at properties this afternoon for my bookstore."

"Would you be able to have luncheon with me first?"

"I'd enjoy that," Caroline replied.

They dropped Leah off first and then drove a few blocks further and left Rachel at home before traveling another block to the Everton's London residence.

As they entered, she asked, "Is the duke home?"

"No. He's at his shipping business today."

Caroline couldn't help but react. "His . . . business?"

The duchess chuckled. "Oh, I know. The *ton* frowns upon any talk of business. Gentlemen are to refrain from dirtying their hands by it and never discuss it." She led Caroline into a small parlor and indicated for her to take a seat. "Jeremy is different, though."

"How so?"

"His father almost bankrupted the family. When Jeremy became the Duke of Everton, he had very little wealth. He was forced to use his business acumen in order to restore the St. Clair fortune. He found he was quite shrewd at investing and almost everything he touched turned to gold. Within a few years, he'd repaid all his father's debts and his investments had tripled. Even quadrupled. We are quite comfortable now. He understands the *ton* disapproves of flaunting business connections and so he tries to be discreet in visiting his businesses. He has a wonderful manager and solicitor who both act on his behalf but he is still the one in charge, making the decisions."

The duchess studied her. "I know you must have wondered why Jeremy did not leap at the opportunity to invest in your bookstore, as the other three did."

Caroline had thought that very thing. Now hearing how the duke was so wise regarding business, it disappointed her that he didn't feel her venture to be a solid investment.

"If Jeremy had become involved, Luke, Evan, and Alex would have sat back and deferred to his experience. He and I discussed how he wanted the three of them to begin to learn about business on their own, without any direct influence from him."

The duchess leaned forward. "My husband very much believes in you and what you are wanting to accomplish. He told me how very much he admires you and your fortitude. You have had to deal with disappointment and death. Instead of succumbing and crumbling, you have remained strong and confident."

She felt tears sting her eyes. "Thank you, Your Grace, for sharing that with me. It means a great deal, knowing how successful the duke is in his finances, to think so highly of me."

"You must call me Catherine. I am about as unduchesslike a duchess as you will find."

"Then I am to be Caroline to you."

"Agreed." Catherine smiled. "I have a surprise for you. I think you'll rather like it."

"What? You've already done so much for me. Helping me with my wardrobe. Agreeing to come to my bookstore. Offering me your friendship."

Catherine rose. "There's a guest waiting for you at luncheon. He's quite eager to meet you."

# CHAPTER NINE

LUKE DIDN'T THINK Caroline would be busy an entire day at Catherine's modiste. She didn't seem very interested in her clothing, other than wishing to look presentable in order to fit in at *ton* events. He didn't think it mattered what she wore. Caroline Andrews' maturity and beauty would speak for itself.

At least with the gentlemen of the *ton*. They would be attracted to her for her looks, first and foremost, but a good portion of them would also enjoy her wit and intelligence. He realized their opinions didn't hold any water with Caroline because she needed the women of the *ton* to like her. They were the ones who would make up her clientele. Buy her books. Pay for a subscription to the lending library. Consume her tea and baked goods. And hopefully, buy merchandise from what was offered. That's why this morning was important. Caroline needed a wardrobe to go into battle with the dragons of the *ton*, one that would make her still seem humble but feel victorious.

In the meantime, while she gathered her armor of corsets and parasols and hats which would accompany her gowns, he could aid her in ways she would notice. His first stop would be Catarina's. Though he'd hoped never to see his former lover again, this was too important. Luke would put aside his reservations and see if he could reason with the fiery courtesan.

He knocked at the door and saw the startled look on the butler's face.

"Lord Mayfield. You . . . were not expected."

"I know. May I come in?"

The butler couldn't very well deny Luke entrance to the home he'd purchased and so he stepped aside.

"I'm here to speak with Mrs. Withers first," he said. "I'll see myself to the kitchen."

As he hurried away, he wondered if the butler had the nerve to interrupt whatever Catarina was doing and tell his mistress that her former protector had returned uninvited.

He found Mrs. Withers rolling dough. She was covered in flour, wisps of graying hair peeking out from under her cap.

"Lord Mayfield!" she exclaimed, her surprise evident. "I never thought we'd see the likes of you again."

He pulled out a stool from under the table where she worked and seated himself "It's good to see you, Mrs. Withers. How have you been?" he asked with a smile.

Her face softened. The St. Clair smile never failed to work. He'd also learned from Cor to treat all servants with respect, showing an interest in them and their lives. It had paid off in loyalty over the years.

"I've been well. My sister, though, lost her husband a week ago."

"I'm sorry to hear that. Are you close?"

"We are."

"Is she a cook as you are?"

"She is. Don't tell her I said so but she's probably more skilled than me."

"Where is she?"

"Here. In London. It's not much of a challenge for her. The old earl she works for is all that's left in the house and he can only gum his food. Bessie's stuck preparing soft, bland foods. She's bored silly."

Things were definitely looking up.

"I'd come to offer you a position," Luke confided, "but perhaps your sister would be better suited."

Anger sparked in Mrs. Withers' eyes. "Now, why would you being doing that, Lord Mayfield? I would love to come cook for you."

"It's not for me, actually."

Her face fell. "Oh. Then I suppose it would be best if I stayed here."

He let her feel sorry for herself a moment and then mused aloud, saying, "This opportunity could actually use two cooks, I suppose."

Mrs. Withers perked up. "Really? For Bessie *and* me?"

"Yes. Let me tell you about it."

He explained how he had a friend who wanted to combine the ideas of a bookstore and tearoom together, where customers could flow between the two establishments.

"There would also be access to other customers from off the street, as well, ones who merely want a spot of tea and something sweet to eat. Your cakes and scones are the best I've ever tasted, which is why I thought of you. Business would be brisk, though, so it might take two of you to bake everything needed."

"What if customers wanted a full tea?" she asked. "More like a meal?"

He considered her words. "That's certainly a possibility down the line. For now, I think Lady Caroline would only be interested in serving sweets with tea."

"Lady Caroline?" the cook asked.

"Yes. It is her enterprise, though I and two of my friends are investors in her new business. She owned a bookstore in America and now that she's returned to London, she's eager to open something similar here."

"Is that even allowed?" Mrs. Withers asked, doubt on her face.

Luke held back his mirth. "Lady Caroline is far smarter than most men of my acquaintance, Mrs. Withers. She has experience running a bookstore and a strong will."

"You seem to think a lot of the lady," she noted.

"I do. And of you, as well. Would you consider coming to work for her? I know her tearoom would be a success because your scones alone will draw people from far and wide."

His flattery had worked, though Luke wasn't exaggerating. He could see he'd won her over.

"When would I start?"

"Most likely within the next two weeks. I'd be happy to meet with your sister and explain to her."

"No, if I'm wanting to do it, Bessie will, too. No worries there, my lord." She frowned. "There's the mistress to tell, though."

"Why don't you let me take care of that?"

"Would you?" she asked hopefully.

"Go pack your bags, Mrs. Withers. I fear once I've spoken with Catarina, she'll throw both of us out," he said cheerfully. "You can have a room at my townhouse. Bessie, too."

"Oh, thank you, Lord Mayfield," the cook said, beaming from ear to ear as she dusted her hands against her apron. "It won't take me long. I'll meet you out back with my bag. Good luck to you."

She left the kitchen and Luke braced himself for the confrontation ahead. He headed from the kitchen and as he reached the bottom of the staircase, he caught a whiff of Catarina's strong perfume. He remained where he was, deciding how to approach her.

Suddenly, she appeared at the top of the stairs and swore when she saw him, rushing down to face him.

"What are you doing here?" she hissed. "I have someone here."

"I needed to speak with you."

"He's a *duke*. And he's already given me my own carriage and horses." She looked over her shoulder. "He cannot find you here, my earl. I have told him we are through. If he thinks I lied, I am doomed."

"Give me Mrs. Withers and I'll never set foot in this house again."

"You want my *cook*?" she asked.

"Yes."

Catarina shoved him. "Go. Take her. Just get out," she whispered, her rage obvious.

"Thank you," he said, hurrying away and out the front door.

Luke told his driver to move around the corner, not wanting to cause trouble with Catarina's new duke. He waited outside less than five minutes until Mrs. Withers appeared. Taking her bag, he led her to his carriage.

Their next stop claimed Bessie Baker, who was eager for a new opportunity that would allow her to work alongside her sister. She resigned on the spot, leaving the housekeeper with her jaw hanging to her knees. Luke dropped the sisters at his townhouse and told them his housekeeper would see them made comfortable.

"When will we meet Lady Caroline?" Bessie asked.

"Soon," he promised and then hopped back inside the carriage.

His next step was the office of Mr. Sanderson, his solicitor. Though he had no appointment, Sanderson made time for him. Luke explained his newest investment opportunity and that a location for the bookstore needed to be found quickly.

"In a fashionable area. I'm not worried about the rent." He described the dimensions he needed, based upon what Caroline had revealed she required, and added that if a place for the tearoom was available next door, the size of the bookstore could be slightly smaller.

"I don't care if it's an existing bookstore or somewhere large enough to start a new business. Time is of the essence," he concluded.

Mr. Sanderson nodded. "I understand, Lord Mayfield, and I may have exactly what you are looking for. A client of mine recently passed. His widow is ridding herself of all of his rental properties and retiring to the country. I have an appointment in half an hour but I am free from two o'clock on. Might I show you and your investors the property then?"

"Place us on your calendar, Sanderson. Give me the address and I'll meet you at two with Lady Caroline and possibly the other gentlemen involved in this venture."

"Very good, sir."

Luke left the solicitor's offices. Since it was close to eleven, he doubted Caroline would be finished. He decided to go to White's, where he hoped to find Evan and Alex. Both men were there, reading the paper and drinking coffee.

"Just the two I needed to see," he said, taking a seat. "We're going to see where I believe Evie's Bookstore and Tearoom will be located."

Alex grinned. "Give us the details, man."

Luke told them first about the property and then how he'd stolen away Mrs. Withers from Catarina.

"You're lucky Catarina was entertaining," Evan said. "She never would have agreed to give up her cook under different circumstances."

"She must really want to hold on to this duke," Alex said. "I wonder who it is."

"I don't know or care," Luke said. "Let's order some luncheon and then go to Jeremy's. Hopefully, the ladies will be through with their shopping by then and Caroline will be free to accompany us to view the prospective property."

They ate and discussed their new investment. Evan wanted the bookstore to carry a large stock of military history.

"Of course you would," Alex teased. "You're a former military officer, Major Merrick."

"And gardening books for the ladies," Evan said. "Rachel is fond of gardening. Architecture, as well."

"Don't forget if it's to be a true success, Caroline will need to stock plenty of romance novels," Alex reminded them. "I found one of Leah's the other day and opened to where she'd placed a bookmark." He rolled his eyes. "You wouldn't believe what my wife had been reading."

Luke laughed. "I'm sure whatever it was, it livened up your time in the bedroom."

"If every woman in London read what Leah reads, there would be far more satisfied husbands," Alex said. "I speak from experience."

They finished their luncheon and left the club, ascending into Luke's waiting carriage. He hoped the property was as promising as Sanderson made it seem. More than anything, Luke wanted to please Caroline. As they journeyed through the teeming streets of London, he thought back to last night when he'd spontaneously taken her hand after Jeremy's toast. Merely joining their hands together had affected him deeply. He'd also seen desire in her eyes, probably something new and unexpected to her. He doubted she had much experience with men. She'd never made her come-out. She'd lived with her aunt in Boston and worked in her bookstore and had put in even longer hours once her aunt passed. It wouldn't have left much time for a social life.

Luke wondered if Caroline had even been kissed—and decided she hadn't. The thought pleased him immensely. He planned to be the first man to kiss her.

And the last.

# CHAPTER TEN

THE DUCHESS LED Caroline to the dining room. The small dining room, she noted, still thinking the room quite large to be classified as small. A man wandered about it, his hands in his pockets. He moved their way when he spotted them. She was immediately drawn to his merry, blue eyes and open, friendly face.

"Lady Caroline, may I present you to Mr. John Bellows," Catherine said. "Mr. Bellows, this is Lady Caroline Andrews."

"I'm delighted to meet you, Lady Caroline." The man looked fondly at the duchess and bowed. "It's always a pleasure, Your Grace."

"Come, luncheon is awaiting us," Catherine said, taking her place at the head of the table and motioned for them to sit on either side of her.

Within moments, soup appeared, along with hot bread. The aroma of the freshly-baked bread caused Caroline's mouth to water.

"I asked Mr. Bellows here because I wanted you to meet my publisher."

Caroline gave the man a warm smile. "I owned a bookstore in Boston until recently."

"Ah, I have a cousin who lives there. He paints portraits. Have you heard of Winston Warren by any chance?"

"I have. Though I've never met your cousin, I've seen his work. My aunt, Evangeline, commissioned Mr. Warren to paint her husband. He was an American sea captain. The portrait hung in her bookstore, which she left to me. When I decided to return to England once the war concluded, I sold the store. I left Captain Morton's portrait behind. It hung in a place of honor at Morton's Book Shop. I thought it should remain."

"What a small world," Bellows exclaimed. "It's always nice to meet someone who loves books."

"I certainly do. Enough to open another bookstore here in London," she said.

"Will you specialize in selling any particular type of book? Fiction? Children's literature? You know, my publishing company sells a large variety."

"I didn't know that."

"Mr. Bellows bought my very first book. His grandchildren love my stories," Catherine said. "How many do you have again?"

"We're up to ten with another two on the way," he said proudly. "My grandchildren begged for C. E. Lawford stories from the beginning. I knew buying Lady Catherine's books would be a good investment because of how entertained my grandchildren were by them."

"C. E. Lawford?" Caroline asked. "You're C. E. Lawford? We carried your books in Boston. Aunt Evie was despondent when the war began because we could no longer get shipments of them. They were our best selling children's stories."

"I wrote under that pen name when I first began," Catherine said. "I'm Catherine Elizabeth and my maiden name was Crawford. Lawford was close to that. I didn't know if my writing would be acceptable to the *ton*, which is why I wrote under a pen name in the beginning."

"And now they gobble up your books," Mr. Bellows said. "His Grace encouraged Her Grace not only to keep writing but to publish under her true name. I'm happy to say that the Duchess of Everton's books are not only my biggest sellers for children but they comprise my most popular books overall. Everyone in the *ton* and beyond wants their children to read what Her Grace has written."

"I'm eager to read the ones you've authored that I've missed," Caroline said.

"I find children to have active imaginations. They enjoy that I usually write about animals who speak just as people do," Catherine said. "Even my own children read my books, though I've never given any to them. That is Merrifield's doing. He seems to buy my books by the dozens and gifts them to our children and others. You will meet him soon. He's always underfoot. A quite likeable gentleman. Rachel's hoping to help marry him and Luke off."

Caroline's belly tightened. She had no idea Luke was ready to marry. Why should she? She'd only just met him. They'd talked mostly about her new business. She knew little to nothing about his personal life although she'd met members of his family. It wasn't any concern of hers that Rachel wanted to play matchmaker for her brother.

*Then why did the thought of him marrying make her heart ache?*

They continued with their meal. Mr. Bellows told some amusing stories about the publishing business. Caroline decided to take advantage of the opportunity before her as they began eating their dessert.

"Mr. Bellows, in my research, I've discovered that some publishing houses in London actually run bookstores and circulating libraries, stocking them with their own books. Do you have any affiliations with local bookstores?"

He shook his head. "No. I provide copies of books to all the ones that order from me. Why?"

"Maybe it would be to our advantage to come up with an agreement that would be of mutual benefit."

Intrigue lit his eyes. "Go on."

"I'm sure most—if not all—bookstores in London carry the latest books authored by the duchess. What if... we hit upon an elite arrangement where your publishing house allowed my bookstore to be the first to stock any book written by her? I'm not asking for exclusive rights to carry her books, just the opportunity to be the first bookseller in the city to offer them for a short period of time. It would certainly draw customers to my shop. It might even result in increased sales for you. Then, say after a month or so, you would make her books available to other bookstores in the city. What do you say?"

"That's a fascinating idea, Lady Caroline. One that would be easy to manage. What about outside of London, though? I wouldn't want to limit my sales in other places."

"That would be up to you, Mr. Bellows, to keep in place your current arrangements. I'm merely looking for a way to set Evie's Bookstore and Tearoom apart from other establishments."

"And you say a month. No more than that?"

"That would be an adequate amount of time to draw clients in, I believe."

"Then we have a deal," he said, offering her his hand. She shook it as he said, "I'll give you the name of my solicitor and he can meet with yours. In fact, I think the both of us should also be at this meeting. I'm not one to leave details to others."

"Let me concentrate on where my establishment will be located and then we can meet to draw up the papers." Caroline looked to Catherine. "Is that agreeable with you?"

She laughed. "Anything to sell more books. Jeremy and I donate all the profits to several orphanages in the area."

They finished eating and Mr. Bellows left them, eager to get back to work. Caroline promised he would hear from her within the next week so they could arrange their meeting.

After he left, Catherine embraced her enthusiastically. "You have a marvelous mind for business, Caroline Andrews."

"She does?" a familiar voice asked.

Caroline turned and saw Luke coming toward them. "I saw Mr. Bellows leaving," he said. "What have the three of you been up to?"

She started to speak and he held up a hand. "Do you have any more engagements today?"

"None that I'm aware of."

"Good. I think I've found a home for Evie's and I've already hired two delightful cooks to provide goods for the tearoom. Evan and Alex are waiting in the carriage, hoping you could accompany us to view the site. You can tell us all about your conversation with Bellows on the way."

"I'd be delighted to see it. And hear about these cooks. I didn't know you'd be hiring employees for me, though." Caroline didn't want any man, much less her three investors, to take over from her.

"You may hire all the rest. Someone to manage the teahouse and take customers' orders. Clerks to stock the shelves and ring up purchases. I've made my contributions. I know good food. Mrs. Withers and her sister, Mrs. Baker, will delight you with their concoctions. The rest will be up to you."

She turned to Catherine. "Would you like to come along?"

"No, thank you. I want to spend some time with the children and I've some writing to do, as well. I'll be eager to hear about everything, though, as will Jeremy. If you're free, why don't we discuss everything over dinner tomorrow night?"

"That would be lovely," Caroline said.

"Good. I will invite your investors and their wives and we'll talk business and then pleasure. I'd love to get your input on the buffet I'm serving for the opening of the Season."

"I have a better idea, Catherine," Luke said. "Invite everyone to tea at my house tomorrow. I can have Mrs. Withers and Mrs. Baker bake a host of items for us to taste. It could help establish the menu Caroline wishes to use in the tearoom. After tea, we can come to your house if you wish or even stay at mine for dinner and conversation."

Catherine looked to Caroline. "Is that agreeable with you?"

"I'm eager to meet these two women and sample their goods. Having a large group test what they bake and provide feedback is a wonderful idea."

"Then I will send the notes now," Catherine said. "Tea at Luke's, followed by dinner here tomorrow night."

Luke held out his arm to Caroline. "Your chariot—and two other gladiators—await you."

She took his arm, tamping down the rush of emotion that went through her as they touched. Once again, she told herself she needed to put some distance between them. Not just physically, but emotionally. She was already becoming far too fond of Luke St. Clair. If this property turned out to be suitable, she would be swept up in so many details that she would have little time to spend with him, much less think about him.

But she could always dream about him.

LUKE MADE SURE he exited the carriage first so he could help Caroline from it. More and more, she consumed his every waking moment. It wasn't just her beauty. That was fleeting. It was her disposition and character. She was very much an optimist and he enjoyed being around someone so positive. Helping her with this project had given him something to look forward to. He didn't miss his usual haunts—and he certainly hadn't missed Catarina or any of his other lovers.

He realized he wanted Caroline to see him in the best light possible. Not as a bored member of the nobility but as someone bright and hardworking. Someone like she was. He was beginning to understand why Jeremy and Rachel thought of their spouses as their equals.

Luke wanted that kind of relationship with Caroline. Desperately.

He lifted her from the carriage, his hands easily spanning her waist, despite the fact that she wore a thick, plain cloak. Alex and Evan followed her out. All four of them turned slowly in a circle, observing the block and surrounding establishments.

"It has the plate glass windows that I requested," she noted. "They will make it easy to display books and wares from Madame Toufours' shop."

On the way there, Caroline had explained to the men her plan to offer the modiste's merchandise. Since the goods would be exclusive to Evie's—and since the modiste designed for the Duchess of Everton—the merchandise would move quickly. She'd also explained how she'd made an arrangement with Catherine's publisher so that Evie's would be the sole carrier of her children's books for the first month of their release. Luke found his admiration growing for her business sense and knew his friends felt the same way by their enthusiastic responses.

"Lord Mayfield!" called Sanderson as he stepped from a hackney.

Luke bent and said into Caroline's ear, "This is Sanderson, my solicitor. He helped find the property we're visiting."

When Sanderson joined them, Luke introduced everyone. He saw the way the solicitor eyed Caroline and didn't like it.

Moving slightly in front of her, he said evenly, "Tell us about the property and area, Sanderson. I hope you brought keys so we could see inside."

The solicitor received the unspoken message and didn't glance in Caroline's direction again. He indicated the position of several nearby, well-to-do shops and then explained how the entire row was for sale.

"Originally, four business were located here. As the leases began to run out, my client had recently passed. His widow wishes to leave London for a quieter life in the country. I feel you could get a very good deal here."

Caroline spoke up. "Please take us inside, Mr. Sanderson. And from now on, speak to me directly. I will be the proprietor and will pay the bulk of the money for the land and its buildings. These kind gentlemen are simply minor investors. I plan to make all of the decisions."

Luke saw Sanderson was taken aback but recovered quickly. "Of course, my lady. If you'll follow me."

He led them to the door in the center of the block and inserted a key.

"After you, Lady Caroline," the solicitor said.

She entered the building, Luke following closely behind.

"The windows allow good natural light but we would need additional lighting," she said.

Their party walked every inch of this store and Caroline began laying out plans aloud, telling them where she would place things. She asked to see the store to the east and decided it would be ideal for the tearoom, indicating where she would want part of a wall knocked down in order to allow bookstore patrons easy access to the tearoom. She showed the men where she would set up reading areas and how she would divide books.

"This area would be for books to be sold, both new and used. You'd be surprised how many people buy used books if they're in good condition. Over here would be all the shelves containing those that would be lent to subscribers."

"How will you know the difference?" Alex asked.

"I can request certain binding to be used. Clerks can also mark books accordingly. I have a plan in place. Don't worry. There won't be any confusion. If I hire the right staff with the correct knowledge, things will flow smoothly."

Caroline wanted to see the shop to the west as well. Once again, they went outside and into it.

"If I have enough funds, this could serve as a warehouse. Inventory could be delivered here. Catalogued and marked. Repairs to binding could occur. The space is small but could be extremely useful."

"What about the small store on the other side of the tearoom?" Evan said. "Ovens could be brought in there for baking and racks set up to cool the baked goods. Also, supplies such as sugar and flour could be kept there."

"That's an excellent idea, Evan." Caroline smiled broadly.

Luke wished he would have thought of that.

They returned to the main store and Sanderson looked at Caroline expectantly. "It does seem to meet all of your needs, my lady. Do you think you'd be interested in purchasing the entire row? You couldn't ask for a better neighborhood."

"What is the widow asking for the lot?" she asked.

Sanderson quoted her a price.

"Bloody hell," she murmured, endearing her even more to Luke. "I wasn't thinking to pay that much."

"Mayfair property doesn't come cheap," the solicitor pointed out. "My client is asking below market value because of her desire to leave London. If you don't snatch up the property, it will go quickly to another."

"I will offer ten percent less than the asking price," Caroline stated. "In cash. No banks need be involved. Surely, your client could put all that cash to good use?"

"You drive a hard bargain, my lady, but I will suggest to her that she accept your offer. I will go and see her now. I'd already sent a message that a prospective buyer was looking over the property this afternoon. She is expecting a report from me. If she agrees, I can draw up the papers and they can be signed first thing tomorrow morning."

"I'm agreeable to that, Mr. Sanderson," Caroline said.

"Very good then. I'll take my leave. You're welcomed to keep the keys and look around a bit longer if you choose. I can always collect them tomorrow if we cannot come to terms."

"Good day, Sanderson," Luke said. "Thanks for your help."

The solicitor left. Evan and Alex continued to wander about, discussing Caroline's ideas, and then Alex thought to measure the size of the other shops so they would know how much room they had to deal with for storage, ovens, and the tearoom itself. Luke preferred to stay by her side.

"Do you have enough funds for the sale?" he asked quietly once his friends had left.

"Barely. It will take almost everything I have, especially once I place my order for books and buy up stock from other local sellers. I will depend upon my investors to help with renovations. Removing walls. Paint and cleaning. Ordering furniture for the reading areas. Helping to pay the staff for the first few months. It will most likely take a year or more before I can turn a profit."

Disappointment flashed across her face. "I'd hoped there would be an upper floor. I'd planned to make those rooms into a home for Davy, Tippet, and me."

"Rachel and Evan are more than happy to host you indefinitely," he pointed out.

"I know. They have been most gracious. Still, I'd hoped I could do more."

Luke placed his hands on her shoulders. "You have accomplished more in a handful of days than most women do in a lifetime, Caroline. You are a force of nature. A woman to be reckoned with."

He saw how his words pleased her as a slow smile lit her face. Suddenly, the urge to kiss her proved greater than his willpower. Luke felt drawn to her mouth like a moth to a flame. Slowly, he moved toward her, giving her a chance to stop him.

She didn't.

# CHAPTER ELEVEN

C AROLINE KNEW THE instant Luke decided to kiss her. The air surrounding them changed, suddenly charged with energy. His emerald eyes darkened with hunger. His fingers tightened on her shoulders. As his mouth gradually sought hers, she knew he was giving her time to turn her head. To say no. To shrug away.

She did none of those.

She wanted this kiss. Her first kiss. She'd been drawn to Luke St. Clair since she'd seen him from a distance when she'd arrived in London. Caroline instinctively knew that this moment had been destined to come. She wasn't one to fight fate. Besides, her natural curiosity had her yearning to learn what it would be like for a man like Luke to kiss her.

And then he did.

It was nothing Caroline thought it would be. She thought a man pressed his lips to a woman's and, after a few moments, they separated. Luke's kiss was far different from her expectations.

First, his mouth hovered over hers, not touching it, merely building the anticipation between them. When he did make contact, he slowly brushed his lips against hers, increasing her longing. Then the exploration began. He would kiss her and then his tongue would come into play. Caroline had no idea tongues were involved in kissing but what Luke did caused her body to come alive. His tongue slowly outlined her mouth, causing her to shiver. He nipped lightly at her bottom lip and then licked away the sensation, soothing her. Her hands moved to his chest, her palms pressed flat against the hard mass.

Suddenly, he changed the game they played by dragging his tongue along the seam of her mouth, urging her to open to him. Caroline had no idea why but she trusted him enough to respond as he wished. His hands released her shoulders and moved up to cradle her face as his tongue entered her mouth.

*Heaven . . .*

The kiss now heated up considerably as his exploration continued. His tongue swept inside, tickling the roof of her mouth and gliding along her tongue. Her breasts grew heavy and she felt her nipples tightening. She latched on to his waistcoat to anchor her as she responded, allowing her tongue to mimic what he did. Luke emitted a low groan and his hands slid from her face and seized her waist, drawing her near.

He deepened the kiss, delving more into her, causing her heart to beat erratically and her bones to melt. If he hadn't held on to her, Caroline feared she would have puddled at his feet. His intoxicating cologne filled her senses. From her scalp to her toes, a tingling sensation erupted. The place between her legs tightened and began to pulsate.

*What was happening to her?*

She couldn't fall for him and be the woman she wanted to be. She wasn't a typical woman of the *ton*. Her experiences in America had changed her in ways too numerous to name. Her father losing all of his money and virtually turning his back on his family had also shaped her outlook. She didn't know if she could trust a man. Any man. Even one who held her so lovingly.

Caroline released her hold on Luke and nudged him away. Reluctantly, he broke the kiss and stared deep into her eyes. She saw raw need burning in them.

"This can't happen again," she said, her breathing rapid and shallow.

---

"Why?"

"I must focus on opening Evie's. It will be my livelihood. I can't throw away the opportunity I've been given to use Aunt Evie's inheritance. I don't want to disappoint my investors. I need to do this for myself."

He gave her a crooked smile, stealing her breath—and a bit of her heart.

"Don't you want more than a business, Caroline?"

Before she could answer him, Evan and Alex returned. She heard them come through the door and wheeled away from Luke, hurrying to meet them. Immediately, she peppered them with questions about the dimensions. Anything to ignore Luke and what had just happened between them.

"We can finish talking about business in the carriage," Luke told them and exited the store.

The three followed him after he locked the door. The footman saw them coming and set the stairs down and helped Caroline into the carriage. Evan followed behind her and took the seat next to her. She blew out a long breath, relieved that Luke wouldn't be sitting beside her.

Unfortunately, it proved worse because he sat opposite her. She averted her glance and focused on her other companions, who'd asked to be dropped back at their club.

"You should consult Rachel on the renovations you wish done," Evan volunteered. "She redid our London townhome and has experience directing a crew. I'm sure she can recommend a manager to you to oversee what little construction you need."

"I'm eager to share the details of today with my man of business," Alex said. He looked as gleeful as a small boy who'd stolen cookies from a jar without being caught.

"We haven't gained the property yet," she reminded them. "If Mr. Sanderson's client doesn't accept my offer, we will be back on the hunt again."

"She will," Evan said with confidence. "If she's that eager to leave London and you're offering all that cash, she won't have a choice. And Sanderson said it had just come on the market. You'll be the first bid. He'll encourage her to take it and save them both time."

"I should hear from him soon," she said. "He mentioned being able to sign papers in the morning. If so, I'd like all of you to be at the signing with your solicitors or business managers."

They pulled up at White's and the pair exited the carriage, Evan promising to see her later at home. He closed the door and she was left alone with Luke, who hadn't contributed to their conversation the entire ride. She averted her gaze and looked out the window, wondering if he would kiss her again. Wishing he would. Hoping he wouldn't because it would further complicate things between them.

When they arrived at the Merrick residence, he jumped from the carriage and handed her down.

"Let me see you in."

"That's not necessary," she said quickly.

He gave her a long look. "It is to me."

Reluctantly, she placed her hand on his forearm, knowing how her body would react. Even though her hands were covered by gloves and he wore both a shirt and coat, she could feel the heat generated between them. Idly, she wondered what it would be like to glide her gloveless fingertips up his bare arm. Heat filled her cheeks at the thought and she kept her head down, not wishing for him to see her blush.

Kent admitted them and after he closed the door he said, "Lady Caroline, a Mr. Morrow is waiting to speak to you. He knows he doesn't have an appointment but he was most insistent, claiming he has urgent business with you."

She could think of no business that would bring her in contact with her father's solicitor. He'd already gruffly booted her from her family home and let her know she had no rights to be there or the ability to take even a trinket to remind her of Mama or Cynthia. Yet something told her that it would be in her best interest to meet with the solicitor to hear what he had to say. Though he'd been rude during their only encounter, Caroline determined she would act with civility.

"Very well. I'll see him."

"He's in the small greeting parlor," the butler shared.

"I'm going with you," Luke said.

She nodded her acceptance, thankful that she wouldn't have to see Morrow on her own. She believed him to be one of those petty men who enjoyed running roughshod over women. She doubted he would be so tyrannical toward her with a peer of the realm present.

Kent led them to a small room off the foyer and Luke escorted her inside. Caroline saw Morrow pacing nervously. He looked up and started, seeing Luke with her.

"Mr. Morrow, I believe you requested to see me on some matter." The solicitor approached and she added, "This is Lord Mayfield." She didn't bother identifying her relationship with him.

Morrow nodded deferentially and said, "Lady Caroline, I bring interesting news to you. You know your father's title and country seat have reverted to the crown, while an estate sale was held yesterday in order to auction off the London property and all its contents."

"What does that have to do with me? You've told me that all monies will be used to pay off my father's debts and that my dowry was protected since it came from my mother and her marriage settlements. What more do we have to discuss?"

"Something most unusual occurred at the auction." Morrow presented her with a sheaf of papers, pressing them into her hands. "The first buyer became the only buyer," he continued. "A single offer was made for the residence and all its contents. This included everything on the grounds, even the coach and horses. Frankly, I've never seen anything like this during my many years of practice."

His lips twitched nervously. "The offer was so great that I immediately closed the sale. To have sold everything in one fell swoop is unheard of."

She frowned. "I still don't see what this process has to do with me, Mr. Morrow."

"The documents you hold give you the answer, my lady. The papers I drew up did not name the purchaser, who wishes to remain anonymous, as the new owner. Instead, he demanded that *you* be named on the deed."

Caroline's eyes dropped to the pages she held. She skimmed the first one and quickly saw that Morrow told the truth. The property her father's house sat upon, along with the residence and everything contained within it, were hers. The notion flabbergasted her.

*Who could this anonymous benefactor be?*

"Thank you, Mr. Morrow," she said, trying to keep both her hands and voice from shaking.

"If you have any further questions, my lady, please do not hesitate to contact me." He withdrew a key from his pocket. "You'll need this."

The solicitor left the room, closing the door behind him. Now that they were alone, Caroline turned to Luke.

"Are you responsible for this?" she asked.

He shook his head, dumbfounded. "I had no part in this. I am as clueless as you appear to be. Though I must say, my admiration has grown for you, Caroline. Any other woman of the *ton* would have fainted at the news."

The last thing she needed was for him to admire her. She needed to put distance between them.

Before she flung herself at him and begged him to kiss her senseless.

THE FIRST THING Caroline needed to do was locate Stinch. In the whirlwind of activity, she had neglected to write a reference for the butler. She only hoped he would be willing to work for her in a different capacity. She'd sent Luke home and gone to her room to write a message, asking the former butler to come to the Merrick residence to speak with her. She rang for a maid and asked that a footman see immediately to its delivery and then sat down and read through the papers Morrow had left with her.

It was all there. She owned everything. She had a place for her and Davy to live. Tippet, too. He could return to sleeping with her, warming her when she longed for someone else to be doing that very job. No, she wouldn't think of him. She couldn't. She had too much to do and he would never be a part of her life.

She didn't have the funds to live as grandly as her father had, though. Too much was tied up in her new venture. For now, she would limit the rooms she used. A bedchamber. A small parlor for seeing others and possibly dining in. The kitchen. That would be all she required. From the state of the foyer, she imagined many of the other rooms had already been stripped of their contents and those items sold. This way, she wouldn't have to refurnish them but instead live frugally.

Caroline didn't need a lady's maid. She hadn't had one since she'd left London. Bathing and dressing herself and arranging her hair were simple tasks. She would need a single maid to clean and wash. A cook to feed them. Both of those servants could live elsewhere. If she only used a handful of rooms, it would be possible. She wouldn't do any entertaining. If she watched things carefully, she could manage to pay her very small staff.

The time might come where she would consider selling the house. Whatever profit she made could then be used to find rooms to live in. The rest could be poured back into Evie's. That would be much more practical. She would have to take that into serious consideration.

Caroline decided to clear her head and walk to the stables to check on Davy. Brimley, the head groom, gave her a ready smile.

"Come to see young Davy again, my lady?"

"Yes, if that's possible."

"He's grooming a horse in the next to last stall on the left," the groom said helpfully.

She walked down the long row of stalls and smiled when she heard Davy whistling. Glancing over the closed half-door, she spied him as he combed the black beauty inside.

"Hello, Davy," she said.

The boy stopped whistling and grinned up at her. "Hello, my lady. How have you been?"

"I'm doing well. I came to see how you are getting along."

His eyes lit up. "As much as I hated the sea, I love horses. They're ever so good and calm. Mr. Brimley says I'm the best lad who's ever worked under him."

"You've always been a hard worker, Davy, no matter what the task."

"I'm practicing my reading every night, Lady Caroline. There's another boy who likes to read. We do it together."

"I'd enjoy if we had another lesson together soon," she told him. "How about tomorrow? I'll speak to Mr. Brimley about it."

"As long as it doesn't interfere with my work in the stables, my lady," Davy said seriously. "I can't let Mr. Brimley down." He paused. "I should get back to work now."

"Very well. I'll see you tomorrow."

Caroline found the groom and arranged a time for Davy to meet with her.

"The boy's right bright, my lady," Brimley told her. "He's lucky to have you in his corner."

"Davy thinks quite a bit of you, too, Mr. Brimley," she told the groom.

Returning to the house, Caroline drew up a list of the types of books she wished to carry and the furniture she would use to create the small reading circles for patrons to use. She then wrote a new list of meetings that must occur. With solicitors to firm up the sale of the building. With Mr. Bellows to draw up contracts for not only ordering books from his publishing house but to exclusively sell Catherine's newest book for a short time. With Madame Toufours to narrow down what merchandise would be carried at Evie's. There was so much to do. Instead of feeling overwhelmed, though, Caroline felt invigorated.

A maid knocked and entered, informing her that Stinch had arrived. Eagerly, she went downstairs and greeted the butler.

"Have a seat," she told him. "I haven't written your reference yet and I want to tell you why."

He looked perplexed but sat, waiting for her to speak.

"I'm going to open a bookstore, Stinch. I helped run my aunt's bookstore in Boston and took over management of it upon her death."

"That's quite impressive, Lady Caroline," the butler said, still looking confused as to why she was sharing this information with him.

"My bookstore is going to be quite large. It will also have a tea-room next door. I fear it will be too much for me to handle all of the day-to-day things. While I wish to be in charge of the accounts and ordering, I will need someone I trust to oversee the employees at both establishments. To draw up their schedules. To supervise them on the job."

She smiled. "I can think of no better person than you, Stinch, to take on this position. You are the most organized person of my acquaintance and I have known you from the cradle. Would you be interested in changing professions? It wouldn't be quite what you've done in the past but it would require a great deal of responsibility and managing capabilities."

Stinch fairly glowed hearing her praise. "My lady, I can think of nothing I'd like to do more."

She asked how much he'd been paid, remembering that he'd mentioned their servants not receiving any wages during the last several months of her father's life. He told her and she offered him a substantial increase, which he found more than acceptable. They spoke of some of his acquaintances that could possibly serve as book clerks and he suggested two of their former maids who hadn't yet found work who would be excellent as servers in the tearoom.

Kent arrived with a letter on a silver tray and Caroline opened it, hoping it was the news she expected. She read through the note and looked to Stinch.

"My offer for the Mayfair property has been accepted. I will be signing the papers tomorrow morning," she informed him. "I'll give you the address. Speak to those you have in mind to employ and we can meet the day after tomorrow at nine o'clock so I may interview them."

Caroline waited until the door closed behind Stinch and collapsed into the nearest chair. Her vision would become a reality. She'd returned to London and found death and despair. Only days later, thanks to the new friends she'd made and the investors supporting her, she'd bought a large property and would open her own bookstore in the most fashionable part of town. Moreover, her childhood home had miraculously been restored to her by some unnamed angel.

She should be ecstatic.

"I am happy," she stubbornly told herself.

But Caroline knew she would be overjoyed—if the Earl of Mayfield kissed her again.

# CHAPTER TWELVE

S UDDENLY, CAROLINE REALIZED she had no solicitor. All thoughts of kisses fled her mind as her heart began racing in panic. She left the parlor as the grandfather clock in the foyer chimed six o'clock. Rachel usually served dinner at seven. Quickly, Caroline went upstairs to retrieve her cloak. She would turn to the one man who could give her a solid recommendation.

The Duke of Everton.

Without telling anyone where she went, Caroline left the Merrick residence and briskly walked the two blocks to the duke's residence. Barton, the butler, answered her knock.

"Good evening, Lady Caroline. Her Grace did not tell me you were expected." He waved her inside.

"Actually, I'm here to see His Grace," she said. "Is he available?"

Ever the British butler, no surprise showed on the servant's face. "His Grace is in his study. I'm sure he would make time for you, my lady. If you'll follow me."

Barton led her to a room on the ground floor and knocked.

"Come," a deep voice said.

The butler opened the door. "Your Grace, Lady Caroline Andrews is here to see you."

The duke rose. "Please, come in, Lady Caroline."

She did, feeling a bit of trepidation at the air of authority the duke projected. It still amazed her how much the St. Clair siblings resembled one another, with their coal black hair and lively green eyes.

"Have a seat." After she did, he seated himself behind his desk and said, "My duchess told me of the deal you struck with Mr. Bellows." He gave her a smile. "A very clever move. Customers clamor for her books as it is. Having access to them before other booksellers do will certainly set your bookstore apart."

"Thank you, Your Grace. I have also arranged with the duchess' modiste, Madame Toufours, to carry a selection of her goods on the premises. I'm hoping that, too, will distinguish Evie's from other establishments."

She saw admiration in his eyes. "It's nice to be in the company of such an astute businesswoman."

She acknowledged his compliment with a smile.

"What brings you here?" he asked.

"Things moved more rapidly than I expected, and I find I'm in dire need of a solicitor. I'm closing on a Mayfair property tomorrow morning and lack representation. Evan had suggested I use his solicitor but he is one of my investors. I need a man I can trust that will solely represent my business interests."

"A wise move on your part. Who found the property?"

"Mr. Sanderson, Luke's solicitor. He also represents the seller and I don't want to use him. It would be too great a conflict of interest in my opinion."

"I agree. And you've come to me for a recommendation."

"Yes, Your Grace. Catherine shared with me how shrewd you are in business matters. I believe a recommendation from you would suit my interests."

"Then I will suggest you use my own man. Higgins represents me in all matters, both business and personal. I am his sole client but since you have only the one enterprise, I think he would be willing to take you on as a client."

Caroline was stunned. "Are you certain, Your Grace?"

"Absolutely. What time will the deed be signed over?"

"In Mr. Sanderson's office tomorrow morning at ten."

"Then if you will allow it, my coach will pick you up at hour before. That will give you time with Higgins so that you may ask him whatever you wish and fill him in on the details of the transaction and your other proposals."

"That would be agreeable," she said, her spirits boosted.

"Might I attend? I have no role as an investor but I'm sure you'll wish for Higgins to see the property once it's in your possession. I'd like to view it, as well."

"You are most welcomed to come," she said with enthusiasm.

"I have another suggestion. Matthew Proctor serves as my secretary and man of business. With the Season about to start, you will be busy attending many events, as well as trying to launch your bookstore. Would you like for me to loan Matthew to you?"

"That won't be necessary. An hour ago, I hired my father's former butler to manage both the bookstore and tearoom. He will deal with the workers while I concentrate on inventory and managing the ledgers. We are both very organized individuals and will work well together."

The duke frowned. "That's still a lot to accomplish while the Season begins."

"I don't plan on attending that many events," Caroline revealed. "I will go to some in order to get a sense of what women are reading and what they might purchase from Madame Toufours. Once the *ton* realizes I am a businesswoman, I doubt I'll receive as many invitations to events. By then, I will have the information I need, though."

"But what of the social aspect of the Season?"

"If you're referring to my trying to find a husband, I won't be placing myself on the Marriage Mart, Your Grace."

One eyebrow rose. "Why not?"

"Although I have been gone from society for several years, people will still know I am the Earl of Templeton's daughter. From what I've heard since I returned, my father had huge gambling debts and a less than savory reputation. I doubt any bachelors would seek my hand in marriage. Besides, I am already three and twenty. Most women my age are already wed."

"Catherine was the same age when we wed."

That startled her. "Truly?"

"Yes. She cared for her ill father for many years. He was injured in a carriage accident. As you can see, we are most happy together and the proud parents of several children."

She shook her head. "The inheritance from my aunt will be used to establish my bookstore and tearoom, leaving me with little to live on. In order for it to become a success, I feel all of my waking hours will be devoted to my business. I won't have time to consider a family, even if a gentleman did wish to marry me."

His emerald eyes searched hers. "If I may give you a last bit of advice, Lady Caroline, I would ask that you not close the door to love. I know I am a better man in every aspect—even in my business dealings—because I have Catherine and our children in my life. You, too, may find everything in your life enhanced if love comes your way."

She rose to her feet and he followed suit. "I will keep that in mind, Your Grace. Now, I must return to Rachel's so I can send messages to my investors, notifying them of tomorrow's closing."

The duke escorted her into the foyer. "Where is your maid?"

"I came on my own."

"I suppose that's a part of the independent streak you gained while in America. London is a large city and, unfortunately, it can be a dangerous one, especially when it grows dark. I will see you home."

"Caroline? I didn't know you were here," Catherine said as she came down the stairs.

She went to her husband and he kissed her. Not the all-consuming kiss that Caroline had witnessed between them but a brief, tender one that bespoke of their love. A pang of jealousy hit her, knowing she would never have what this couple did.

"I came to seek business advice from His Grace," she said.

"I'm going to escort Lady Caroline back to Merrick's," the duke said. "Could you ask Cook to hold dinner for half an hour?"

"It's an excellent night for a stroll. I'll accompany you." Looking to Barton, who'd appeared magically, she told the butler, "Please see that Cook is informed that we'll dine a little later than usual."

"Yes, Your Grace." He opened the door for them and the trio went outside.

It only took a few minutes to reach the marquess' townhome and Caroline thanked them both for seeing her home.

"I'm looking forward to seeing your establishment, my lady," the duke said.

"And tea tomorrow," Catherine added. "I hear that we're going to be sampling items that will be served at Evie's Bookstore and Tea-room."

"Yes, that's what Luke has planned," Caroline confirmed. "Until tomorrow."

LUKE HAD SPENT most of his day disappointed. He'd arrived at his sister's in time for breakfast, with Alex in tow, assuming they would all ride to Sanderson's office to sign the papers on the Mayfair property.

Instead, he'd learned that Caroline would go separately from her three investors. She informed them that she would be meeting with her new solicitor on the way to Sanderson's office, explaining how she didn't want to entangle any of her interests with theirs by using one of their three solicitors. While Luke understood—and actually agreed it was a wise move—he'd wanted to ride across London with her for selfish reasons.

All he'd thought about was their kiss in the bookstore. He'd been right in assuming she'd never been kissed. He'd also been correct in thinking that a passionate woman lay buried within her. Though inexperienced, she quickly caught on. He knew, with time, she would come to understand her sensual nature. Even now, he could still taste her. He wanted Caroline Andrews more than he'd ever wanted any other woman.

Now, his job was to convince her that she needed him.

Luke didn't think she'd allow any more kisses, at least for now. She'd totally ignored him after the one they'd shared, though he'd been pleased when she allowed him to stay with her while she met with Morrow yesterday afternoon. He was still stumped as to who her benefactor might be. It would take someone with great wealth to sweep in and purchase an entire London townhome and all of its contents. The thought caused jealousy to flare within him.

If kisses wouldn't be allowed, he would have to reach Caroline through other means. Obviously, that meant her bookstore and tearoom. She was investing almost everything she'd inherited in these two businesses. If they succeeded, she would be happy. If Luke helped her thrive in this venture, it would be to their mutual benefit.

Thus, his presence now with Mrs. Withers and Mrs. Baker.

Luke had told the cooks what they prepared for today's afternoon tea would be a preview of the teahouse's menu.

"Your audience will be my family. They all are lovers of good food and highly critical. On top of that, you'll be meeting Lady Caroline for the first time. I want her to know I made the right decision in hiring the both of you."

"We'll do you proud, Lord Mayfield," Mrs. Baker said.

He'd already sampled a few items they'd baked this morning and found all to his liking but asked, "Could you make another chocolate roll and add walnuts to it? I'm fond of nuts and think others would like the addition, as well."

"Of course, my lord," Mrs. Baker told him. "I'm a nut lover myself."

Mrs. Withers cleared her throat. "I know you said no sandwiches but I believe if Evie's becomes as popular as I think it will, a full tea service will be desired. We should be prepared for that."

"That makes sense." He consulted his pocket watch. "We have only an hour before all arrive, though."

"That's not a problem, Lord Mayfield." Mrs. Withers grinned. "Bessie and I have prepared enough sandwiches for a small army. Just in case you agreed to my proposal."

"You are too clever for me, Mrs. Withers."

The cook blushed at his praise and then her eyes grew wide. She and Mrs. Baker suddenly curtseyed, causing Luke to look over his shoulder. His grandmother stood there, coolly surveying the area.

"Cor, I didn't know you'd be coming. I thought you didn't arrive in town for a few more days."

Luke went to embrace her but the dowager duchess held up a hand to stop him.

"I don't want flour all over my gown, Grandson." She looked him up and down. "When did you start baking?"

He glanced down and saw flour dusted all along the front of him. "I've been supervising. And tasting."

"The tasting part doesn't surprise me," she said dryly. "Why the other? Jeremy told me a horde is expected and that today's tea is important, which is why I came early to speak with you."

He dusted off his hands and placed them on her shoulders, brushing a kiss on her cheek.

"Allow me to change and then I'll tell you why."

Retreating to his bedchamber, he tossed off everything above the waist as his valet redressed him. Making his way to the drawing room, he found it empty and went back to the kitchen. His grandmother was sampling a macaroon.

"The secret to a delicious macaroon is adding a few drops of rose water," she said. "I also find a handful of slivered almonds to be a nice addition. Prepare a new batch but keep them separate from these. We'll let those at tea decide which they prefer."

"Cor, let's leave our cooks to the kitchen," Luke suggested. "Come, let me catch you up on all you've missed."

He brought her to the drawing room and made sure she had a cushion placed behind her back. Though still in good health at seventy-five, sometimes she tired if she stood for too long and her back would begin to ache.

Once she was settled, his grandmother got to the point. "Who is this Lady Caroline that Jeremy mentioned? He told me it would be her and the family for tea today."

Luke grinned. "She's the woman I plan to wed."

# CHAPTER THIRTEEN

AROLINE SPENT AN hour with Davy, amazed at the improvement
he'd made since their last session. The boy told her he read
aloud every night with his friend once they'd finished the day's tasks
and she encouraged him to continue the practice. She gave him two
new books to share with the other stable lad and then changed her
gown for tea before joining Rachel and Evan in the carriage. Once they
arrived, Evan escorting the two women to Luke's front door. A second
carriage pulled up and out spilled Jeremy, Catherine, Leah, and Alex.
They joined the others just as the butler admitted them.

Leah linked her arm through Caroline's. "I was visiting my sister
before we came. All we could talk about was your new bookstore and
tearoom. We wanted to come early. In fact, Cor already came."

"Cor?" Caroline asked, stumped at the unusual name. "Who is
that?"

"Our grandmother," Rachel replied as the butler led them upstairs
to the drawing room. "She is the Dowager Duchess of Everton and a
force within the *ton*. If Cor supports you, the *ton* will follow suit."

Nerves rippled through Caroline. She needed her ventures to become a success. Not only did she have investors that would need to be
repaid but it was important to earn enough money to put back into the
bookstore and pay her own bills. What if everything boiled down to
one elderly woman giving a yea or nay to society?

As she entered with the large group, she immediately spotted the dowager duchess seated in a large wing chair. Luke had pulled his own chair close and talked animatedly with his grandmother.

"Come and meet her," Rachel said, pulling Caroline in the direction of the woman who had the best posture she'd ever seen.

"Cor, this is Lady Caroline Andrews," Rachel said breezily. "She's about to open a fashionable bookstore and tearoom. We're going to be talking about it over tea."

Dark eyes scrutinized Caroline carefully. The older woman had to be at least sixty. Possibly, even seventy, yet her timeless beauty shone through as she smiled kindly at Caroline.

"My dear, come and sit with me." She reached out her hands and took Caroline's. "I'm delighted to meet you. Call me Cor. Everyone does." She turned to her grandson. "Luke, give Lady Caroline your seat. We must become acquainted."

"Of course, Cor," he said smoothly and offered her his seat. "I'm off to check on tea."

She sat and the older woman said, "Tell me why you want to go into business, my dear. It's not every day a woman of the *ton* chooses to do so."

"I'm not your average society woman, Cor," Caroline said. "Living in America changed my perspective on a few things. I was also influenced by my Aunt Evie."

"Evie?" Cor mulled the name over. "Was she Evangeline Andrews by any chance?"

"Yes. Only family called her Evie, or so I've been led to believe."

Cor patted Caroline's hand. "Evangeline Andrews caused a bit of a scandal in her day. She was a most beautiful girl. Danced like a dream. All the men fawned over her. Let me think." The old woman frowned, her lips pursing. "Ah, yes. She broke her engagement to some silly fool. I heard she ran off with an American."

She nodded. "Yes, that's my aunt. She married a sea captain and became Evie Morton. They never had children and when Captain

Morton passed, she sold his ship and with the proceeds opened a bookstore. That kept her plenty busy."

"So you went to visit this aunt?"

"I did. I even worked in her bookstore while England and America were at war." Caroline quickly explained the rest of her short history and how she'd come home with the dream to do the same in London.

"Luke tells me you're adding a tearoom?"

"Yes. To me, reading and tea go hand in hand. It seemed natural to offer a bite of something sweet to eat with a cup of tea. Also, if I can attract women to my bookstore and circulating library, they might decide to meet and shop first and then stay for tea afterward. Many conversations have occurred over a cup of tea. Men have their clubs. Women have circulating libraries. Evie's Bookstore and Tearoom will offer a chance to socialize and purchase a book, as well as exclusive items from Madame Toufours."

"Catherine's modiste?" Cor asked, her eyes lighting up. "Oh, tell me about this part."

Caroline outlined the details of the arrangement and included drawing buyers in with an autograph session from the Duchess of Everton and her latest book.

"You are a shrewd businesswoman, Lady Caroline," the dowager duchess noted. "I would like to see this bookstore's location if I'm going to recommend it to my friends."

"I want to come, too," Leah begged. "I know Alex has already been there."

"You'd better include Rachel and me in that invitation," Catherine said. Looking at Cor, she added, "I'm thinking about doing a reading from my latest book. Mr. Bellows is working to have it published by the time Caroline's shop opens. Can you imagine how many sales will occur that will benefit our orphanages?"

Luke appeared with two women. They rolled tea carts in.

"Time to sample and give your opinions," he said, directing the women where to place the carts.

Caroline saw everything needed to make tea on the first tea caddy, including a hot water urn and heater and a plethora of teacups. It surprised her that three teapots had been brought, though.

"We have three blends for everyone to try today," Luke said. "Catherine, will you serve as hostess for me? The blends have already been mixed for you."

"Certainly." Immediately, she poured hot water into all three teapots in order for it to sit a few minutes so the pots were warmed.

After Luke described the various blends and why he'd chosen them, Catherine poured the water into a waste bowl on the lower shelf and placed a different blend into each pot, following it with boiling water.

"While we're waiting for the tea to steep, I'd like you to meet the cooks who will run Evie's Bookstore and Teahouse. This is Mrs. Withers and her sister, Mrs. Baker." Luke introduced everyone present to the servants, saving Caroline for last.

"This is Lady Caroline, your employer."

"I am pleased to meet you both," she said enthusiastically. "I also cannot wait to try what I see on the other caddy. Would you tell us about what we will be served, Mrs. Withers?"

"We've prepared an assortment of various sweets—cakes, scones, pastries, and biscuits. Lord Mayfield had us try different variations on some items, such as the chocolate roll. You'll find one with nuts and one without. Everything on this tea caddy is what we'd like to place on the menu to start, with your approval, my lady."

"I'm definitely in favor of nuts," Alex said. "In chocolate? Even better."

"I see sandwiches on the bottom level," Rachel said.

Mrs. Baker stepped up. "Normally, sandwiches need a knife and fork to eat them. My sister convinced Lord Mayfield that you also needed to sample some of her sandwiches. They're not in the usual triangle. These are crustless sandwiches cut into long strips. They are to be eaten with your fingers."

"An excellent idea," Leah said. "Oh, I can't wait. Are we ready to begin?"

"Almost," Catherine said as she strained out the tea leaves and poured cups from the first pot. Rachel helped pass them around while Leah and Luke made sure everyone had a plate for their sandwiches and sweets.

Caroline asked the two cooks to remain in order for them to hear the comments. "We can all learn from what's said today. My eyes have already taken in this feast and I can tell you I'm most pleased."

"Lord Mayfield hoped you would be," Mrs. Withers said.

"I'm glad I trusted his lordship with this part," she said, smiling at the women she'd spend a great deal of time with over the next few years if all went according to plan.

She not only ate a sample of everything but tried cups of each blend of tea. She listened carefully as everyone discussed the food and which items were their favorites. It surprised her when Mrs. Withers and Mrs. Baker wheeled in two more carts filled with food. Besides more cakes and tarts, they'd brought a variety of cheeses and fruit.

Everyone present ate until they thought they might burst. Jeremy and Evan favored the fairy cakes with butter icing and the macaroons, which Caroline learned Cor had instructed the cooks to make with a bit of rose water. Alex liked the nutty chocolate roll and Leah preferred the lemon-cheese tarts and trifle. Catherine and Rachel liked the cakes best, especially the currant, walnut, and sponge ones.

"We've heard from everyone but you, Cor," Luke said. "Do you have a favorite sweet or sandwich?"

The elderly duchess smiled. "You know my sweet tooth, Luke. I enjoyed the pound cake and chocolate roll best, though the macaroons were most delicious."

Caroline asked them to rank which items were a favorite with everyone, calling for pen and ink so that each item was assigned a number rank.

"These top choices will go directly onto the menu. The others with a lower rank I'll allow Mrs. Withers and Mrs. Baker to tweak a bit. We may go with a feature of the week or month and only offer certain sweets for a limited time."

"Excellent idea," Jeremy said. "What people can't get, they'll want even more. You could even advertise when a beloved item is coming to draw in a crowd."

"Do you think we should stick with sweets or include sandwiches from the start?" she asked the group, noting Mrs. Withers leaning forward with interest.

"These sandwiches were by far superior to most," Luke declared. "I think at least a half-dozen should go on the menu."

Once again, they discussed which sandwiches they preferred, using Caroline's method to rank their favorites. After much discussion, she had a list of every item to carry. They all agreed serving a variety of teas would be another draw, though Caroline expressly wanted it limited to no more than three blends.

"If we carry too many selections, it will cause confusion. Some customers will become too fussy."

"I like the idea of choice—but not too much choice," Leah said. "Men will eat or drink whatever you put in front of them but women like the idea of picking from a variety offered."

"I agree," Catherine said. "Oh, this has been most exciting. I'm afraid, though, that none of you will want dinner."

Everyone agreed that dinner on top of everything they'd eaten would be too much.

When Caroline saw that things were going to break up, she gave Mrs. Withers the list and said, "Lord Mayfield will help you order the supplies you'll need to be up and running in three weeks. You'll need to also let him know the number of ovens and racks to be purchased.

In fact, I'll have him bring you to the property tomorrow so you can look over the space."

The cooks thanked her and she told Luke what task she'd assigned him.

"I want to contribute something," Evan said. "After all, I'm also an investor."

Caroline thought a moment. "You told me that Rachel was in charge of the renovation of your townhome. Why don't you go with her to the site tomorrow and explain my vision of the place? You know where I wish to put shelving and furniture, as well as where the door needs to be cut and a few walls knocked down."

"I can do that," Evan agreed, smiling at his wife.

"You'd allow me such a huge role?" Rachel asked.

"Of course. I trust you. And I only have so much time and quite a bit left to do."

"When do wish to open?" Evan asked.

"My goal is three weeks from now. A month at the latest. That's a couple of weeks into the Season. By then, I will have attended a few events, which will help me build my inventory."

"Remember, I want military histories," Evan said. "And Leah wants romances."

"I want books on architecture and gardening," Rachel reminded.

"I will try to please patrons with a wide variety of tastes," Caroline promised. She paused and then said, "Before everyone leaves, I have something else to share with you."

"Good news?" Catherine asked. "I know you signed the contracts this morning on the property."

"This is in regard to another property." She swallowed. "My father's house."

Rachel reached over and patted her hand. "I know the auction was held. Remember, you may stay with Evan and me as long as you wish."

"Actually, I have a place to stay now."

"Did you rent rooms?" Leah asked.

"No. I'll be staying in my father's house."

"What?" all three women cried.

Quickly, Caroline explained how some generous benefactor had purchased the home and contents and deeded everything her.

"And you have no idea who did this?" Alex asked.

"None whatsoever," she admitted. "I wish I could thank the person that did so. I only plan to use a few of the rooms. A bedchamber. A parlor. The kitchen. I'm too busy with getting Evie's up and running but as soon as I have time, I'll hire a maid and cook that can come in a few times a week."

"It's a large place for you to be all alone," Catherine said. "Are you sure you want to live there by yourself?"

"In time. And you're right. It is quite large for me, Davy, and Tippet. I don't believe Evie's will make a profit for a good year or more. If it looks as if it will be longer than that, I want to make sure my investors receive their return and a profit. In that case, I'll sell the house and use the proceeds to keep the bookstore operating."

"What of any furniture within the place?" Luke asked. "If you're only going to use a handful of rooms, perhaps instead of purchasing new furniture for Evie's lounging and reading areas, you could use what you already have. That way you'll only need to order small tables and chairs for the tearoom."

Caroline nodded her approval. "An excellent idea. It would save money and time."

"Why don't we go look at it now?" Luke suggested.

# Chapter Fourteen

Luke prayed none of his very helpful family would invite themselves along, especially since everyone present knew how he felt about Caroline. Thankfully, no one spoke up and offered to accompany them.

Instead, all the women made plans on when to stop by tomorrow morning to see Evie's. Even Cor was eager to go. Before Luke and Caroline left, Cor pulled them aside and motioned Jeremy over to join them.

"If you don't find furniture to your liking, you might want to check with Jeremy," his grandmother said. "The attics at Eversleigh are filled with unused furniture."

"I'd forgotten about that," his brother said. "I used to go up and play in the attics when I was young. I was always up to some sort of mischief," he told Caroline.

"I don't think I've ever been up there," Luke said.

"You had Rachel. You were closer in age," Jeremy said. "I was the only sibling for a good while. I had to find ways to entertain myself. Cor's right. All the pieces up there are sitting. See what you have now and then you can always make a trip to Eversleigh and pull some of that and put it to use. Or if you'd like Rachel to do so, I'm sure she'd be willing to help. You must have quite a bit left to do in order to see to opening so soon."

Caroline nodded. "With Rachel supervising the changes to the interior and Luke and our two cooks working on creating the menu and purchasing supplies, my main task will be assembling the inventory and seeing it properly catalogued for either sale or circulation. That is a daunting task."

"Why not start with your father's library?" Luke suggested. "It would give you a foundation to work from."

"An even better reason to go check it out now," she agreed.

They said their goodbyes and when Luke wanted to send for the carriage, Caroline refused.

"We are but a few blocks. Besides, I could stand to walk off some of that tea."

He laughed. "I think we all overindulged."

As he led her down the street, they talked about which sweets ranked highest with everyone and ways to feature a special every couple of weeks. By the time they reached the former Earl of Templeton's house, they were in high spirits.

Caroline paused at the door and reached inside her reticule, withdrawing the key.

"I never needed a key," she shared as she unlocked the door. "I was always with Mama and Cynthia. A footman or Stinch would let us in."

He closed the door and asked, "Where to first?"

"The library, I think. It's a logical place to begin. It's this way."

As they went, he noticed blank spaces on the walls and figured the earl had sold off some paintings, trying to ease the crushing burden of debt that beleaguered him. Once they reached the library, he noticed more empty spaces.

Caroline glanced around and said, "I'm sure you've noticed the bare walls. Father must have sold much of the artwork. I also have noticed a few missing vases. At least there's still some furniture left. But let's get to what's important—the books."

They took some minutes skimming the shelves.

"I'll need to make a list of everything here but this gives me a good idea of what I have." She indicated two shelves. "These are all first editions. If Father would have realized how valuable they were, they would have been the first to be gone."

"Was your father a great reader?" Luke asked. "He's got a large collection of Shakespeare. Chapman's translations of *The Iliad* and *The Odyssey*. Milton. Pope. Congreve."

She eyed him with interest. "You sound familiar with all of those works."

"I am. Remember, I told you I enjoy reading. I wasn't interested in literature as a schoolboy but when I went off to university and could follow my own interests, I took a liking to reading and have kept up with it ever since. Plays. Poetry. Novels." He laughed. "Even pamphlets on farming techniques and livestock breeding."

"You're interested in that?"

"I am a landowner. My estate is called Fairhaven. I'm responsible for a large group of tenants. I'm always experimenting, seeing if we can get a greater yield of crops from the land."

"You surprise me, Luke. To the world, you present a devil may care image. You are much deeper than what you let on."

"And that's a good thing?" he asked softly.

"Definitely."

"Then I'm glad for your approval. Of course, I would assume you would approve of my voracious appetite for reading since I will be a frequent customer at Evie's."

She frowned. "Don't think you have to do that. You or any of your family."

"We all enjoy reading. Cor taught the three of us how to read before we ever had a governess or tutor. And you've heard how Leah is a subscriber to a circulating library. Be glad we are such a large bunch and will patronize Evie's. We can talk it up with all of our friends."

"Thank you." Sincerity shone in her warm, brown eyes. For the first time, he noticed the flecks of amber in them.

"Are there any other books in the house or should we search for pieces of furniture now that would be appropriate for the bookstore?"

"There may be a stray book or two. I'm sure I left a couple in my room while packing for Boston." She paused. "I haven't been to my room since I left."

"It was cruel of Morrow not to let you claim your personal things. At least you have access to them now."

"Let's go upstairs."

Luke went with her and Caroline pointed out things missing from the corridor. They reached her room and entered. She was quiet as she looked about, running her hand along the bed and opening the wardrobe.

"Just as I left it," she murmured.

She led them across the hall to another bedchamber. When he opened the door and then entered, she gasped.

"Everything's gone!" she cried, spinning in a circle.

Without being told, he determined this was her sister's room—and that her father had sold all the contents.

"How could he have done this?" she said angrily. "I have nothing left to remember Cynthia by." Her hands fisted and her cheeks heightened with color. "I don't know if I'll ever be able to forgive him."

"He must have been in dire straits to strip the room in such a fashion, as well as sell off other pieces throughout the house," Luke said, trying to soften the blow.

"Sometimes, I don't think he cared a whit for any of us. Me. Mama. Cynthia. He was a very selfish man who only cared about himself and his pleasure. His card games. His mistresses."

Guilt filled Luke. Caroline could have been describing him a short time ago. But that was before he decided what was important in life and rid himself of things—and people—he didn't want in his life.

"I must go to Mama's room," she said and hurried away.

His longer strides easily caught up to her and they entered a chamber that was larger than the ones they'd been in. From the looks of it, about half of the furniture had been taken away.

Caroline went to the dressing table and opened a jewelry box.

"Empty," she said dully.

He could feel the waves of disappointment emanating from her and wanted to comfort her, deciding to speak of something he'd buried deep within.

"I'm sorry your father was so rotten, Caroline. I can relate—for mine was cut from the same cloth."

She slowly closed the jewelry box and met his gaze.

"My father's life revolved around being merry," Luke revealed. "He gave no love to his children and devoted not one whit to the three of us. He would only partake in whatever gave him pleasure. That meant drinking to excess and bedding every available woman he could find. And gambling—the same as your father. When Jeremy inherited the title, the estate was almost bankrupt, thanks to Father's losses at the tables. It took years for Jeremy to pull us out of debt."

"I had no idea. I'm sorry, Luke."

"We don't talk about it," he said. "It's in the past."

"I wish I could say the same," she replied. "Having only come home and now being confronted with all of this is disheartening. I feel so alone."

Luke hated the hurt in her voice, all due to a despicable man, one just like his sire. To witness such a lack of love in Caroline's life brought him deep pain.

"Jeremy became a father to me and Rachel once our father passed. I am fortunate that he and Cor lavished us with attention and love. I cannot fathom you returning to England and feeling so isolated, with no loving family members to turn to."

Caroline shrugged. "I've been on my own so long. I don't really know any other way."

She went to the bedside table and picked up a small painting. Luke came and stood behind her, looking over her shoulder. He saw two girls on the cusp of womanhood and instantly knew them as Caroline and Cynthia.

Caroline gazed at the portrait for a long time and finally said, "This was painted just before Cynthia came ill that last time. I'd decided to postpone my come-out so we could do it together." Her finger touched her own image. "It's hard to think I was once this girl. A naïve, shy thing who kept her nose in a book, trying to learn as much as she could to impress a father who always ignored her."

He placed his hands on her shoulders. "I like you better now. You've matured into a beauty that's only promised in this portrait. You are outgoing and outspoken. Strong and determined." Luke brushed his lips against her hair. "You have become a thoughtful adult, Caroline. One who will never act as selfishly as your father did. You will cherish your family and love them well."

She rested the portrait against the table and he heard her choke back a sob. Luke turned her in his arms and brought her close. Her fingers clutched his coat as she buried her face against him. Even through the material, he could feel the hot tears. He stroked her back, murmuring soft words to soothe and console her.

The heaving sobs subsided and she stilled. Luke relaxed his grasp on her without totally releasing her and Caroline lifted her tearstained face. Her gaze met his and his heart broke at the sadness he saw. Without thinking, he leaned down and kissed her, wanting to comfort her. That's all the kiss would have been. Brief. Light. Reassuring.

Until she opened her mouth to him.

It was as if someone lit a match. Something sparked instantly between them. His tongue delved into the rich velvet and tasted her yearning. Her heat. Desire flared within him. His hands spread on her back and brought her against him. He wasn't the only participant in the kiss. Caroline's arms went about his neck, her hands locking together and pulling him toward her. Her tongue did battle with his, engaging in a strategy that overwhelmed him. Her light, floral perfume wafted about him and he delved even deeper with his kiss.

Her fingers pushed into his hair and fisted there as their kiss became more urgent. His hands slid down and cupped her rounded bottom, kneading it. He broke the kiss and allowed his lips to travel down her throat, finding where her pulse pounded wildly. He nipped and licked at the place, hearing her moan as she tossed her head back, giving him all the access he needed.

Her breasts, crushed against his chest, suddenly called out to him. Luke's lips burned a path down her neck and went lower as his hands came round and cupped her breasts. He squeezed gently and dragged his thumbs across her nipples, slowly circling them as she whimpered. His mouth closed over one breast, his tongue finding the erect nipple through the thin material of her gown. As he licked at it, her fingers tightened in his hair, pulling him closer to her. Luke's heart raced wildly. All he wanted was to strip her of her clothes and take her.

The thought took him back to reality.

That was the last thing he would do. He wanted her to want him but he couldn't let their passion spin out of control and make the all-important decision for her. She must be clearheaded and determined to pick him to spend their lifetimes together without desire clouding her judgment. Luke wanted Caroline to feel confident and get her business off to a strong start. She must stand on her own and be comfortable with who she was before he could ask to be a part of her life.

Though how he was going to keep from blurting out that he loved her might be the greatest test he'd ever faced. In that moment, Luke accepted the fact that he did love her—and because of that, he would keep silent. For now.

Reluctantly, he pulled his mouth away. He saw her glazed eyes and fevered cheeks and couldn't resist one final, quick kiss, hard and possessive. Then he released her.

"I'm sorry," he said, grabbing her elbows when she swayed.

"Why?" she asked, her eyes pleading with him to continue.

"I meant merely to comfort you. You've faced such disappointment and loss. I'm afraid I took advantage of you in a weak moment. You're a lady, Caroline. I'm a gentleman. I value our friendship. I would never compromise you."

Hoping she was steady on her feet now, he let go. Reaching for the portrait, he picked it up and handed it to her, knowing it would give her something to focus on.

"You should take this with you back to Rachel and Evan's. Place it by your bedside. Talk to your sister each night. Tell her all that you accomplished that day and how much you love her and wish she could see you. Know that she's always proud of you, even if she can only look down from heaven at you."

Caroline wiped away tears with the back of her hand and clutched the painting to her breasts.

"Let me see you home," Luke said quietly.

They didn't speak the entire way to his sister's house. When they arrived, he said, "I will work with Mrs. Withers and Mrs. Baker tomorrow. I'll see that the right ovens are purchased and that they finalize the menu so we can order some of the staples they'll need in baking."

"When will I see you again?" she asked.

*Whenever I can keep my hands off you*, he thought.

"Soon," he promised.

Luke rang the bell and Kent answered almost immediately.

"Goodnight, Caroline," Luke said and hurried away.

# CHAPTER FIFTEEN

C AROLINE'S MIND WANDERED. Her eyes felt grainy from lack of sleep. She'd tossed and turned all night long, thinking of the kiss she and Luke had shared.

*Why had he stopped?*

He'd told her. She just had trouble accepting his reason.

Because they were . . . friends.

He'd said he'd taken advantage of her and valued their friendship. That he'd never compromise her.

Frustration filled her. *She'd* been the one who'd taken advantage of him. She knew he was trying to comfort her with an innocent, brief kiss. She was the one who'd felt desire flame within her. And she was the one who turned the kiss from sweet to one full of heat. Even now, her blood sang with his name.

How would she live with the fact that he only wanted to be friends? Was it even possible for men and women to be friends, with no passion between them? Just being in the same room with him caused her to come alive. Her senses seemed sharper. Her body tingled, longing for his touch. She hung on every word he spoke. Yet knowing he didn't think of her as she did him made her think she should avoid him. She'd thought to do that when they'd first met, thinking him a dangerous rogue who would trifle with her heart. She hadn't wanted that, especially with her focus on establishing her own bookstore.

Caroline supposed that if Luke truly were to look for a bride this Season, as she'd been led to believe, she would be the last woman he'd ever choose. First, she had a father who'd fallen out of favor with the *ton*. Gambling and mistresses were tolerated to a certain point but the Earl of Templeton had gone over the edge, losing money hand over fist, so much that not only was he financially ruined, but he had shamed the only family he had left.

The fact that Caroline was now a businesswoman would also be a strike against her. A family as old and distinguished as the St. Clairs would not want someone frowned upon by the women of the *ton* to become Luke's wife. She already knew she would be judged even more harshly than a titled gentleman who might dirty his hands in trade.

She didn't think it would affect the new friendships she'd made though she doubted she would be able to socialize with Rachel, Leah, or Catherine in public. Once word got out about her bookstore and tearoom, Caroline knew social invitations would dry up. She would not want her friends' reputations maligned by her presence. She hoped she would still see them in their homes. The three women already meant a great deal to her, as if she'd been welcomed to their sisterhood.

Stinch cleared his throat. "Do you agree, Lady Caroline?"

Oh, dear. She hadn't heard a word her new manager said. Wanting to support him, though, she smiled and said, "I certainly do, Mr. Stinch. You are rarely wrong about anything."

He smiled, pleased with her praise. "Then I think I will let those waiting know what our decisions are."

"Yes. It would be best if news of their hiring comes from you since you will be in charge of everything regarding our employees. Have them report first thing in the morning. By then, I'm hoping to have some inventory available. And let any former servants of Father's know that I will write them references even though they won't be working at Evie's."

"Yes, my lady."

She watched him go to deliver the news to those who would be working for her. Two of their former maids would be taking orders and serving customers in the tearoom. They were both in their mid-twenties, young enough to stand on their feet long hours and yet with enough experience to be steady on the job. They'd also hired one of the former footmen as a driver. Not for the coach but for the large cart that she knew was in the stables. It would be used to ferry books to Evie's from other bookstores and possibly even directly from a few London publishing houses. That's what she would look into next.

What had surprised her were three clerks they'd hired for the bookstore itself. None of the former Templeton servants who'd come to interview seemed qualified to act as clerks who recommended books and waited on customers. A few of them hadn't even been able to read, which had knocked them out of the running. She and Stinch had hired three young men this morning from other booksellers, though. Two of them had previously worked at rival bookstores she'd visited and were men she'd asked many questions. The third man had worked in a nearby circulating library and had heard gossip about what establishment would fill the empty space she'd purchased. He'd taken a chance and come by two days in a row and was granted an interview when he saw them inside. She thought the trio all well qualified since she'd asked them not only about various types of literature and nonfiction books but assessed their speech skills and mannerisms. They all would do well working with the public.

A fourth young man, barely twenty, had also come on board. He'd apprenticed with a bookbinder and knew quite a bit about how to repair books. He'd told them that his master had a son who also apprenticed under his father. The young man knew when the time came, the son would be favored and receive a job in the family business. He decided to take the initiative and strike out on his own.

He promised to be a hard worker and had also worked a few hours a week in a local bookstore. His familiarity with how books were labeled and shelved would be invaluable.

Stinch returned and gave her a list of four names.

"These are those who wish for you to write them a reference, Lady Caroline. I told them they could return tomorrow to receive them. They all asked that I thank you. Finding a job in London without a reference is almost impossible."

"I'll take care of it," she said, placing the list in her reticule.

She was ready to leave the bookstore when a familiar face walked through the front door.

"Mr. Walton. I'm surprised to see you."

He tipped his hat to her. "Lady Caroline. It's nice to see you've returned safely from America." He glanced about. "So the rumors I've heard are true. You're opening a bookstore."

"I am."

"Then you'll need an assistant."

Walton had served as her father's secretary for many years. He'd always taken time to ask Caroline what she'd learned from her governess that day and occasionally slipped her a peppermint from a jar he kept in a drawer.

It hurt her to say, "I don't think I have anything for you, Mr. Walton. Mr. Stinch is serving as the bookstore's manager. I've already hired sales clerks."

"Who'll keep the ledgers? Order your books?"

"I'd plan to do all of that," she said gently. "I inherited my aunt's bookstore in Boston and am quite familiar with how to run one."

Disappointment crossed his face. "I see." He paused. "It's just . . . so hard finding another position at my age. Your father dying suddenly left me without any references. Even then, I feel others are reluctant to hire me because of the sad state of the earl's affairs. I am blamed merely by my association with him, though none of the debt was my doing."

He nodded brusquely. "Thank you for your time, Lady Caroline. I wish you the best of luck in your venture."

Her heart ached as she watched him walk away. "Wait!" she cried before he reached the door.

Walton turned and came back to her. "Are you willing to write a reference for me, my lady? That would certainly be appreciated."

"I can offer you something temporary," she began, formulating in her mind what he might do. "I need to acquire a list of bookshops in London, especially the smaller ones. I must find out if any sellers wish to be rid of some of their inventory. I'll need helping buying inventory, a good variety because I want Evie's to be known for having whatever a customer needs and if we don't, getting that particular book as quickly as we can. I also need a list of publishing houses and which ones sell direct to booksellers. And if they give a discount if a large volume is purchased. It would require a great deal of investigation."

Walton's face brightened at the prospect. "It sounds exactly like something I could do."

"Once I have it and I begin buying, I'll also need someone to record each book and the number purchased. Some books will be designated for sale, whether new or used, while both new and used volumes will become part of my circulating library. It will take a great many hours to get all of this done."

"Time is something I have on my hands, my lady."

"Once that's done, I can take over since I won't be buying in such great volume. Would this temporary job suit you, Mr. Walton?"

"It would, indeed, Lady Caroline." He smiled shyly. "I may even make myself so indispensable that you might want to keep me around. Especially if your bookstore becomes a success."

"That would be ideal for both of us," she said, returning his smile.

"I'll start now, making the rounds," he proclaimed. "Shall we meet here tomorrow morning?"

"Yes, Mr. Walton. That would be a fine idea. Concentrate on booksellers first."

"I will. A very good day to you." This time, the former secretary left with a spring in his step.

Caroline hoped she would be able to keep Mr. Walton on.

"THAT'S CUT A little low, don't you think?" Caroline asked Catherine.

Immediately, Madame Toufours tsk-tsked her comment. "Lady Caroline, you have a wonderful bosom. It should be shown."

She looked to Catherine, her eyes pleading.

"I agree with Madame," the duchess said. "Besides, you can always wear a fichu to fill in the low neckline if you're uncomfortable."

"I suppose. I've just never shown so much of my bosom before."

"The women of the *ton* will be envious," the modiste said and then smiled. "And the men will be enamored."

Caroline felt her face flaming.

"Not all are cut so low," the modiste assured her. "Let's try another. Marie-Therese, bring the lavender."

The assistant went to fetch the next gown and the Frenchwoman helped Caroline from the garment she wore. After another hour, her fitting was completed.

"I must say, I didn't even recognize some of my former gowns," Catherine said. "You are a genius, Madame Toufours."

"I am," the modiste agreed. Looking to Caroline, she asked, "Do you have time to stay behind, my lady, and discuss the merchandise to be placed inside Evie's? I'm ready for it to be moved."

She looked to Catherine, who said, "I must return home. Mr. Bellows is coming to show me the final version of my book. I'm to check it for any errors before it goes to press. It will definitely be ready for the opening of your bookstore. Let me send the carriage back for you since you may be here a while."

"That's very thoughtful of you, Catherine."

"Keep it for as long as you need today. I will be home for the rest of the day."

"Thank you."

"Let me have Marie-Therese and Genevieve carry out your gowns, Your Grace," Madame Toufours said.

As the assistants took the gowns to the waiting carriage under Catherine's supervision, Caroline said, "I have several gowns to donate to your shop. They belonged to my mother, who passed away. Perhaps you would be able to remake some of them as you have the duchess' gowns for me. If not, I'm sure you could use bits and pieces of them as material for other gowns you create."

The modiste's eyes lit with interest. "When can I have them?"

"As soon as you'd like."

"May I send a wagon tomorrow morning?" Madame asked eagerly.

"What time? It's at my father's house, the Earl of Templeton's. I'm staying with the Marchioness of Merrick. Her townhome is directly across from my former home."

"Is nine too early?"

"Not at all," Caroline said easily. "If anything, it's late for me."

She'd been busy day and night for the past week. Already, she'd purchase many books, including the entire stock from a bookseller that had planned to retire early next year. Caroline had convinced him the opportunity to rid himself of the contents of his bookstore wasn't to be passed up and they'd struck an agreement on the spot.

In a week, Rachel had seen to the minor construction projects at Evie's, including having the wall knocked down to join the bookstore with the tearoom. The entire place had been cleaned and painted and, only yesterday, furniture had been delivered. This afternoon, Rachel and Leah were meeting Caroline at Evie's to organize the placement of various reading areas. They were using furniture from her father's townhouse to begin and would see if more would be needed.

"What of the goods you wish me to carry?" Caroline asked.

"They are ready to be transported, as well, once you give your approval."

"Then let me see them."

The modiste led her down a hallway and through a door to a storeroom. She turned to her left and indicated a large group of items.

"These are what I wish to bring. Marie-Therese has a list of everything, along with the prices to be charged."

"I'll go to Evie's now and send my driver and a clerk to load them. Marie-Therese can come with them and arrange things. If you'd like to stop by after your shop closes, you can see how things were laid out and make any suggestions on placement."

"These are exciting times," the modiste said, a satisfied look on her face.

"They are, indeed," Caroline agreed.

She left in the ducal carriage, which now waited for her with her own gowns from her fitting. It conveyed her to Evie's. She asked the driver to deliver the gowns inside to the Merrick townhome and then dismissed him. She spoke to Stinch about picking up the wares from Madame Toufours and he told her he would see to it immediately. Her friends arrived and with the help of two clerks, they arranged and rearranged the furniture to their liking, deciding what they had was adequate for now. Shelving would come in tomorrow and be placed. That was a good thing since, next door, stacks of books filled the small warehouse and she still hoped to purchase more before the grand opening.

Marie-Therese arrived with the goods from Madame Toufours and Rachel and Leah decided to help the clerk arrange the wares for sale. Caroline let them know the modiste would be by in a few hours to approve of their work.

Mrs. Withers came and asked if everyone in the bookstore might like to sit for a spot of tea. Nobility and workingmen alike filed into the teashop, where the cook and her sister lavished them with sweets and hot cups of tea. Caroline looked around, glad they'd finally gotten in the tables and chairs she'd ordered. Everything was falling into place nicely.

Everything—except her heart.

It, unfortunately, dangled from a precipice of her own making. It didn't help that Luke, once the ovens had arrived, had made himself scarce. She'd only seen him once. He'd informed her that he was working on the font to be used for the teahouse's menu and how items would be grouped and priced. He assured her he had everything in hand and had found a printer for the work.

After that, nothing. She'd seen the three husbands, as she'd begun to call them, several times. Evan and Alex dropped by with helpful hints, while Jeremy had asked to meet twice with her, wanting updates on her progress. He'd made a few subtle recommendations that she'd pounced upon, knowing his experience in business far outweighed hers.

"Lady Caroline, a message has come for you," Stinch said, handing her the note.

"Thank you."

She opened it and saw it was from another bookstore owner that she'd tried to meet with. He'd been out of town on a buying trip and, now, he agreed to see her if she were currently free. With the furniture already placed and Rachel and Leah aiding Marie-Therese, Caroline decided she wasn't needed for the rest of the day. She told her friends goodbye and explained to Stinch and Walton where she'd be and that she would see them in the morning.

"May I come with you, Lady Caroline?" Walton asked. "This is one of the few shops I haven't investigated yet."

"Of course."

Outside, Walton hailed a hackney and told the driver, "Netherby's

Bookshop," and then helped her into the vehicle.

She was curious to meet Leland Netherby. Walton had told her the man had a reputation among the book community for being persnickety and demanding. Most booksellers avoided dealing with him when they could. Caroline didn't mind.

She liked a challenge.

# CHAPTER SIXTEEN

NETHERBY'S WAS ONLY five blocks from her own bookstore, which would make him one of her chief competitors. Caroline and Walton entered the bookstore and Walton peeled away to look the place over. She went to the desk and a clerk asked if he could help her.

"Lady Caroline Andrews to see Mr. Netherby," she said crisply.

"Ah. Let me see if Mr. Netherby is available."

Before she could inform the clerk that she was invited—even expected—he hurried away. As Caroline waited, her eyes roamed the store. Experience told her there were between eleven and twelve hundred books available on the shelves. She began moving through the store, estimating that a little more than half of the available books were new and the others used. The small corner devoted to children's books was poorly stocked. She took that as good news since she planned a large area for children's books.

Suddenly, it hit her that women of the *ton* would be shopping for books for their children. They might even bring their children along on occasion. What if she created a reading nook and play area? It could have books for them to read and puzzles to play with while their mothers shopped. She could even hire someone experienced with children to watch over the area so mothers could browse on their own and even have a cup of tea.

Excited by the idea, she returned to the desk. The clerk was still missing. She joined the line with two customers in it and waited patiently until her turn came.

"I have an appointment to see Mr. Netherby," she said.

"Don't worry, Sims. I'll take care of this."

Caroline saw the clerk she'd spoken to earlier had finally returned. She didn't know if he'd been waylaid by a customer or if Mr. Netherby had kept him but her time was valuable.

"Is Mr. Netherby ready to receive me?" she asked pointedly.

"He is. If you'll come this way."

The man led her through stacks of books, where she saw Walton browsing, and then through a door and down a corridor. They reached an office with an open door and the clerk left her without a word.

Leland Netherby concentrated on a sheaf of papers. He was mostly bald, with tufts of graying hair bunched above his ears.

When he failed to acknowledge her presence, Caroline cleared her throat. Netherby looked up, almost bored, and slowly removed his spectacles, placing them on the desk before him. He rose slowly to his feet.

"Lady Caroline Andrews?" he asked languidly.

Her temper flared but she tamped it down. She had a suspicion this man was testing her.

"Yes," she said and smiled graciously. "You must be Mr. Netherby. I'm pleased to make your acquaintance."

"Come in." He indicated a chair before his desk and she took a seat.

"Thank you for inviting me to meet with you," she said. "I've become acquainted with some of London's booksellers already but it's nice to meet you since our shops are so close. Has Netherby's been here long?"

"Yes," he said, pride evident in his posture. "I am the third generation to operate it. My grandfather began the store. My father ran it after him and then passed it along to me. It has been in this location for decades."

"My, that's impressive. Do you have a son who will take over from you someday?"

Displeasure filled his face. "My son has chosen to . . . follow another path."

"I'm sorry to hear that," she said politely.

"Tell me about your little bookstore."

Something spiked inside Caroline. Instinct told her he'd deliberately kept her waiting. This man was her rival. She decided to only give him the barest of information.

"It will be named Evie's Bookstore, after my late aunt," she began.

"And what makes you think you have the capability of running a bookstore?"

Immediately, his tone made her think of the verbal battles she'd participated in with her father and she grew wary.

"Because I ran one in Boston," she said succinctly.

He shrugged. "A provincial little town."

"Actually, Boston is a thriving city," she informed him. "One of the largest in America. I assisted my aunt in running the place and managed it on my own after her death."

"You're playing at being a businesswoman, Lady Caroline," Netherby said flatly. "No one is going to accept a woman bookseller. Oh, there are some women who run a business in London. Milliners. Modistes. No one is going to take you seriously, though." He paused, looking her up and down. "You are a woman of the *ton*. You'll be ostracized by that very *ton* for dirtying your hands in business. They won't shop at your little store. And no one will recommend it, either."

He crossed his arms. "If a customer wishes for a book I don't have, I tell him I'll get it for him. If I'm unable to within a reasonable amount of time, I send him to a fellow bookseller. I—and others in London—will never send them to your establishment."

She started to speak but he held up a hand.

"Yes, you've purchased some stock from other sellers in the past week but that will not be the case in the future. You won't be able to build any more inventory. I'll see to that. This is a man's world, my lady. Run by men. You aren't wanted here. We shall close ranks and make sure—if you continue this foolish venture—that you fail."

Caroline rose, knowing her cheeks blazed in anger. "Evie's Bookstore is my livelihood, Mr. Netherby. I don't have the pleasure of having a father who left me well off because mine was a gambler who lost everything. I have the wherewithal and determination to stake a claim and create a haven for women to buy their books and socialize a bit. I understand that we are competitors and that you have little regard for me. I am sorry for that. It's your loss, though. Not mine. Good day, sir."

She left the office, hearing Netherby shout after her, "You'll fail! So will that tearoom of yours. You'll be a laughingstock."

Caroline burst through the door and stormed through the bookstore. Walton quickly joined her and they left the premises.

"What happened?" he asked.

"Mr. Netherby doesn't have a high opinion of women going into business. Especially women who might compete against him. He's going to try and turn other booksellers against me."

Walton swallowed. "So, it's war, is it?"

"It is, indeed. This visit to Mr. Netherby has only increased my resolve. I am determined to make a success of Evie's simply to spite him," Caroline declared.

THREE DAYS LATER, Caroline realized how dire her situation was. Suddenly, no one would sell to her or any of her representatives. Everywhere, booksellers gave her the cold shoulder. Still needing a great deal of books, she tried not to panic. She had too many people she'd hired depending upon her for her to fail in this endeavor.

The problem led her once again to the Duke of Everton.

Barton admitted her and asked, "His Grace? Or Her Grace?"

"His Grace," she said and followed the butler to the duke's study.

Everton welcomed her warmly and introduced her to his companion.

"This is Matthew Proctor, who serves as my eyes and ears and advises me in business."

"A pleasure to meet you, Lady Caroline," Proctor said. "His Grace has told me of your venture. I'm eager to see it—and shop there."

She frowned. "There won't be any shopping or any store if I can't get my hands on more inventory." She looked to the duke. "May I sit?"

"Of course." He steepled his fingers. "It sounds as if you have troubles. Share them. Together, Matthew and I might be able to come up with a solution."

Caroline told him of what she'd accomplished since his last visit and how everything had changed after her meeting with Leland Netherby. Everton said nothing but a muscle in his cheek twitched as she told him how the bookseller had threatened her.

"He's going to drive me out of business before I can even open my doors," she said, exasperation plain in her voice. "Netherby has rallied other London booksellers around him. The tearoom is ready to open now but I still lack in books."

She sighed. "That's why I've turned to you, Your Grace, for advice. I'm sure as often as I show up here, I should be paying you as my financial adviser."

"There will always be petty Netherbys in the world. We cannot let them win." Everton rose. "Come with me to my library. You, too, Matthew."

The three of them went upstairs and into a large library.

"Look over the shelves, Lady Caroline," the duke encouraged. "See what you think of my collection."

As she did so, Everton asked, "Do we have a list of all the books contained here, Matthew?"

"We do, Your Grace."

"Let me see it."

Proctor excused himself. Caroline continued to peruse the shelves until he returned and handed the list to the duke. Everton, in turn, gave it to her.

"Here is a list of books to be added to your bookstore and circulating library."

Shock filled her. "Your Grace . . . I cannot . . . I mean . . ." Her voice trailed off.

"You can pay me a fair price." He paused, a devilish smile crossing his handsome face. "A pound, let's say."

"What?" she exclaimed.

"I have three thousand books in my library at Eversleigh. I can transport some of those volumes here. Or perhaps, I may just buy books for a new library here in London. At a new establishment that I will patronize and recommend to all of my friends."

Tears welled in her eyes. "Your Grace, you're being far too generous. Let me pay you for your library. You have so much here that with what I've already accumulated, it will be more than enough to open Evie's. I want to buy it at fair market value."

"No. I'll sell it all for a pound. Not a penny more." His jaw set in determination.

"I can't—"

"If you don't buy it, I'll sell it to Netherby for that same price."

Caroline gasped. "You wouldn't."

He grinned. "Oh, I would."

She brought fisted hands to her waist. "You are fighting quite dirty, Your Grace. And very proud of that fact."

The duke chuckled. "I am, aren't I?"

"Then I suppose you've left me no choice." She opened her reticule and withdrew a pound note, handing it to him. "My driver and wagon will appear first thing tomorrow morning to begin transporting my purchase to Evie's."

"I can have my—"

"You may not, Your Grace," Caroline said firmly. "I've bought the books. I will see them delivered to my store. Even if you decide you're going to buy every single book back." Her chin rose a notch.

He nodded in approval as he pocketed the note. "As you wish, Caroline. And please, no more of this 'Your Grace'. I am Jeremy."

She blinked back the tears that threatened to fall. "Thank you, Jeremy."

"You look as if you could use a cup of tea."

"Tea would be lovely," she said as she folded the list he'd given her and placed it inside her reticule.

"Matthew, care to join us?"

"No, Your Grace. I have other things to attend to." Proctor excused himself.

Jeremy led her from the study and they came across Catherine.

"Did your book pass muster?" Caroline asked.

"It was perfect," her friend said. "Do you have time to stay? I've a few things to discuss with you. First, though, I was going to go see the children. You haven't met them yet, have you?"

"No. I'd like that very much."

"Then let's go visit them a bit and then we can have some tea." Catherine looked to her husband. "Coming?"

"I'll be up in a few minutes. I need to finish something first."

"Something I interrupted," Caroline said, chuckling. "I seem to be doing more and more of that."

"You are a delightful interruption," he said.

Catherine led her up the stairs to the next floor. "The nursery is this way."

They approached the open door and Caroline immediately heard laughter, followed by a happy squeal coming from a child. She glanced inside and saw Luke there, holding a girl of about four by the waist, his back to them.

"Into the crow's nest you'll go, Lady Delia," he said gruffly.

She playfully swiped at him. "No, you pirate. Put me down."

"I'll save you," a young boy cried and ran across the room, a toy sword in his hand.

Luke set Delia down and she and the boy pounced on him. Luke grabbed another sword resting on the ground. They fought one another with shouts.

"Let me, Timothy," Delia cried and took the sword from her brother, stepping into the fray against her uncle.

Once more, Luke engaged in battle and then a girl who'd been reading in a window seat calmly put aside her book and ran toward Luke. She grabbed his legs, wrapping her arms around him.

"Get him!" the newcomer cried.

Luke collapsed in play and all three children swarmed him. Caroline's heart melted seeing him with his nieces and nephew, knowing this was no show. He had no idea others were present. She was seeing the true Luke St. Clair.

The children began tickling him, giggling all the while as he floundered and laughed.

"I give up!" he cried. "No more torture, I beg you."

"The price is a story," the oldest child said. She pushed herself off him and retrieved the book she'd been looking at, bringing it to him.

Luke's back was still turned to her and Catherine as he pushed himself upright and reached for the book.

"Thank you, Jenny."

He opened it as Jenny sat next to him. Timothy snuggled up on his other side, while Delia climbed into his lap.

"I'll hold it, Uncle Luke. So you can make the voices."

"Must I?" he asked and all three children pleaded for him to do so.

"If you insist," he said.

Luke began reading and the children sat enraptured. Catherine crossed to the left and lifted a baby from the nursemaid who held him and brought him back to Caroline.

"This is Philip," she said softly, not wanting to interrupt the story.

"Hello, Philip," Caroline whispered, stroking the baby's hand. He reached up and grabbed her finger and held on, giving her a gummy smile.

She let him continue to hold it as she turned her attention back to Luke and the story he read. Caroline recognized it as one of Catherine's, a favorite of Aunt Evie's. As the children had demanded, their uncle used different voices for various characters, drawing them into the story. She could have watched him forever but the story finally came to an end. Luke closed the book and rose, Delia in his arms.

Catherine said quietly, "He stops by a few times a week to play with them. I didn't even know he was here." She paused. "Luke will make an excellent father someday. Once he finds the right woman."

At that moment, he turned around, his hair mussed from the horseplay and a beautiful smile upon his sensual lips. His eyes met hers. If Caroline hadn't realized it before, she knew it now beyond a doubt.

She was in love with Luke St. Clair.

# CHAPTER SEVENTEEN

CAROLINE SAT STILL as Rachel's maid finished arranging her hair. She gripped her hands in her lap, feeling like one large bundle of nerves. Here she was, at twenty-three, only now making her debut into society. She tried to remember the lessons with her dance master years ago and found everything she'd practiced with him had fled from memory. What if she got out on the dance floor and couldn't move? The thought chilled her.

"There, my lady. You look right nice," the maid said, offering her a hand mirror.

She looked at her image, pleased that at least, on the outside, she appeared ready to conquer the world. Her caramel-colored hair was artfully arranged and her dark blue gown complimented both her hair and fair complexion.

"Thank you," she told the servant, who quietly exited the room.

Caroline couldn't help but wonder what tonight would be like. She'd never been to a ball before. She and Rachel had visited Catherine this morning and seen the ballroom. Servants scurried about with potted palms and decorations, giving her a small idea of what the room would look like tonight. Still, she had to factor in hundreds of guests in their finery. Especially since this was the opening event of the Season, everyone invited would want to look their best.

Rachel entered, looking lovely in a green gown that matched her emerald eyes. Diamonds sparkled at her ears, throat, and wrist.

Caroline knew from their previous conversation that these were the Drake diamonds, which Evan had bought especially for her.

Caroline had no jewelry to wear. Once again, she knew the women of the *ton* would judge her for that.

"You look beautiful," Rachel exclaimed. "Madame Toufours outdid herself on your gown."

"She is very talented. Though I'm a bit self-conscious about the neckline." She fought the urge to yank the gown up. In her opinion, too much of her bosom showed.

Rachel placed her hands on Caroline's shoulders. "You will shine tonight."

A servant appeared in the doorway. "My lady, Lord Merrifield is here. Lord Merrick is with him now."

"Thank you. We'll be down shortly," Rachel said.

"I'm looking forward to meeting Lord Merrifield."

"He will be one of several gentlemen you'll dance with tonight," her friend revealed. "The St. Clairs will introduce you to all of our friends in attendance. In fact, I'm putting Merrifield in charge of you while we're in the receiving line. Jeremy insists that Evan, Luke, and I join him. He is a strong proponent of family. While we're receiving guests, you'll be in good hands."

"Then I suppose I should go meet him."

"I think you'll enjoy Merrifield's company quite a bit," Rachel said. "He's articulate and handsome and puts others at ease. I feel you would have a lot in common, especially since he's mad for books. Not only is Merrifield a gentleman—but one of the best men I know." She grinned. "*And* he's looking for a wife."

A hot blush flooded Caroline's cheeks. "Rachel, I'm not—"

"You're not going to commit to Merrifield or any other man tonight," her friend agreed. "But he's definitely someone to keep in mind. I've promised to help him look for a wife since he's done such a pitiful job up until now. Who knows? You might be Lady Merrifield one day."

They went downstairs and Caroline saw Evan talking with a man. He had his back to her but she could see he was tall and had broad shoulders.

"There they are," Evan said, and the man turned.

My, the earl was awfully handsome.

Merrifield had dark blond hair and high cheekbones. As they came closer, Caroline was drawn in by his penetrating blue eyes. He smiled, revealing white, even teeth. She couldn't imagine why he'd had such a difficult time finding himself a wife.

"So, this is the mysterious bookstore owner." He took her gloved hand and kissed her fingers. "I'm surprised it's taken us this long to meet."

Rachel snorted. "This is Merrifield, Caroline. He's a terrible flirt. Get used to it."

The earl's eyes gleamed at her with interest. "Rachel has told me so much about you, Lady Caroline. I understand you've been busy night and day, preparing for the opening of your bookstore and tearoom."

"I have," Caroline replied. "I was able to accumulate my stock more quickly than I'd expected so Evie's will open this coming Friday."

"Let's get to the carriage," Evan said impatiently.

"We can take mine," Merrifield said. "It's already out front. It will be convenient for us to go together." He offered Caroline his arm and led her outside.

Once inside the carriage, he said, "I will be one of your most loyal customers, Lady Caroline. I am a great lover of books and buy them often for myself and friends."

"I hear you purchase many children's books," she said.

He laughed. "All of my friends seem to be married with children. I enjoy spoiling the little ones."

"Books are a great window to the world. You are doing these children a favor with such a thoughtful gift."

Rachel said, "You're to introduce Caroline around while we're in the receiving line, Merrifield. Make sure you have her meet the right people."

"Of course, Rachel. Heaven forbid that I don't do your bidding." He looked to Caroline. "She's a bit of a tyrant, don't you think?"

Caroline couldn't help but chuckle.

"Enough of that," Rachel said, swatting Merrifield playfully. "We're here."

As she entered the ballroom, it looked like a spring garden. Flowers abounded, their sweet scent filling the air. They went to greet Jeremy and Catherine.

"It's good to see you all," the duke said.

"You've done a magnificent job with the ballroom, Catherine," Caroline told her friend.

"Rachel helped with the overall design. She has a good eye for decorating and arranging things."

"She's done the same at Evie's," she confided. "Moved a few chairs. Changed the angle of some of the bookshelves. Brought in a few knickknacks to personalize the place."

"And don't forget the fresh flowers," Rachel added. "Once you open on Friday, I believe having those at the circulating desk and where purchases are tallied up will make for a nice touch."

"I'm eager to see Evie's," Merrifield said. "It seems everyone has but me."

Caroline thought a moment. "I have an idea. Everyone should come tomorrow afternoon at three, not only to see the bookstore and help me make any last-minute decisions, but I could have Mrs. Withers and Mrs. Baker serve tea. We could order from the menu as customers will, in order to give them and the girls waiting some experience before our grand opening."

By now, Luke had joined them. She was aware of his presence the moment he arrived. Her nose recognized the sandalwood soap he used. He looked beyond handsome in his dark evening clothes.

"That's a capital idea," he proclaimed. "It would allow the clerks and staff to work out any kinks." He gave her a warm smile. "Excellent idea, Caroline."

She nodded and lowered her eyes, not wanting to meet his for fear her true feelings toward him might show.

Cor joined them, using a cane. "Fetch me a chair, Evan," she commanded. "The receiving line will be long. I don't intend to stand for the duration."

"At your service, Cor." He left to find one.

"You're joining us, Caroline," Jeremy said. "You may stand here."

His words took her aback. "What? No. Of course not. I'm not family."

"You're staying with family, though. You are a dear friend to us all. It will be a way for you to meet others. I insist."

"And just as firmly, I'll decline," she said. "Lord Merrifield is going to accompany me as I meet your guests."

As Jeremy scowled, Luke laughed aloud. "I don't know the last time anyone told my brother no. Bravo, Caroline."

She blushed at his praise.

"Don't worry, Caroline," Catherine said. "It's good for my duke to be put in his place every now and then."

"You better watch yourself, Duchess, or I will find a private place and put you in yours," her husband warned playfully. Then to Caroline, he said, "I've already mentioned to some of my friends that you will be here. They know to sign your programme. Look for Morefield. Aubrey. Neville."

"And she must meet Amanda," Luke said. "She's Aubrey's sister. They've both been friends of the family for years."

"I look forward to meeting them. Outside the receiving line," she said with a smile.

Catherine laughed. "Oh, Duke, I do like this girl."

"Will Amanda even be here?" Rachel asked. "She only gave birth last week."

"Amanda loves to dance," Luke said. "She would have to be on her deathbed to miss the opening event of the Season."

With that, Merrifield led her away from the boisterous St. Clairs. They walked the length of the ballroom, taking in the decorations, as he asked questions about her new businesses. By the time they started back, she saw the first guests arriving, noting that Leah and Alex had also joined the receiving line. A footman handed her a card and her escort immediately took it from her.

As he wrote his name beside the second dance, he said, "I've been told I may only have one dance with you tonight. Rachel insisted you meet as many people as possible." Then he began writing again.

"Whose name are you writing in then?" she asked.

He chuckled. "I had my instructions. You're to dance the supper dance with Luke and sit with him and his family at supper."

"I see." She hoped she didn't betray her excitement at that news.

He wrote another name. "That's Everton's dance. You should be honored. He never partners with anyone other than his duchess."

After that, Caroline met so many people that she knew she would never remember all of their names. Her dance card filled quickly with names of gentlemen that Merrifield introduced her to.

"You must be Lady Caroline," a woman said and moved close to her. "Luke told me Merrifield would be introducing you around. I'm Lady Stanley but you must call me Amanda."

Caroline noted not only the woman's friendliness but her great beauty.

"I'm pleased to meet you. All the St. Clairs speak of you fondly."

"My brother, Marcus, and I have been friends with them for years. I hear from Leah that you're about to open a bookstore in Mayfair.

Where is it?"

Caroline told her the location and then said, "I'm having a small preview tomorrow at three, followed by tea. Would you and Lord Stanley like to attend?"

Amanda beamed. "That would be lovely. I look forward to it." She paused. "Oh, it looks as if Jeremy and Catherine are ready to open the ball."

She glanced at her dance card and saw her first dance hadn't been claimed. Then she realized no one would be dancing but the Duke and Duchess of Everton. They went to the center of the ballroom and the orchestra struck up a tune.

"Jeremy likes to dance with Catherine alone. He's a great romantic at heart," Amanda said. "They are the perfect couple."

She had to agree. Catherine's rich, auburn tresses and lilac gown were a nice contrast to Jeremy's dark looks and evening wear. The pair moved with ease, never taking their eyes from one another as they swept around the ballroom. It was obvious this was a couple deeply in love. A tug of longing pulled at her, wishing it were her and Luke out there and that he gazed at her with such affection.

That was impossible, though. Her mind had accepted that a romance with Luke St. Clair would be impossible. It was taking her heart longer to realize that, though.

The dance ended and Merrifield appeared. "Ready for our dance, Lady Caroline?"

"Lead the way," she said bravely, though her insides wobbled like jelly.

Luckily, it didn't matter. Her partner was a superb dancer, moving her about the floor with ease. She found herself relaxing and even enjoying the dance.

It ended and she said, "Thank you, Lord Merrifield. That was my first dance at a ball. My first time at any *ton* event."

"Truly? I would never have guessed. You are very graceful. Why haven't you danced before?"

As he returned her to Rachel and Leah, who awaited her with smiles, she told him she'd been stuck in Boston as the war raged and had only returned to England with the signing of the Treaty of Ghent.

"I hope you will enjoy this Season, Lady Caroline. I look forward to seeing Evie's tomorrow—and dancing with you again." Merrifield bowed and left her with her friends.

She danced numerous times after that, knowing in the back of her mind that Luke would claim her for the supper dance. When he arrived at her side, her heart began beating wildly, like a small butterfly trapped in someone's hands.

"I believe this is our dance. At least it is if Merrifield wrote my name beside the right spot," he teased.

"Thank you for dancing with me," she said as he took her to the center of the floor.

"Of course, I wanted to dance with you." He took her in his arms as the strains of a waltz began. "I've looked forward to this all night."

Caroline seemed to float through the air. She was aware of his hand pressed to the small of her back, feeling the heat of it through her gown. He held her a bit closer than her previous partners had, her breasts grazing his chest, causing them to ache for his touch. She licked her lips nervously.

"You're a success tonight," Luke said. "Just as Evie's will be a success."

"I hope so."

"I know so," he said firmly. "You've worked diligently to make it so."

She smiled. "I've had quite a bit of help from the many friends I've made since my return to London. Including you."

"Including me," he agreed happily. "I hope you're pleased with my contributions regarding the tearoom."

"You've hired the best cooks in London. I'm sure of that. You—

and Cor—have helped tweak the dishes that will be served. And I love the idea of bringing in the blackboard which lists the special desserts offered each week. I wouldn't have been able to open the tearoom at the same time as the bookstore without all of your help. I am in your debt."

He grinned. "I rather like that. Should I get that in writing so I may call the chit in?"

She sensed her cheeks heating and glanced away.

"I know how I can claim my reward for all my hard work."

Caroline glanced back at him. "How?"

"Accompany me to the theatre tomorrow night."

# CHAPTER EIGHTEEN

CAROLINE REGRETTED TELLING Luke she would attend the theatre with him. She didn't want to encourage more than friendship between them, knowing he needed to find a suitable bride from the Marriage Mart. A young, fresh girl with a spotless reputation. By the end of the week—when Evie's opened and word got out who its proprietor was—Caroline would be looked upon differently by the *ton*. Luke needed a wife who would support him and cause no controversy in society.

Lady Caroline Andrews was definitely not that woman.

She also knew the more time she spent in his company, the harder it would become for her to hide her feelings. Already, she'd given him her heart. She must start distancing herself from him before the broken pieces became obvious and her unrequited love embarrassed the both of them. It was important to steel herself for the day when Luke did find the appropriate woman to wed. Though it would pain her to see him gaze lovingly at someone else, she had to prepare for that eventuality. If he were anything like his brother and sister, Luke would fall deeply, madly in love and proclaim his feelings to the world.

Even worse, as a friend of the family, Caroline would be expected to make friends with his bride, who would be swept into the bosom of the St. Clair family with her marriage to Luke. Catherine, Rachel, and Leah would welcome a new female into their tight sisterhood. If Caroline were wise, she would start now and subtly remove herself from her friends. She had the bookstore and tearoom to focus on, along with Davy and Tippet. Running her new enterprises would be the perfect excuse to give her friends as she gradually withdrew from them. They would all understand that she must devote time to both ventures in order to make them succeed, long hours that didn't involve afternoon tea, garden parties, and balls.

It would be lonely, though. She already cherished the time she'd spent with these three women. To cut them from her life would be difficult. In the long run, though, it was the only solution. It would protect their reputations.

*And her heart.*

Tomorrow afternoon's gathering at Evie's would be the last she would attend with them all. Gradually, she would pull away discreetly. They'd be caught up in their lives. They all had husbands and children to tend to and social events that would keep them busy. They would think of her less and less as time progressed.

That would mean selling her father's London townhouse sooner rather than later. Its proximity to the Merrick household would make it far too easy for Rachel to drop by, bringing the others with her. Besides, it would go for a pretty penny. She'd be able to reimburse Luke, Evan, and Alex immediately and not make them wait for a return on their investments.

Satisfied with her decision, she left the retiring room and returned to the ballroom. With supper now ended, she was scheduled to dance with her host and didn't want to slight him by not showing up. Caroline joined Amanda and her husband. Lord Stanley was an affable man and had danced with her earlier, full of news about their newborn, their third child.

Immediately, Jeremy and Catherine joined them.

"Are you enjoying yourself?" the duchess asked. "I know it's your first ball. You look spectacular. Madame Toufours went on and on about your stunning figure and how she enjoyed designing this gown for you."

"Oh, Madame Toufours created your gown?" Amanda asked. "Several women asked me if I knew who your modiste was. Now I can tell them."

"Madame is most talented," Caroline said. "And yes, I've enjoyed tonight very much."

Catherine looked to her husband. "Duke, the musicians are awaiting your signal so they may begin."

He lifted her hand and kissed it. "Then I must not keep them or our guests waiting, Duchess." Jeremy turned to her. "I believe this is our dance, Caroline."

The Duke of Everton led her onto the dance floor and nodded at the orchestra, which immediately struck up a lively tune. By the time they finished their dance, Caroline was out of breath, her cheeks flushed from the exertion.

"May I get you some ratafia?" Jeremy asked.

"I would appreciate that," she replied.

He led her back to Amanda and excused himself. Caroline noticed her new friend looked tired.

"Have you thought about leaving the ball early?" she asked.

Amanda nodded. "I have. Tonight is the most activity I've had in a week since giving birth. I adore the St. Clairs, though, and wanted to support them by coming to this first event of the Season."

"I'm sure they would understand if you and Lord Stanley slipped away early." Caroline looked and found Amanda's husband talking to someone nearby and motioned him over.

He came at once, a worried look on his face. "Are you all right, dearest?" he asked his wife.

"I'm weary. Perhaps we should leave. I want to get enough rest to go to Evie's tomorrow and sample the menu."

"Then we wish you a good night, Lady Caroline," Lord Stanley said, tucking his wife's hand through the crook of his arm. "We look forward to seeing your shops tomorrow."

She waved goodbye to them and realized, for the first time to-night, she was alone.

Not for long.

Immediately, a trio of women standing close by moved in on her. For a moment, she felt like a fox trapped by hounds as she looked at the gleam in the women's eyes.

The first woman smiled ingratiatingly at her. "Oh, I'm sorry Lady Stanley left so suddenly. I was hoping she would be able to introduce us. I hope you don't think me forward to come up to you in such a way. I am Lady Bethany." She indicated her companions. "This is Lady Betsy and Lady Bettina."

"Lady Caroline," she murmured, though she knew this woman already knew full well who she was.

"Delighted to meet you, Lady Caroline. My, you've had quite the night at this first ball of the Season. You've danced with Aubrey, Stanley and Neville. All of the Duke of Everton's friends. Not to mention Lord Merrifield, that handsome devil. The Marquess of Merrick and the Earls of Mayfield and Alford."

She wondered why this woman would have kept such close notice of whom Caroline partnered with and decided this had to be one of those horrible gossips who looked for things to talk about.

Politely, she said, "I am fortunate that I've gained so many partners this evening since I'm attending my first ball. The Duke of Everton was kind enough to see that I didn't sit out many dances by encouraging his friends and family to dance with me."

Lady Bethany sniffed and said, "Yes. Even Everton danced with you. That's a rare happening. He only makes time for his duchess. What have you done to gain his attention?"

Caroline hated the women's rude tone. "I am friends with his sister, Rachel, and his brother, Luke."

The moment she used Luke's Christian name, she knew she'd

erred. The two subordinates squealed, *"Luke?"* as their ringleader said condescendingly, "Friends? You're *friends* with the Earl of Mayfield?"

"Yes," she said evenly. "I've grown close to the family. I'm staying with the marquess and marchioness. Rachel's brother is a frequent visitor."

Lady Bethany snapped her fan. "No lady of quality is friends with any man, especially Mayfield. That one is a rogue, through and through. Do you know how many mistresses and married lovers the man has had? Too numerous for anyone to count. That man has spent more time lurking in bedchambers and drawing pleasure from women than any gentleman of the *ton*. They say he takes a lover every night of the week. Sometimes, even two in one night. At the same time."

Lady Bethany's friends tittered nervously at such bold conversation, waving their fans and turning away, looking as if they knew their friend had gone too far. The woman's words gave Caroline pause, knowing she'd lost her heart to Luke St. Clair. Though the man Lady Bethany described seemed nothing like the Luke Caroline knew, the sting of the gossip made her think she knew only one side of him and she told herself she should be more wary of the time they spent in one another's company.

Lady Bethany continued. "The Earl of Mayfield won't bother to settle down for a good decade or more and will most likely break a string of hearts along the way. You'd be wise to acknowledge that of your *friend*, Lady Caroline. Only when he thinks about needing to pass his title and lands down will he deign to take a wife. Even then, she better be prepared to spend many nights on her own. A man such as the Earl of Mayfield will never change his wandering ways. Once a scoundrel, always a scoundrel."

Anger threatened to spill from Caroline as this woman continued to speak of Luke in a derogatory fashion. She could feel the dark, heated splotches staining her cheeks as she reined in her temper. Lady Bethany was someone who delighted in spreading rumors. For all

Caroline knew, the woman merely repeated hearsay about Luke and had no actual knowledge of his behavior. She might even have been attracted to Luke and he hadn't returned her interest. It wouldn't do to have ugly words with this stranger and cause a scene that would embarrass her hosts.

"I think it's more than friendship between her and Mayfield," Lady Bettina said slyly to her companions, who finally turned back and joined the conversation once again.

"Definitely," Lady Betsy agreed. "Do you think you're more than friends with Mayfield, Lady Caroline?"

When she held her tongue to contain her fury, Lady Bethany said smoothly, "Of course Lady Caroline has designs on Mayfield, foolish as they may be. She's wormed her way into being friends with the St. Clairs. And who is she? A no one."

"Caroline?"

Relief filled her. She turned and saw the Duke of Everton standing there, a cup of ratafia in his hands. He passed it to her.

"Thank you, Jeremy," she said evenly, gloating when she saw Lady Bethany's jaw drop with her familiar use of their host's first name.

"I'm sorry I was detained. Could I draw you away from your present company? My duchess has need of your advice. You're the only one who will do, she said." He offered her his arm and Caroline took it, grateful to have his solid frame supporting her weak knees. "Ladies," he said, his deep voice both polite and yet judgmental.

She saw fear in the three women's eyes. They knew they had crossed the powerful Duke of Everton and would have to pay the piper.

Jeremy led her around the ballroom and as he did, he apologized. "I'm sorry I was gone so long. I thought you would be fine with Amanda."

"She was feeling tired and I encouraged Lord Stanley to take her home."

As they reached Catherine and Rachel, he said, "You should never have been left alone with those vipers. They won't be invited to any future events any St. Clair family member holds."

Rachel's eyes widened and she scoured the ballroom. "I see them. Oh, bloody hell. I should have warned you about them, Caroline. The Three B's. They're vicious gossips and to be avoided at all cost."

"I meant what I said," Jeremy said firmly, as Luke joined them. "None of those women is to be invited to any social event we hold." He glared at them across the room and they turned away in retreat.

"Not the dreaded Three B's," Luke said. "Did they attack you, Caroline?" he asked, worry evident on his face.

"A bit. Jeremy rescued me, though."

"They aren't to be trusted," Luke said, his eyes narrowing as he watched the women from across the room. "None of them has landed a husband yet, mostly due to their sharp, forked tongues. Stay away from them."

"I will," she promised, still feeling shaken after the encounter.

"There are only a handful of dances left," he said. "I'm sure your partners would understand if you excused yourself and left."

Caroline lifted the programme dangling from her wrist and skimmed over the names that remained. "I hate to disappoint anyone, Luke. Besides, I don't want the Three B's to feel victorious. If I left now, it would be as if they'd won. I'd rather stay and dance and enjoy myself until the last song has played."

He gazed down at her, nodding his approval. "Very well then. I will see you tomorrow afternoon at Evie's and then, tomorrow night, we'll attend the theatre and supper afterward."

A gentleman joined them and Luke greeted him. "Morefield. Your partner awaits you."

The newcomer smiled and held out his hand. "I believe this is our dance, Lady Caroline."

CAROLINE READIED HERSELF for the day and then wrote a quick note to Higgins. In it, she asked her new solicitor to see about putting her father's house on the market immediately. Very little furniture was left in it after she'd used what hadn't been sold to populate her bookstore. What remained, she could take with her once she found rooms to let or even leave it for the next owners as she started anew.

As she went down to breakfast, three new books in hand for Davy, she gave the message to a footman and asked that it be delivered to Higgins at once. She entered the small breakfast room and found a mountain of mail beside her plate. Evan was the only one present, sipping tea and perusing the newspaper.

"What is this?" she asked, indicating the large stack.

"Invitations," Evan replied. "It seems you made quite an impression on the *ton* last night. The fact that Jeremy danced with you—when he doesn't dance with anyone but Catherine—let the *ton* know how favored you are with him and his wife. That one dance opened the door for you. The drawing room awaits you, as well. It's filled with flowers from your many new admirers."

She glanced at the invitations ruefully. "I'm afraid to respond to any of these. By week's end, Evie's will be opened. I doubt anyone will want me at their social gatherings once that news gets out."

"Why?" he asked, clearly puzzled by her remark.

Gazing at him steadily, she said, "You're a man of the world, Evan. You know what will be said of me once it's known I'm a woman in business. I may have garnered some brief attention last night but I'll be set aside just as quickly by the fickle *ton*."

Caroline saw understanding dawn in his face. He placed his hand atop hers. "It won't change how your friends feel, Caroline. You are the same person to us."

Tears misted her eyes. "Thank you."

She pushed aside the stack and ate a little breakfast before excusing herself and going to the stables. Mr. Brimley told her that Davy was knee deep in mucking the stalls.

"I'll be sure the boy gets the books," he promised Caroline, and she left them in the groom's safekeeping before heading to Evie's. Just walking through the doors filled her with pride. The bookstore didn't have the number of volumes that the Temple of Muses held but it was much larger than the average London bookstore, thanks in large part to Jeremy's contributions. The duke had been overly generous with her and she wanted to make sure she paid him back, both monetarily and by showing him how his advice and her work ethic paid off in making Evie's a success.

She went first to the tearoom to tell Mrs. Withers and Mrs. Baker of the afternoon visitors.

"Have every item on the menu available, even the sandwiches," she advised. "This will be our last time to tinker with the items we'll serve on opening day and throughout the first week of business."

Caroline left through the open arch that connected the tearoom to the bookstore and saw that Stinch and all her clerks had already arrived.

Gathering them around, she said, "Today, I want to work on the display windows. They will be what passersby see and we want them to lure customers into our store. Tell me what you've seen around London."

Yesterday, Caroline had given them all assignments, dividing up the number of bookstores between them and having her staff visit each one, paying particular interest to any displays in windows or within the shops themselves. They discussed what they'd viewed and then began trying out some of the ideas, coupled with ones of their own. The morning and into the afternoon passed pleasantly, ending with every window being arranged to perfection, as well as several display tables throughout the bookstore.

"I want to go outside to see our work from that angle," she told Stinch. "Everyone's worked so hard. Give them the rest of the day off, including yourself. We'll all be working long hours soon. Might as well rest while we can."

"Certainly, Lady Caroline. I'll inform the others." He hesitated a moment.

"Is something wrong, Mr. Stinch?"

He shook his head. "Not a thing, my lady. I hope you don't think me too forward, but I must say that I feel it is a great honor working for you and being a part of Evie's. To have seen you grow from a young, curious girl to a mature woman with a strong work ethic, one who has accomplished so much on her own, why—it's remarkable."

Warmth filled her hearing his compliments. "You have always been so kind to me, Mr. Stinch. I'm blessed to have you working for me in a new capacity. I see you flourishing in a way I'd never imagined. Evie's will be a success, thanks in no small part to your contributions."

The manager blushed. "Thank you, my lady. You've given me this unique opportunity. I'm very grateful and so pleased at all you've accomplished in such a short time. I admire you greatly."

She placed a hand on his arm. "The feeling is mutual."

Stinch blinked back tears. "You've risen above and overcome your father's terrible reputation. He left you destitute but you have blossomed because of your intelligence and good character. Forgive me for saying so, Lady Caroline, but I feel like a proud papa watching the woman you have become."

Caroline threw her arms around him, squeezing him tightly, then giving him a peck on the cheek. "Thank you."

She went outside to admire their handiwork and saw her clerks and manager file from the building. She waved goodbye and walked from the window on the far right to the ones in the middle and finished at the far left, studying each carefully and making notes in her head of small details she wanted to change. Glancing up, she saw the sign that had been hung while they were at work today and smiled, pleased at how everything was coming together.

"So, this is Evie's Bookstore," a condescending voice said.

Caroline turned and saw Leland Netherby standing behind her.

# CHAPTER NINETEEN

LUKE SET OUT early for Evie's Bookstore and Tearoom, wanting to arrive ahead of the large group expected for a tour and tea. He stopped along the way and made arrangements for a late supper after taking Caroline to the theatre tonight. The place was small, intimate, and exclusive. Fortunately, he'd frequented it over the years and they were happy to accommodate him.

A few blocks from the bookstore, he saw Stinch coming his way. The former Templeton butler had impressed Luke with the ease in which he handled the staff. Though the world of books was new to Stinch, he'd become knowledgeable, admitting to Luke that he'd always spent what little free time he had with his nose in a book.

"Mr. Stinch," he greeted. "What brings you out on this fine April afternoon?"

The bookstore manager stopped. "Lord Mayfield, it's a pleasure to see you. Lady Caroline released the entire book staff a few minutes ago. We've been working on the display cases all day. Everything was to her lady's liking and she dismissed us, knowing we'll soon be putting in long days."

"I'm eager to see the window displays. I'm surprised my sister wasn't there, directing you where to place things."

Stinch smiled. "Lady Merrick has a fine eye for detail, my lord. She has made adjustments, both large and small, and they've all added to the overall ambience of Evie's."

"I'll pass along your compliment to Rachel. I won't keep you. Good afternoon."

Luke continued through Mayfair and turned the corner where the tearoom was located. He spied Caroline down the block in front of the bookstore, engaged in conversation. As he drew near, he saw it was none other than Leland Netherby. Luke had bought a handful of books at Netherby's over the years, but he found the clerks as surly as its owner and finally quit going there. He wondered why Netherby was here.

Then he saw Caroline's pale face and the angry, dark red blotches on her cheeks and quickened his pace.

"What's going on here?" he demanded.

Netherby whirled. "Ah, Lord Mayfield. How nice to see you. Why, we're just two booksellers, comparing notes."

Ignoring the older man, Luke turned at Caroline. "Are you all right?"

"Yes, thank you, Lord Mayfield," she said formally, looking as if she might explode at any moment. She glanced at Netherby. "Lord Mayfield is one of my investors."

Interest sprouted on Netherby's face. "Is that so? Did your brother also choose to invest in Lady Caroline's little ventures? The Duke of Everton seems to have the Midas touch and knows when a business will succeed—or fail."

Knowing what the man was after, Luke reluctantly said, "No. My brother is not an investor but Lord Merrick and Lord Alford are."

"A pity. If Everton chose not to invest, it was for a good reason." Netherby shook his head sadly. "I hope you won't lose too much on this enterprise, Lord Mayfield. You might ask the duke's advice the next time you choose to make an investment so he can steer you in the proper direction." He looked to Caroline. "Remember what I said, Lady Caroline. Any time. Any time."

With those cryptic words, the older man sauntered away.

"Wait here," Luke told Caroline and strode after the bookseller. "Netherby!" he called out, his blood boiling.

The man turned and warily said, "What do you want, Lord Mayfield?"

Luke glowered at the figure he towered over. "What I want is for you to behave as a gentleman should. I know the book community is a small one and usually supportive toward one another. If you can't be helpful or encouraging to Lady Caroline, then leave her the bloody hell alone."

He saw fear spring into Netherby's eyes and added, "And for your information, Everton wanted to invest in Evie's but Lady Caroline already had all the financial backing she needed. Her bookstore will be a tremendous success. Count on it."

With that, Luke turned away and returned to Caroline. He took her elbow and brought her deep inside the bookstore, far away from the windows in case Netherby decided to spy on them. He led her to a comfortable chair. She collapsed in it, an angry growl coming from her.

He took a nearby seat. "What did that bloody fool say to you?"

"Nothing I wish to reveal."

"Caroline, talk to me," he commanded.

She remained stubbornly silent. Luke admired her for that.

"So, you won't tell me what he said to you."

"No. Partly because I'm afraid you'd chase him down again and beat him to a bloody pulp."

His hands fisted in anger but he kept his tone mild. "That bad?"

Caroline grinned wryly. "Worse. But I have friends coming soon. I'll tuck away all my dark thoughts of seeing Leland Netherby's body hanging from a gibbet. Or perhaps, his head parked upon a spike."

He laughed. "You are more imaginative—and far more wicked—than I'd thought."

Naturally, his own thoughts turned wicked, thinking of the things he wanted to do to her.

Anger still sparked in her eyes. "Let's change the subject, Luke. I'm not going to waste another moment on Netherby or anyone like him. I *will* make Evie's a success, I'll guarantee you that."

He took her hand and both of his. "Of course you will. You've created a warm, inviting space. You have a large selection of books. You'll tempt customers with the sweet aromas coming from the tearoom. I have full faith in you. I always have. I always will."

For a moment, their gazes met and he yearned to kiss her again. He fought the urge. She'd just been verbally abused by a man, a competitor who'd shaken her confidence badly. If anything, he didn't want to seem as if he were also trying to dominate her, too, though in a very different way. He wanted Caroline to know she was stronger than anything Netherby could dish out.

Changing the subject, he released her hand. "Are you ready for the theatre tonight? I heard it's an amusing comedy."

All signs of anger dissipated and her eyes lit with excitement. "I've never attended the theatre before. I don't care if it's a comedy or drama. To attend a live production is a dream of mine."

He smiled warmly. "Then I'm glad I can make it come true."

The door opened and the bell tinkled, warning them someone had entered the premises.

"Anyone here?" Leah called.

Caroline stood. "We're over here."

Luke rose, as well, greeting Leah and Alex, as well as Rachel and Evan, who accompanied them.

"Your window displays are so eye-catching," Rachel raved.

"We just completed them today," Caroline said. "I hope they'll draw people in. Would you add anything to them? Or change something?" she asked anxiously.

"Hmm. Let me think," Rachel said. "Leah, come outside with me. Let's look with a more critical eye and not as Caroline's best friends."

Luke saw the blush rise on Caroline's cheeks at Rachel's words. He supposed Caroline's sister, Cynthia, had been her closest friend from what she'd revealed. He knew little of her time in America except that she'd lived with her aunt and worked at Evie's bookstore. Caroline was probably starved for friendship. Luke was glad she'd made good friends with the women in his life. He'd always appreciated strong women, having been raised by Cor.

He thought about Caroline's declaration of not wanting to wed, believing it was because she likely had no dowry after her father gambled the entire family fortune away. Luke didn't care if she had one. He was interested in her as a person, both physically and intellectually. No one interested him as much as Caroline Andrews had. He envisioned a life with her, one in which they'd never be bored. He couldn't wait until the day he could take her in his arms and they begin planning their future together.

One advantage he had was that she didn't want other gentlemen to pursue her. Once that became known, he hoped it would improve his chances with her. He also got to see her outside of *ton* events, another leg up over the other men.

Luke only wished he would've had more time with Caroline today before the others arrived. It stilled troubled him that Netherby had said something to upset her so. It might take a visit to the nasty bookseller to find out what Netherby had been about.

The bell jingled again and Jeremy led Catherine and Cor in as the Stanleys and Aubreys followed them inside. Merrifield showed up with Morefield and his wife, completing their group. Caroline gave them a thorough tour of the premises, pointing out certain features and why she'd planned things the way she had. Luke noted how pleased she was at the many compliments she received about the bookstore's layout and the large stock available in a variety of topics.

Merrifield insisted she put several books on reserve for him to pick up on opening day. Caroline took the stack he gave her to the storage room, promising the earl the books would await him when he arrived.

"When will Evie's open?" Amanda asked. "I want to be sure and attend on the first day."

"This coming Friday," Caroline told her. "We'll be open from ten in the morning until five in the afternoon. The tearoom will serve from eleven o'clock until six in the evening."

She looked to Luke. "Why don't you guide everyone to the tearoom? I'll lock up here and join you."

"Follow me," Luke said, leading everyone through the archway into the tearoom.

Mrs. Withers and Mrs. Baker awaited them, both sisters beaming from ear to ear.

"These are the lovely cooks who will prepare tea for you." He motioned Daisy and Kitty over, hoping the former housemaids were ready. "This is your greatest test yet," he said quietly. "The clerks have been coming from next door and eating and drinking whatever you've put in front of them. This time, people will be ordering specific items. Remember everything we've talked about."

"We're ready, Lord Mayfield," Daisy assured him and stepped forward. "I'm Daisy and I'll be helping seat you today, along with Kitty. Who'd like to sit together?"

Luke watched as Daisy and Kitty made sure everyone had a place and then offered them a menu. The two women wrote down the orders and took them to the kitchen, handing over the slips of paper to him for inspection. He saw they'd used the abbreviations he'd worked out in order to save time, noting each customer's selection. The two older women were also familiar with the system. He gave Mrs. Withers the orders and stepped back into the tearoom.

Caroline joined him and he explained the process to her since they hadn't spoken of it.

"So 'PC' is pound cake."

"Yes, plain pound cake," he said. "And 'LPC' is lemon pound cake.

The women all know what to use."

"It's brilliant, Luke," she praised.

"I've also mapped the room, placing the tables on a page, and the chairs there, as well. It will help Kitty and Daisy keep straight what order is to be delivered to which table and even chair position."

"I can't believe you thought of all of this."

"I'm happy to have been of service."

Everyone ordered a full tea, including sandwiches. Luke knew Mrs. Withers now wore an "I told you so," look upon her face back in the kitchen. He was glad he'd given in to her demand to serve more than sweets.

As they watched, Caroline said, "I think everyone is enjoying their tea and the food."

"Once they've finished, you should ask again which items were favorites and why. And the same for anything that doesn't strike their fancy. Those few items could be stricken from the menu," he suggested. "For now, you need to sit, though. You've been working all day and could use some refreshments."

"Only if you join me. I insist."

He smiled. "I've never been one to turn down a scone or cup of tea."

Luke led her to a table for two and held the chair for her.

Kitty came over, her smile in place. "Good afternoon, my lord, my lady. What may I get you to eat and drink?"

Luke decided to challenge the girl and asked, "What would you recommend?" thinking she might become flustered with the question.

Smoothly, she said, "I'm partial to the bread and butter pudding with currants. And if it's a sandwich you want, I'd try either the roast beef or ham."

He nodded approvingly. "Good girl. You may get questions like that sometimes. You answered perfectly."

He and Caroline placed their order and received it in a handful of minutes. He looked about and saw the smiles and lively conversations at the other tables.

"Is this another dream come true?" he asked. "Seeing tables full as people chat and sip their tea?"

"It is," she said softly. "You have been a big part of this, Luke. By taking over the tearoom, you've allowed me to concentrate on the book side of things. I can't thank you enough."

"Maybe I'll be able to get a free cup of tea once a week?"

"And a scone. No, two," she said, laughing, taking a last bite.

Luke glanced around. "It looks as if everyone has finished."

He looked back and saw a small bit of clotted cream in the corner of her mouth. Before he could say anything, Caroline dabbed her mouth with a napkin. Immediately, he wished he'd been able to lick it from her lips.

*Soon*, he promised himself. Once Evie's opened and became a success, he would woo Caroline, sweeping her off her feet. He decided they would honeymoon after, just the two of them, no one else. He greedily wanted her all to himself for a good two weeks or more. He idly wondered how many times he could make love to her in that amount of time.

She addressed the group and asked for their opinions. Luke noticed Mrs. Withers and Mrs. Baker had come out from the kitchen to listen to the comments. Everything was positive, though both the blueberry scones and all of the cakes were definite favorites.

Caroline was swarmed as everyone told her goodbye, showering her with compliments.

"I will definitely purchase a subscription to your circulating library," Amanda said.

"So will I," Catherine chimed in. "Mr. Bellows also said he will have my latest book delivered to you tomorrow morning. He's hoping you'll sell out of the copies he provides."

"That's exciting news," Caroline said. "Let me show you the area you'll do your reading at and where you'll sign the purchased books afterward."

Everyone had filed out by then, leaving Luke with Jeremy.

"She's quite a woman," his brother said. "Determined. Intelligent. Kindhearted. And quite beautiful."

"Caroline is that and more," he agreed.

"Have you told her of your feelings?"

"Not yet."

"Why are you hesitating?" Jeremy pressed. "If she doesn't know, you could lose her to another."

"I don't think she's kissed anyone but me," Luke confided with confidence.

Jeremy's brows arched in ducal fashion. "Oh?"

"I'm the first to have kissed her. I will be the last." Luke placed a hand on Jeremy's shoulder. "I'll know when the time is right, big brother. Trust me."

"We all like her a great deal. She'll make a wonderful St. Clair."

Luke smiled. "I think so, too."

# CHAPTER TWENTY

LUKE SPENT MORE time watching Caroline than he did the actors on stage. She delighted in every line spoken in the inane comedy. Sometimes her lips twitched in amusement; other times she laughed aloud, deep and hearty. Those were the times he liked best, seeing her abandon herself to the silly moment on stage.

Rachel poked him with her fan in his left ribs and he turned, frowning at her.

Leaning close, she whispered in his ear, "Have you heard a single line uttered in this play?"

Grinning shamelessly, he said, "Not one."

She glanced over his shoulder. "She's entranced."

"She's never seen a play before. God only knows what she did for entertainment in Boston."

"I assume you don't want Evan and me to accompany you to supper afterward?"

"Not a chance. You are here solely so that we are chaperoned in front of the masses. I don't need—or want—you at supper. It's my time with Caroline. Not yours."

"Be glad I'm your loving sister or I would be wounded by your words." She leaned back in her chair.

Luke turned his head toward the stage again but continued to study Caroline. Her thick, brown hair was piled high on her head this evening, leaving her lovely, swanlike neck exposed. He longed to nibble his way up and down it and daydreamed about doing so for a few minutes. Loud applause brought him from his reverie and he saw the comedy had ended. Caroline applauded enthusiastically and turned to him.

"That was fabulous," she declared and immediately returned her attention to the stage where the actors were taking their curtain calls.

Finally, the cast disappeared and the audience rose from their seats. He helped Caroline from her chair.

"I can't wait to see a drama next," she declared.

"Wait for something Shakespeare," Evan said. "I believe Drury Lane has an upcoming production of *Hamlet* next month once this play finishes its run."

"Would you like to come back for it?" Luke asked as he took her hand and placed it on his arm.

"Yes," she said with enthusiasm.

They returned to their carriage and as they settled themselves, he watched Rachel begin her own little drama. His sister frowned a moment and put a hand to her head. Evan asked her if something was wrong and she said nothing. Then, a moment later, she sighed, both hands going to her head this time.

"Are you not feeling well?" Caroline asked, concern in her voice.

Rachel raised tired eyes. "I'm afraid a sudden headache has come on. I thought I could fight through it but my temples are starting to throb."

"My poor baby," Evan said convincingly, pulling Rachel against his chest and stroking her hair. "I'm afraid we won't be able to accompany you to supper. I want to see Rachel home and in bed."

"Oh, we wouldn't dream of going without you," Caroline assured him.

Luke flashed Evan a warning look, but it was Rachel who said weakly, "No, please. Go without us. Supper after the theatre is all a part of the experience. I wouldn't wish to rob you of that." She sighed dramatically and closed her eyes.

He wanted to kick her, thinking she'd overplayed her hand.

"Are you sure?" Caroline asked softly.

Rachel nodded. "Yes."

"Let me inform the driver," he said.

"No," Evan said quickly before Luke rapped on the ceiling to give the driver new instructions. "The supper club is only a few blocks away. Let us drop you there and then the carriage can take us home. I'll send the driver back to wait for you."

"That's very considerate of you, Evan," Caroline said politely.

The coach halted after a few blocks and Luke handed Caroline down, both of them wishing the other couple goodnight. He led her to the entrance, where a doorman ushered them inside. The sound of a violin played softly in the background.

"Oh, this is lovely," Caroline said, taking in the ambience of the club.

They were seated immediately at the table Luke had requested. Actually, the table had to be pulled away so they could sit beside one another on a banquette, and the table was swept back in front of them.

"Do you trust me to order for you?" he asked.

"Yes. Go ahead."

He did so and then inhaled her floral perfume. "That's a lovely scent you're wearing."

"Do you like it? I borrowed it from Rachel. I have no perfume of my own."

Luke promised himself that when they wed she would have a hundred perfumes to choose from. Caroline had been denied many of the finer things in life a lady of her rank was accustomed to, all thanks to her profligate father.

A tray soon arrived with two glasses of Madeira and a limited assortment of cold meats, cheeses, fruit and cake.

He held up his wine glass. "To you—and the success of Evie's."

They sipped the wine and nibbled on the goods from their tray, talking about people she'd met at last night's ball and how kind everyone had been to her.

"I'm not surprised, though. Your brother made it clear that I was to be treated well. I heard he only dances with Catherine so I felt very honored to partner with him."

"As the Duke of Everton, Jeremy commands instant respect. Not everyone in the *ton* is enthralled with him, though. He has done a few outrageous things to show how much he loves Catherine. If anything, the ton can be quite stuffy. They don't like the unconventional but, as a ranking duke, Jeremy can get away with things others can't."

A couple swept past their table and Luke cringed the moment he caught a whiff from the cloud of perfume that lingered.

*Catarina.*

Of all the places for her to turn up, why did it have to be here?

He saw her newest protector, a duke with a nefarious reputation, seat her. Luke cut his eyes away, returning his gaze to Caroline.

"I've had an idea for another investment," he said quickly.

"I'm afraid I don't have the income to pursue anything else," she said. "But I'd love to hear your idea."

"I was thinking of buying a boarding house where the rooms would only be let to employees of Evie's," he began. "Mrs. Withers and Mrs. Baker have been staying in my servants' quarters and they've spoken of finding a place of their own, closer to the tearoom. If something near Evie's could be located, it would only be a short walk for them to arrive at work. The same for the others. Mr. Stinch. Daisy and Kitty. The book clerks and binders."

"That's a very good idea but I'm tapped out. If you care to pursue it, I think several of the others would be willing to move in. Perhaps Mrs. Withers and Mrs. Baker could also serve as cooks and provide a morning meal before the work day began and another once they returned at night. They would need to be paid extra, though." Worry filled her face.

"That wouldn't be your responsibility," he reassured her. "That would be the landlord's. Mine. If you don't mind, I'll speak to the others tomorrow and see if they're happy with their living arrangements or if they'd be interested in something of this nature."

Suddenly, the air grew dense again and Luke looked up to find Catarina standing in front of them.

"My earl. What a pleasant surprise finding you here."

Catarina shouldn't be surprised at all since Luke had brought her here a handful of times, usually while other social events such as the opera and theatre took place. He hadn't wanted to flaunt her presence in public but, at the same time, he'd wanted her to get out every now and then.

"How nice to see you again," he said politely, not introducing her and hoping that would make her go away

Instead, she looked to Caroline. "I was going to the retiring room. Might you wish to come, my lady?"

Curiosity filled Caroline's face. "I was needing to visit it." She looked to Luke. "If you don't mind."

Gritting his teeth, he nodded. "Be my guest."

A waiter appeared and moved the table back. Luke helped Caroline rise and watched her leave with his ex-mistress.

This would not be good.

CAROLINE FOLLOWED THE exotic beauty, wondering who she was. Luke hadn't introduced them, which made her think he'd possibly forgotten the woman's name. She had met so many people at the Everton ball last night and could see how easily not remembering a name might be. She did know with certainty that she hadn't met this woman last night because she would remember such an attractive woman.

Both women stepped behind a screen and made use of the chamber pots provided and then returned to a large mirror. Since no servant was in attendance, Caroline poured water over her hands as she held them over a bowl and then offered the same for her companion.

"Thank you," the woman said. "I am Catarina."

She replaced the pitcher and reached for a small towel to dry her hands, wondering how to introduce herself. Was this Lady Catarina? Should she mention her own title? She'd abandoned it in Boston but was unsure what to do here.

"You are Lady Caroline Andrews," the woman said, studying her a moment and then turning to the mirror to fluff her hair.

"How do you know me?" she asked.

"I hear things," Catarina said vaguely and then added, "from my protector."

*Oh . . .*

Now, Caroline understood who this woman was. A sick feeling washed over her as she realized how Catarina knew Luke.

"You were his mistress," she said, their eyes meeting in the mirror.

"I was his lover. He was very good to me."

"Were you . . . together long?" Caroline asked, hating that she did.

"Almost a year," the dark beauty said and then faced her. "He tired of me. He will tire of you. He has a roving eye. He is not one to settle down yet. By the time he's ready, you will have wed and had a good three or four children."

Irritation swept through her. Did no women ever speak kindly of Luke? The Luke she knew was sweet-tempered and generous. Kind to a fault. He might have been a rogue in the past but she knew he was looking for a wife now. He was a man who loved children. She'd seen it firsthand when he played with his nieces and nephews.

Or was that the man his family saw? Was Luke different away from them? Was he actually the scoundrel other women proclaimed him to be? The woman before her claimed to have been his mistress. Caroline had no doubt she spoke the truth. But had Luke ever revealed his true self to Catarina?

Whether he had or not, Caroline knew she didn't hold a candle to the alluring woman beside her. This stunning beauty was the kind of woman Luke St. Clair coupled with. Caroline felt pale and washed out standing next to Catarina. She'd only fooled herself by thinking Luke had been slightly interested in her when he kissed her. After all, Luke himself had told her they were only friends. No other kisses had followed.

She pushed aside any notion of ever kissing him again. No more fantasizing. No more daydreaming. She was Caroline Andrews, businesswoman. Levelheaded and focused on everything *but* Luke St. Clair.

Her shoulders went back and her chin rose a notch. "First, I am not interesting in Luke that way. We are merely friends, out after an evening with other friends at the theatre. And as for marrying and having children, that is the one thing I don't plan on doing, Catarina. You see, I'm a businesswoman. About to open my own bookstore and teahouse. Luke is one of my investors. I will have no time for any husband, whether he's faithful or has a wandering eye. And I certainly won't have children."

Caroline smoothed her own hair and then said, "Good evening."

She returned to their table, an anxious-looking Luke pushing the table back and rising.

"It's been a long evening. I think I'm ready to go home now," she told him.

He grimaced. "Let's go to the carriage."

They rode in silence on the way home. When the horses stopped in front of the Merrick townhouse, Luke handed her down and kept her hand in his.

"I'm sorry."

"For what? Not introducing me to your lover?" she said more sharply than she should have.

He winced. "I never claimed to be an angel, Caroline, but Catarina is in my past."

She patted his arm and pulled her hand from his. "It's fine, Luke. I told her you were my investor and that I had no claim on you."

With that, Caroline marched to the front door and entered. Kent closed it behind her and she hurried up to her bedchamber. Once there, she flung herself on the bed.

She had no claim on him—but he'd claimed her heart without even knowing it. Caroline was more determined than ever to break ties with Luke.

For good.

# CHAPTER TWENTY-ONE

C AROLINE DRESSED FOR her second ball, again in another original creation from Madame Toufours. She had attended a garden party yesterday afternoon, meeting several new women and making sure she brought up the topic of books so she could hear what they had to say. Many of her new acquaintances had strong opinions on what they liked to read and she was pleased that she carried all but one of their suggestions.

The topic of the Duchess of Everton's books had come up. They seemed to be a favorite of children, making Caroline eager to see if sales of them at Evie's would be tied to the popularity the books seemed to have in the *ton*. Before the garden party, she'd spent the morning supervising the delivery of Catherine's books, devoting an entire round table to displaying copies, as well as two large book-shelves of the newest release. She'd made sure to stock all of her friend's previous books, too, hoping they would fly off the shelves when Catherine made her appearance and signed copies on Friday.

Tonight's ball was the only other event she'd accepted an invitation for. With Evie's opening tomorrow, she planned to put in a full day both Friday and Saturday at the bookstore and tearoom. After that, she'd have to gauge whether or not her presence would be accepted or if disapproval of her running her own business kept her away from other events during the Season.

She dismissed the lady's maid that had helped her dress and arrange her hair and sat before the mirror, admiring her reflection. Tonight, she wore a pair of borrowed earrings from Rachel, who insisted the emeralds would go beautifully with Caroline's dress. She'd refused the necklace that matched the earrings. The large stones flashed with fire and would have been too recognizable. It was already bad enough that she lived on the Merricks' generosity. She didn't want to be seen as a hanger-on, using her friendship with the marchioness for personal gain.

A knock sounded at the door and Caroline bade them enter. A footman carried a silver tray with a note on it.

"Thank you," she said and removed it.

Once he left, she broke the seal and opened it. A small part of her wanted it to be from Luke. She hadn't seen him at yesterday's garden party. They'd left with things strained between them. She needed to make it up to him at tonight's ball and then ease away from him on good terms. If he thought problems existed between them, he would pursue the matter. Caroline wanted to end things on a cordial note with Luke. She would delve deeper into her business and he could return to making his choice from the Marriage Mart.

Instead, the note was from Higgins, her solicitor. He wrote that he'd been approached with an offer for her father's home. It was from a well-to-do merchant who offered the price Higgins had advised her to set on the property. He wrote that the merchant would like to meet with her Monday morning at eleven o'clock. Though it would add to the gossip, her selling the townhome to one not of the nobility, it would mean an instant flow of cash. She could reimburse Luke, Evan, and Alex and have plenty left over to rent decent rooms and buy additional books for Evie's.

Caroline wrote a brief response to Higgins, telling him she would accept the offer and informing him he needed to be prepared to complete the sale come Monday. She left the room and went downstairs, giving the message to Kent and asking that he see it delivered to her solicitor.

Evan and Rachel came down the staircase together. He held his son in his arms. They reached the bottom and Evan kissed Seth's forehead. Rachel covered the baby's face in kisses of her own and then the nursemaid who'd followed them down took Seth and returned upstairs with him.

"He smiled at me today," Rachel told her. "Don't believe it when others say that babies that young don't smile because Seth did. Twice. He's absolutely brilliant."

Her husband's arm encircled her waist. "Maybe we should think about having another one," he said playfully and kissed her cheek.

"Later, Major," she told him, her voice seductive.

"Did you serve in the army?" Caroline asked Evan, vaguely remembering someone had mentioned him selling his commission.

"I did," he said, his smile fading. "It's seems like a hundred years ago now."

"Have you ever thought about writing a book about your experiences?"

Rachel laughed. "Oh, Caroline. You've got to think of something else beyond books!"

She shrugged. "I can't help it. They are my life."

They arrived at the Teasley ball, going through the receiving line. Once again, her programme filled up quickly. Some faces she recognized while others were newly introduced to her. Luke arrived with Merrifield and asked for her card.

"You may view it but there are no open slots," she informed him.

His eyes darkened. "You didn't save a dance for me?"

"I didn't know I was supposed to."

"May I see it?" Merrifield asked.

Caroline handed it over as he studied it. "Thank you," he said and returned it to her, smiling to himself. "If you'll excuse me."

"Then you must sup with me," Luke said.

Exasperation filled her. "I can't do that. Though I may be new to balls, I know good manners insist I'm to attend supper with my partner from the dance prior to supping."

"Break tradition," he urged, giving her a bone-melting smile.

"No. I won't. Go find yourself some lovely girls to dance with." She glanced around and her eyes locked on the Three B's, who studied her from across the room. "I see Lady Bettina staring at you. Or perhaps you wish to dance with Lady Bethany or Lady Betsy."

He burst out laughing. "I've learned my lesson. Next time, I will arrive earlier." He leaned down and whispered into her ear. "Unless *you* choose to save a dance for me." His breath tickled her ear.

Luke pulled away. "Keep that in mind." He sauntered off.

Her first partner led her to the dance floor moments later and Caroline determined to enjoy tonight, not knowing if this was the last ball she would attend. When the fourth dance started, Merrifield showed up.

"You aren't on my dance card," she chided as he took her to the center of the ballroom.

"I am now," he said, pulling her into his arms.

"How did you manage that?"

"I called in a favor from a friend." He twirled her around and then brought her close. "It will be worth it to see the envy on Luke's face."

"I doubt that," Caroline said.

Merrifield frowned at her. "Why do you say that?"

"Luke doesn't care for me . . . in that way. Ask him. He will tell you we are merely friends."

Her partner grew thoughtful. "I'll do that."

They finished the dance, Merrifield as smooth as ever, making her feel graceful and polished. He returned her to where Leah and Amanda stood together and bowed.

"I'm off to ask that question," he said mysteriously and left.

"What question? Of who?" Leah asked.

"Nothing. Merrifield is merely being silly," Caroline said.

She ate supper with a lively viscount and his friends, thoroughly enjoying herself, and then danced several more times. When her next partner showed up, he asked if they could do so another time.

"My mother has a headache and has asked for me to see her home."

"By all means, go to her," Caroline urged.

After he left, she decided to go to the retiring room for a few minutes of rest. Only a few women were present. She went behind one of the curtains and, moments later, overheard her name. She grew still, knowing she shouldn't eavesdrop, but chose not to reveal herself.

"Have you heard that she plans to open a bookstore? *And* a tea-room?"

Several women tittered with laughter.

"How gauche," one said. "Just think how awkward it will be if you encounter her at a social event."

"If she'll be invited to any. Who would ask anyone in trade—much less a woman—to a *ton* event? She'll never land a husband now."

"That's not all," another said. "I've learned who her father was. The Earl of . . . Templeton."

"No!"

"Oh, yes. No wonder she has to do something for money. Templeton ran through it all and left nothing."

"You heard what happened to him?"

"Something about footpads, I think."

"Not only did he gamble the family fortune away, but he was murdered."

*Murdered?* Caroline felt a wave of nausea sweep through her.

"I did hear about that. Wasn't he robbed and then stabbed?"

"Yes, he's the one. They dumped his body in the Thames. It was found the next day, all bloated, his face misshapen. The fish had had at him, you know. I even heard . . . he was . . . a sodomite. That it wasn't thieves but an enraged lover who had at him when the earl wouldn't pay up for services rendered."

Bile rose in her throat.

"I can't believe she was even invited to the Teasley ball. The viscountess must not have heard any of this."

"For some reason, the Duke of Everton and the Marquess of Merrick are protecting her."

"*Protecting* her? Do you mean . . . are they . . ."

"It's what I've heard. Those two publically proclaim to love their wives so much but they're like all men. I'm sure they're passing Caroline Andrews back and forth between them. And it wouldn't surprise me if Mayfield also was dipping his wick in her."

Caroline turned and vomited everything from her recent supper in the chamber pot. Blood rushed to her ears. She felt hot all over and dizzy.

This is what the *ton* was saying about her. That she was some trollop. No one would want to patronize Evie's. She would lose everything.

She pulled back the curtain and saw only one woman stood fussing with her hair. When she saw Caroline, though, her eyes widened. Quickly, she exited the retiring room.

Slowly, Caroline went to wash her hands and her mouth. A servant poured water over them and she cupped some, swishing it in her mouth and then spitting it out. She dabbed the offered towel against her mouth and dried her hands. With as much dignity as she could muster, she left.

She returned to the ballroom but felt eyes everywhere watching her. Her vision blurred with unshed tears. She stumbled toward one of the French doors that led onto the balcony and hurried outside. The cool, midnight breeze rushed at her as she angrily wiped the falling tears from her cheeks. At least with this chill she had the terrace to herself. No gentlemen bothered to romance their ladies in this stiff breeze.

Caroline went to the rail that overlooked the darkened gardens. Misery filled her. Her dream would end before it even began. A plan quickly formulated in her mind. She would return all of Jeremy's books to his collection. Sell as many of the others as she could, although she assumed Netherby would step in and pressure other London booksellers to give her only pennies on the pound for them. The Mayfair property was a good one. She would be able to sell it for a decent amount. The sale of her father's townhouse would also bring in a nice sum. She would repay what she owed—and leave London. There was no sense in remaining. She was a laughingstock. It also would help her quickly severe the connections with her friends. Their names were already being dragged through the mud, along with hers. She hated that this was the way she'd repay their kindness.

With the money she had left, she could find a cottage in the country. Start a new life. Leave all of this ugliness behind.

"Caroline?"

She stiffened.

*No, no, no!*

This was not the time for Luke St. Clair to see her. She ignored him and rushed away, down the stone stairs and away from the terrace.

Within moments, he caught up with her, his strong fingers latching on to her elbow and spinning her around.

"Dash it all, Caroline. What's wrong?" he demanded.

She burst into tears.

He enveloped her in his arms and brought her close to his chest, his hand stroking her back as she sobbed against him. Bit by bit, he pulled the story from her as she blubbered, embarrassed by what she told him. Finally, he had the gist of it—except for the part about her being a strumpet. She couldn't even speak those words to him. She pulled away and he remove a handkerchief, drying her tears.

"You can't give any credence to gossips."

Caroline's jaw dropped. "It was more than gossip, Luke. How could I not have known that my father was murdered in such a grisly manner? It was bad enough being the daughter of a gambler who lost all his money. To learn how he met his end—and to hear what the *ton* is saying about me—and about you and your family for befriending me? It's too much."

Her head dropped in shame.

Suddenly, warm fingers touched her chin, tilting it upward until her gaze met his.

"Forget about it, Caroline."

"How can I?" she asked.

"Like this."

Luke's mouth covered hers.

# CHAPTER TWENTY-TWO

HEAT EXPLODED WITHIN Caroline the moment Luke's lips touched hers. His hands fastened about her waist, holding her in place as he hungrily kissed her. This wasn't the slow, leisurely exploration from before. Instead, it was hot. Demanding. Possessive.

As if he truly wanted her. As a woman.

*Not a friend.*

Her hands pushed into his dark, thick hair, kneading his scalp. She heard a low growl and he yanked her against him, his hands moving from her back to her waist. And then lower. Luke fingers traveled down her buttocks, causing a delicious sensation to build inside her. Then he cupped her rounded cheeks and squeezed, causing her to whimper. She felt no cold. No wind. Only the heat of his body pressed against the length of hers as he kissed her senseless.

She slid her hands to the nape of his neck, playing with the ends of his hair. He broke the kiss, as breathless as she was, his lips sliding down the side of her throat to where her neck met her shoulder. He lingered at the sweet spot, pressing hot kisses there and then grazing his teeth along the sensitive skin. Her head fell back as a shiver darted through her.

Then she felt something new between them, hard, pressing against her belly. Caroline dragged a hand down his chest, all the way to where the pressure occurred. She placed her hand between them and touched it.

This time Luke was the one to gasp.

Quickly, she realized what was happening and moved her hand away.

"No. Go ahead. Touch me, Caroline," he said hoarsely.

Curious, she did as he asked, gliding her hand up and down along the length of hardness pressing against his trousers. He closed his eyes tightly as if in pain. She squeezed it and he moaned, his grimace becoming a smile.

He placed his hand over hers and said, "That's enough," and lifted her hand away. He caught the tip of her glove in his teeth and pulled. The glove began sliding from her fingers. Impatiently, he released his hold on it and used his hand to remove it all the way.

Taking her wrist, he turned her hand palm up and kissed its center, sending chills through her. He kissed each of her fingers, one by one, saving the thumb for last. Luke grazed his teeth along the pad and then his tongue flicked across it. Suddenly, his mouth engulfed it, his tongue dancing deliciously along her thumb.

"Oh!" she cried, as he continued laving and sucking it, causing an odd stirring at where her legs joined.

He slowly pulled her thumb from his mouth, his eyes holding hers.

"Do you know how you affect me, Caroline?"

"No," she whispered, her heart beating rapidly.

"You make me feel strong and yet weak at the same time. I want to hold you. Kiss you. Claim you as mine."

"I thought . . . you considered us friends."

He laughed, low and rich. "Is this how friends behave toward one another?" His arms came about her and held her tight. "There is no other woman in the world for me but you. You are my world, Caroline."

His lips tenderly caressed hers. She felt cherished. Safe. She longed for this moment to go on and on.

But it couldn't. She was a woman the *ton* would never accept.

What she'd overheard in the retiring room made her a pariah. She was no more than damaged goods. Luke was from a distinguished, powerful family. It wouldn't be right for him to sacrifice his reputation, even if he cared for her.

*Even if he loved her . . .*

To save him, she would have to give him up. Forever.

And then leave London, never to return.

Caroline pushed him away. "No. This isn't right."

Luke cradled her face in his large hands. "I know. If anyone saw us now, you'd be ruined. I won't have that. We'll do everything properly. Announce our engagement. Have the banns read. Wed in the chapel at Eversleigh."

He kissed her brow. Her resolve began to crumble. She pressed her nails into the palms of her hands, forcing herself to speak up.

"No," she said forcefully. "There will be no engagement. No wedding."

Confusion filled his eyes. "But . . . I thought . . . the way you responded to my kiss. I—"

"You thought wrong," she said coldly, ignoring the surprise and pain that crossed his handsome face. "I was happy to have your friendship and to have you invest in my bookstore. I want nothing to do with you beyond that. In fact, I've come into a bit of money and will be able to reimburse you, Evan, and Alex early next week."

Caroline stepped back a few paces, knowing if she didn't put some distance between them she might weaken and fall into his arms again. "I'm sorry if I gave you the wrong impression, Luke. My feelings won't change regarding this matter. I think it best if we no longer have contact with one another. I would not want to be accused of leading you on."

She wheeled and hurried away, ignoring him calling after her.

And ignoring her heart shattering with every step that took her further from him.

CAROLINE GATHERED HER employees around her. Both the bookstore and tearoom would open in ten minutes' time. She hadn't been able to eat or drink anything all morning. The aroma of freshly-baked sweets wafted through the arch joining her two businesses, causing her stomach to turn queasy.

She hid her misery with a smile. No one must suspect how she felt today.

Looking out over the small group she'd grown close with over the last few weeks, Caroline lamented that they would soon be out of work. She would make time today to write each of them references, hoping that her name attached to the document would not detract from what she wrote.

She'd already sent word to Higgins, asking that he contact the buyer and have them meet her this afternoon instead of waiting until Monday morning in order for the transaction to take place. The sooner she could cut ties with London, the better it would be. She'd already hurt Luke deeply. Leaving London quickly would be best for them both. He still had the entire Season ahead of him in which to find a bride. She prayed he did just that. He deserved a good life with a woman he could love and the children she would give him.

For now, Caroline addressed her staff, reminding them of small things to do and say. She doubted they would have any business at all, beyond a few curious gossips who might come to browse and see what the fuss was all about. She wished she could cancel Catherine's reading, which was scheduled for eleven o'clock, but didn't see how she could do so without causing more questions than she was willing to answer.

"Everyone is ready, Lady Caroline," Stinch said after she dismissed her employees and they began taking their stations.

"You have done a wonderful job, Mr. Stinch. You should be proud of what you have accomplished."

"I never saw myself in the book business, my lady." The former butler smiled. "I only wish I could have started in it from the beginning. I've never been happier than I have been these last few weeks."

Tears stung her eyes. "I'll be in my office. Please fetch me when the Duchess of Everton arrives."

"Of course."

Caroline retreated to the back and closed the door to the small office. She didn't want to be out on the floor for people to stare at, as if she were some monstrosity.

She decided to write out the references since she had nothing else to do. Everything had been so well organized. It would be a good use of her time.

She'd almost completed them when a knock sounded at her door and Catherine popped her head in.

Her heart hurt seeing this wonderful friend she'd made, hoping her quick departure from town would help save Catherine's reputation.

"What are you doing, hiding here in the back?"

"I had correspondence to attend to."

"You are so disciplined, Caroline. I could never have done so when I had a store full of customers. Why, books are flying off the shelves!"

"Truly?"

"If what I saw continues, Evie's will be a rousing success."

It didn't change anything. Her little venture was a novelty. Something for the *ton* to visit and then gossip about. Even if it did prove successful, which she doubted, she knew she couldn't stay. She couldn't chance running into Luke. When she'd spoken so harshly to him, Caroline had felt a good chunk of her shrivel and die. The best, decent parts. She had nothing left to give to anyone and she certainly would never heal from her emotional wounds, knowing Luke might pop into Evie's at any moment if she stayed.

She rose. "Let's get you situated."

Caroline had taken advertisements in the morning papers for the past three days, wanting to publicize Catherine's reading. When they stepped into the bookstore, shock rippled through her.

The place was jammed full of people. She heard the bell continually ring as the door opened and shut. Clerks rang up purchases to deep lines of customers and she saw Mr. Walton had shown up. Even though she'd told her father's former secretary she had no more need of him, he had come to the opening and now pitched in alongside the other clerks. A huge group of children and their mothers gathered where Catherine would speak.

"See? I told you. I hope we can make our way through this mob."

Suddenly, Jeremy appeared. "Might I lend a hand to two beautiful ladies?"

Gratefully, Caroline took his arm and the way magically parted as the duke led her and his duchess through the throng.

She made sure Catherine was seated and had both her book and a cup of tea within reach. The grandfather clock that Rachel had insisted they bring from the Templeton townhouse chimed eleven times and the restless crowd settled down.

Caroline stepped forward. "I'd like to welcome everyone to Evie's Bookstore and Tearoom. Today, we are especially pleased to sponsor the Duchess of Everton in a reading from her latest book, *The Happy Frog Makes a Friend*, which goes on sale today. Once the duchess has finished, she will sign any purchased copies of the book. All proceeds will go to charity." She looked to Catherine. "Your Grace?"

"Thank you, Lady Caroline. I'm delighted to be here and see all of these wonderful children. Are you ready to hear about the adventures of Freddie the Frog?"

"Yes!" a chorus of children replied.

"Then I suppose we should start." Catherine opened the book and began reading.

Caroline stood to the side and watched the enraptured faces as the children—and adults—present listened to the duchess reading.

"She's quite good at this," a voice murmured.

Turning, she saw the Earl of Merrifield at her side. "She is."

"It's a brilliant opening," he said. "I knew Evie's would be a success."

"Thank you."

Her eyes skimmed the crowd and she saw her friends had come to cheer Catherine on. Rachel and Evan stood with Leah and Alex. Cor and Jeremy. The Morefields and Nevilles. The Stanleys. Amanda waved to her enthusiastically and Caroline waved back.

But no Luke.

She shouldn't be surprised. She'd told him she didn't want any contact between them. He was a gentleman and would honor her wishes. It hurt her not to see him—but it would have hurt even worse if he'd come.

They listened together until Catherine turned the last page and proclaimed, "The End."

"Again!" a young voice cried and the audience laughed heartily.

"Excuse me. I need to get Catherine to a table."

"And I need to purchase my books. Well done, Lady Caroline," Merrifield praised. Then he said, "I'm glad I asked Mayfield my question."

She remembered. It was only last night the earl thought to make Luke envious by gaining a dance with her. She'd told him that Luke wouldn't care.

Caroline had been wrong. Luke did care. And she cared too much.

"I saw him chase after you last night," Merrifield continued. "Hopefully, he straightened out your false impression."

"We settled things nicely between us, Lord Merrifield," she said. "There's no confusion now on where either of us stand."

"Good. I was tired of keeping it all a secret. Good day, Lady Caroline."

As he left, she wondered what he meant. Had Luke shared how he'd felt about her with Merrifield? When would he have done so?

Oh, it didn't matter. She couldn't waste any more time on a hopeless situation. Caroline hurried to rescue Catherine, who had children swarming all around her. She politely shooed them away and moved the duchess to a table near where books were being purchased.

"I'll sit with you."

"You don't have to do that, Caroline. I know you have plenty to see to."

"They must present a receipt in order for you to be able to sign. It will show they've purchased their copy. It's too much to ask for you to check for that and sign. I'm afraid it's already chaotic enough."

"Then I'm happy for your company."

For the next hour, Catherine signed her name to the books customers bought. Stinch came and whispered in Caroline's ear that every copy had been sold but others of Catherine's were being gobbled up.

"Would the duchess consider signing those, as well?"

"Sign what?" Catherine asked the manager.

"We've no more copies of *The Happy Frog*, Your Grace. People are asking if you'd be willing to sign other books you've written," Stinch said.

"Of course. Anything for our orphanages," she said happily.

At that point, Mr. Bellows pulled Caroline aside. She hadn't known he would appear today.

"It seems your plan is working, Lady Caroline," the publisher said. "Mr. Stinch informed me all copies of the duchess' new book have been sold. Would you like more to be delivered?"

"As soon as possible," she replied. "Could they be here by morning?"

"If I leave now, I can have boxes delivered by the end of the day."

"Even better. Would you also include copies of her other books? I see many people in line carrying those."

"I'll see to it," the jovial man said and left the store.

Within the hour, all copies of the Duchess of Everton's books had been bought.

Catherine opened and closed her right hand several times. "I don't think I've ever written my name so many times. Not even on invitations to a ball."

Jeremy appeared and took her hand in his, kneading the fingers and then kissing them. "I would suggest going next door for some tea and a biscuit but there isn't a vacant seat. Let me take you home, Duchess." He pulled her to her feet. "You look tired."

"I believe I have enough energy to do activities beyond writing my name, Duke," she said, a twinkle in her eye.

He slipped an arm around her waist. "Are they activities we might do together, Duchess?"

She cocked her head and pretended to think for a moment. "In fact, several of them are."

"Then we must make our way home with all haste." Jeremy looked to Caroline. "This was an excellent idea. Perhaps we can do this at Evie's each time Catherine has a new book."

Knowing there would be no next time, Caroline merely nodded. "Thank you again, Catherine."

She found Rachel and Leah were still here, in an area of the circulating library, sitting with a few friends and animatedly discussing one of Leah's favorite romance novels. Caroline didn't interrupt them because she saw Higgins enter the store with another man. She went and greeted them.

"Lady Caroline, this is Mr. Studley," her solicitor said.

"Thank you for meeting me here. If you'll come to my office, we can discuss the business at hand."

She led them to the back and Higgins briefly reviewed the transaction, making sure neither party had any questions.

"I'm willing to accept your offer, Mr. Studley. The house has a few furnishings remaining. You are more than welcome to them."

"Mrs. Studley would appreciate that, Lady Caroline. Mr. Higgins told me this is the first day your bookstore has been open. It seems you're off to an excellent start."

"Opening days can be deceiving, Mr. Studley. It's whether patrons will come back in a week. Or a month. And buy, not browse."

Higgins indicated where she was to sign and the solicitor told her the papers would be filed Monday morning. She authorized him to repay her three investors the moment the funds had been transferred.

"I haven't been living in the townhouse so I have nothing to re-move," Caroline told the new owner. "Feel free to move in once you receive the papers from Mr. Higgins. I hope you and your family will create many happy memories in the house."

"Thank you, my lady."

"We'll see ourselves out," Higgins said.

Caroline sat alone for a few minutes. From the looks of it, Evie's had done booming business on its first day. Perhaps she'd been wrong in thinking the *ton* wouldn't patronize the place. She'd noted many customers of the rising middle class had also visited today. They would be solid customers and, hopefully, would return in the near future.

Still, she felt London was no longer home to her. She might have been born to the *ton* but it no longer accepted her. What she'd overheard at last night's ball would continue to spread. No one of quality would want to associate with her, much less invite her to social events. Mr. Stinch had proven to be an excellent manager, someone she trusted. She could leave the running of both shops in his capable hands, though she'd need to hire a bookkeeper. She decided she would ask Mr. Walton if he would be willing to take that position. With the sale of the townhouse, she could pay her three investors in full and still have enough to buy a small cottage. One by the sea appealed to her. She could enjoy long walks on the beach with Tippet as her compan-ion.

Her only regret would be walking away from the only man she would ever love.

Her stomach growled loudly, protesting that it hadn't been fed all day. Caroline decided to go to her tearoom and see how business fared there. She'd been so busy that she hadn't set foot in it all day.

Leaving her office, she headed directly there and stopped in the doorway, gazing across the filled tables. The tearoom was doing as well as its counterpart. For a moment, she wished Aunt Evie were still alive so she could see all that Caroline had accomplished.

Then her body tingled with familiarity as the scent of sandalwood surrounded her.

Luke St. Clair had arrived.

# CHAPTER TWENTY-THREE

L UKE HAD BEEN present the entire day but he made sure to stay out of Caroline's way. He'd spent the first hour in the tearoom. Though some patrons had come from the bookstore through the connecting arch, a larger portion had walked in off the street. He'd gone back and forth between both establishments, noting how each did brisk business on this opening day. His sister-in-law's reading and book signing proved to be popular and he hoped Caroline would think to ask other authors to make an appearance, as well.

In the hours that unfolded, Luke thought about the reasons why Caroline had fled their encounter. He'd intended to speak to her alone at last night's ball when Merrifield informed him Caroline thought she and Luke were no more than friends. He cursed himself, remembering how he'd told her that very thing after previously kissing her. His intentions had been good, wanting to wait and declare his affection for her until she'd gained confidence by standing on the success of her new establishments.

Instead, his silence had only complicated matters. She believed he wasn't interested in her, which was the last impression he'd wished to give. By God, he loved her! He needed to let her know of his feelings.

Before it was too late.

He cursed himself for not telling her the circumstances surrounding her father's death. Learning about the circumstances of Templeton's demise through vicious gossip had undone Caroline. He still ached at the memory of hearing her wrenching sobs last night. It hadn't occurred to him to bring up the matter to her and if he had, what would he have said and when would he have spoken about it?

Luke also knew there had to be more that she wasn't telling him. True, she'd eavesdropped and learned of the gossip surrounding her father's death. She had the impression the *ton* wouldn't frequent Evie's because of it and the fact that she was a woman in business. The failure of her venture weighed heavily upon her—yet it shouldn't have been tied to rejecting him. Something more had been said, something she hadn't shared, that drove her from his arms. The connection between them was too great. He'd kissed a good many women but none of them had the effect on him that Caroline Andrews did. She'd lied about her feelings toward him.

He was determined to learn why.

Biding his time, he waited until near the end of the day before he approached her. The crowd had begun to thin in the bookstore as closing time approached. He'd observed Higgins arrive with a man in tow and then leave half an hour later. Luke wondered who the stranger might be and what business he'd conducted with Caroline. Perhaps it was in regard to the money she said she'd come into though he was reluctant to believe her about that, thinking it was another way she was putting him off.

He watched from behind a tall bookcase as she made her way toward the teashop for the first time today. She paused in the doorway, observing how the room still bustled with customers.

It was time to join her—and find out the truth.

As he came to stand beside her, her stomach growled noisily.

"It seems you're in need of one of Mrs. Withers' sandwiches," he said pleasantly. "Have you eaten anything today?"

"No," she admitted. "I was too nervous before both places opened. Once they did, I haven't had a moment to myself."

"Then it's a full tea for you."

She shook her head. "There are no places to be had. I'm not going to unseat a paying customer merely because my stomach growled."

"I have an idea."

Luke left her and went to the kitchen, where their two cooks bustled about. He took one of the serving trays and set it aside before taking two plates and filling them.

"For Lady Caroline," he told Mrs. Baker when she glanced his way. "Could you also have a pot of tea sent over to her office?"

"Of course, Lord Mayfield," the cook replied.

He returned with the tray. "Your office is the perfect place to end your day."

As they wound their way through the bookstore, Mr. Stinch approached.

"It's almost closing time, my lady. Any instructions?"

"Everyone has worked so hard today. Release the clerks as soon as they tidy up. All unbought books need to be placed back on the shelves and then they can leave for the day. Have them return two hours before opening tomorrow to label and stock the books Mr. Bellows is having delivered."

"They just arrived. I had them taken next door and placed with our surplus inventory."

"Excellent. The only other thing will be to bring the money box to me. Normally, I will let you count it at the end of each day but I'm curious as to how our opening went."

"I'll see it brought to you," Stinch said and left.

Luke carried the tray to her office and placed it on top of the desk.

"Sit. You're famished and look tired."

Kitty arrived with a smaller tray containing a teapot and two cups and saucers, along with cream and sugar. Luke thanked her and took it, setting it next to the tray with food. He poured Caroline a cup and added the splash of cream and one cube of sugar that she preferred and handed it to her.

"Thank you," she said and sat in the chair behind her desk as she stirred the beverage. Taking a sip, she sighed. "This is exactly what I needed."

He fixed himself a cup and started on a sandwich. She did the same and, for several minutes, they chose to eat instead of converse. Once their sandwiches were gone, she nibbled on a sugar cookie while he picked up a macaroon.

"You should be very pleased. It was a very strong opening at both shops."

"A business cannot be judged on a first day alone," she retorted. "The *ton* might have come today out of nothing but curiosity."

"True, but once they saw the variety of books you offer and tasted the delicious sweets? They'll return. Others will, too."

"I can only hope so." A shadow crossed her face.

"I saw Mr. Higgins arrive."

She took a sip of her tea. "Yes, he was here on business. The gentleman that accompanied him has bought my father's townhouse."

Her words surprised him.

"That will enable me to pay you, Evan, and Alex back immediately and give me additional funds to invest in Evie's."

"I see." He wondered if she would continue to stay with Rachel and Evan but didn't want to ask.

"I think I would like to walk through it a final time before Mr. Studley takes ownership on Monday," she revealed.

"I can accompany you there once you finish your tea."

Luke saw her hesitation and then relaxed when she said, "Thank you. I'd appreciate that."

"Then we should finish our pound cake and be off. I don't want to return the tray to Mrs. Baker unless we've finished every bite. She's a bit more sensitive than her sister."

"Any excuse to eat cake?" Caroline teased.

"No excuses are ever needed. Cake is a necessity in life," he proclaimed.

When they'd finished, he took both trays in hand and returned them to the tearoom. It was closing time there and the last customers were leaving. Caroline had followed him and heaped praised upon the four women.

"You did me proud today. My aunt, Evie, would also have been proud."

"We were busy all day, my lady," Daisy said enthusiastically. "Several customers promised me they'd be back."

Luke went with Caroline as she returned to the bookstore and also complimented those employees. By now, the clerks had put the store back to rights, shelving books and straightening the furniture.

Mr. Stinch appeared with the moneybox. "I know you wanted to count it, my lady, but I couldn't resist the urge." He shared the amount they'd earned in the bookstore. "Of course, we must take into consideration the cost of the books and the salaries paid today but, overall, I believe it an excellent start."

"I'll trust your count, Mr. Stinch," Caroline said. "Please collect the earnings from the tearoom, as well, and place the money in the safe in my office. You can remove it in the morning and fill the clerks' tills with enough change. I think we'll want to make bank deposits three times a week, on Mondays, Wednesdays, and Fridays. You'll be in charge of that."

"Quite a day's profit," Luke said, hoping she would begin to believe in herself and the two businesses she'd created.

"Let me get my reticule," she told him.

She was being cordial. He'd give her that. And she was allowing him to accompany her to her former home before he escorted her across the square to his sister's townhouse. It gave him hope that he could break through the walls she'd flung up between them.

They left, Caroline reminding Stinch to lock up. Luke hailed a hansom and gave the driver their destination before helping her into the cab.

As he settled in beside her, she asked, "Don't you have an event to attend this evening?"

"No. Contrary to popular belief, I'm not out until dawn every night of the Season." He didn't add that in the past, many of those free nights had been spent with his mistress or in a rendezvous with a merry widow.

"Are you planning to go the March ball tomorrow night?" he asked. "Or I believe Viscount Linwood is having a card party for the less adventurous at the same time."

"No. After a full day at Evie's, all I'll want to do is come home and soak in a hot bath."

The thought of a naked, wet Caroline had Luke salivating. He better change the topic quickly.

"Do you plan to spend all of your days at Evie's?"

"I'm not sure," she said evasively.

Once again, Luke wondered what she hid from him. He would get to the bottom of it after they were inside Templeton's townhouse. They'd have no interruptions to plague them.

He sensed the cab slowing. Once it came to a full stop, he hopped out and paid the driver and then handed Caroline down.

She opened her reticule as they walked to the door and withdrew a key. "I'll need to have this delivered to Mr. Higgins by Monday."

Luke took it from her and unlocked the door.

They entered the foyer and he asked, "Are there any particular rooms you wish to visit?"

"No. I just wanted to see the place a final time. I doubt I'll be invited to grand homes anymore."

Luke kept silent, waiting for her to see her childhood home a last time before he challenged her opinion regarding how the *ton* viewed her. He knew she had formed it based upon the little gossip she'd overheard in the retiring room. He wanted her to know she had good friends, even powerful ones, who would see that society treated her well.

They visited the library first, which she said had been her favorite room growing up.

"Books were friends to me. I soaked up learning. At first, it was to show my father how much I could learn. The facts I spouted never impressed him, though. By the time I realized that, I was learning because I wanted to, squirreling away knowledge."

"I've told you my father was much the same. His children were nothing but a nuisance to him. He left us in the care of nursemaids, followed by tutors and governesses. Jeremy and I were shipped off to school and largely forgotten by him. Poor Rachel had to stay home. She avoided encounters with him."

"What about your mother?" Caroline asked.

"All three of us never knew our mothers. Each died in childbirth. Father would marry again once he tired of his current mistress or needed a new dowry to fill the family coffers."

She bit her lower lip, causing a surge of desire to ripple through him. "I'm so sorry."

"It's all right. Besides the hired help, we had someone better than a parent. Cor. She made up for any lack of attention by our father. Cor taught us right from wrong and what should be valued. She saw we were well loved and grew up to be strong, independent individuals."

"I've only spoken to her a few times but she's a remarkable woman."

"I think so, too."

They stopped at the drawing room and then her mother's small parlor. A cushion still rested on a settee that Caroline said she'd embroidered when she was ten.

"Will you take it?" he asked.

"No. it's from a past that I don't wish to recall. The only good from that time in my life was being with my sister. Cynthia was a dear companion. When Father was largely absent and Mama ineffectual, Cynthia is who lives on in my memory."

They went upstairs after that. She didn't bother returning to either of her parents' bedchambers and only briefly looked into her sister's. Instead, they crossed the hall and she entered her former room. Walking to the window, she pulled the curtain aside and gazed out on the square below.

"Cynthia and I used to sit in this window seat and look across the way. We didn't know who owned the townhouse opposite us. No one ever lived there so we made up stories about who the owner was and why he and his family were never in residence."

Luke knew the true tale of how Evan's father, the Duke of Winstead, had washed his hands of his only son when Evan was but thirteen. Evan had chosen to remain in the country at Edgemere when not in school, learning from his steward all he could about the estate and getting to know his tenants. The townhouse had remained empty. To this day, Evan didn't speak to his father, especially after the duke had tried to prevent Rachel from marrying Evan. He'd once told Luke he wished he could remain Marquess of Merrick forever instead of one day inheriting his father's title because he didn't want to be known as Winstead.

Caroline dropped the curtain back into place and crossed the room to the bed. She sat on it and looked at him.

"I would like to lie in my bed one last time. With you."

# CHAPTER TWENTY-FOUR

CAROLINE HAD BEEN thinking about how she would never belong to Luke and decided she could.

*For one night.*

Her plan to retire to the country would take her out of circulation from the London gossips and save the reputation of the St. Clairs. She could spend the bulk of her life by the sea, only venturing into town a few times a year to conduct business. She'd made a wise choice in hiring Stinch to manage both places. Once she found someone to keep the ledgers, she could request monthly business reports from him.

Her future life would be a quiet one. Even lonely at times. That's why she'd decided she wanted memories of Luke to fill the empty places in her heart. He'd awakened something within her that she had a need to explore. She was now aware of physical desire simmering within her. That's why she'd allowed him to accompany her here tonight. She hadn't cared to see the townhouse a final time. It was merely a ruse to lure him somewhere private. She knew he desired her. She would use that and ask him to love her this once so she could cherish the memories of what might have been between them had things been different.

He came toward her, so tall and handsome that she began trembling. Taking her hands, he brought her to her feet. A slow smile spread across his face.

"I knew you weren't indifferent to me," he said softly. "That you felt the same way I did."

He gazed at her intently, drinking her in. Caroline did the same. For one glorious night, this man would be hers.

"Love me," she said.

"I plan to for the rest of our lives."

Guilt flashed through her. She knew what she did was wrong but, already, her body burned for him. For once, she would be selfish and take what she wanted, without regret.

His fingers entwined with hers as he bent and pressed soft kisses on her brow. Her temples. Her cheek and jaw. After each kiss, Luke said her name. Quietly. Reverently. As if he couldn't believe they were here, together, alone.

He released her hands and his fingers skimmed up her arms until he cradled her face, his thumbs rubbing back and forth.

"You are so very beautiful. Inside and out."

With that, his lips met hers in a searing kiss that grew longer and hotter, stirring the embers inside her until the flames engulfed her. She wrapped her arms about his waist and pressed her body against his. His hands traveled the length of her back, up and down, the friction heating her until she begged him to undress her. Caroline wanted her skin against his. She wanted to taste him. Touch him. Hold him.

Luke took his time, peeling away the layers she wore, until everything was gone and she stood before him naked. She should have felt embarrassment or shame. Instead, she only felt desire.

His eyes took her in. "You are a revelation. A beauty beyond compare." He wrapped his arms about her and brought her to him, kissing her deeply. The sensation of his wool coat against her bare skin was oddly erotic.

Breaking the kiss, she said, "I want to see you. All of you. Now," she commanded boldly.

He grinned. "I'll work as fast as I can," and began stripping away his own clothing.

When he finished, she thought he was like one of the statues in a book she'd read on Ancient Greece. There was so much to admire. His broad shoulders and bare, muscled chest. The flat stomach and long legs, with calves she longed to stroke.

"Will I do?"

She grinned. "You most certainly will."

Caroline wrapped her arms about his neck and pulled him down to her, taking the lead as she kissed him. She moved from his mouth to his neck, licking the salty skin as she inhaled his sandalwood soap. His hands stroked her back and buttocks, causing a marvelous tinging to shoot through her.

Without warning, he scooped her up and carried her to the bed, placing her on it gently before he stretched out beside her.

"I will kiss every part of you," he promised.

And he did.

Everywhere his hands went, his mouth and tongue followed. His licking and sucking her breasts drove her into a frenzy. She went from stroking his back to raking it with her nails. Then Luke kissed his way down her belly and went lower, toward her womanly core. His fingers encircled her ankles and pushed her legs up until her knees were bent and she was open to him.

He kissed her core, which caused a low pounding to begin. She hid her shock as he continued kissing her there. Then his tongued darted inside and Caroline nearly leaped from the bed.

"Oh! Oh, my! Luke!"

He looked up. "I'm busy."

He went back to what he was doing. Her fingers threaded through his hair, pushing him against her as the drum beat increased in rhythm. She whimpered as his tongue danced inside her, causing something to build. She moaned. She panted. And then she tumbled gloriously as sensations overwhelmed her, an electricity that shot waves of pleasure through her, pleasure that she'd never known existed. It kept on and on until it finally subsided and her hands fell to her sides.

Luke kissed his way back up to her mouth as his fingers went where his tongue had just left. He murmured something against her lips but she couldn't understand it. All her focus was on her core and what his fingers were doing to her. Again, that same odd, wonderful, incredible feeling built up and then crashed as she cried his name, over and over. It finally subsided and now she lay limp, unable to move.

"What have you done to me?" she asked, barely able to form words.

Those emerald eyes twinkled with mischief. "Hopefully, satisfied you. And now I'll make you mine."

He pushed up and she saw his manhood jutting from him, large and long.

"It only hurts once," he said and before she could ask what, he entered her quickly.

Caroline gasped at the pain, clawing at his shoulders.

"Wait, love. You'll see."

She swiped at him twice more and then stilled. The pain was gone but she could feel how he filled her. Then he withdrew and pushed into her again. He repeated the motion. Suddenly, her hips rose to meet him, as if her body knew what to do. She wound her arms about him and he continued the long, slow thrusts.

"Are you all right?" he asked.

"Yes. But . . . can you go faster?"

He chuckled. "I can do whatever you wish."

Luke increased his pace. His hand came between them and found the nub that caused her tremendous pleasure. Suddenly, she was crying his name as he called out hers. Then he collapsed against her. Caroline welcomed the weight that drove her deep into the mattress. She locked her arms about his neck and kissed him soundly.

He rolled until they were both on their sides and they kissed until she thought her lips might bleed.

When he finally broke the kiss, she . . . yawned.

"I'm sorry," she quickly apologized.

"You are tired," he said, smoothing her hair. "This was the biggest day of your life with the store opening."

That might have been the case but what they had just done together would qualify as the most wondrous experience of her life. She would never, ever forget this.

"Let's sleep a while," he suggested, turning her until her back pressed against his chest and his arms held her safe.

THEY DOZED BRIEFLY and then began all over again. Luke made love to her twice more and then told her they should dress.

"I know Rachel and Evan were attending a ball tonight with Leah and Alex. We need to get you home and to bed before they arrive. You can pretend you went home straight after leaving Evie's. They'll never know the difference."

He dressed first and then played lady's maid to her. His knowledge of how ladies undergarments worked let her know she was only one of many women he'd coupled with. It didn't matter, though. She had tonight. She would always have tonight. No one could ever take the memories away from her.

They exited the townhouse and he locked the door, returning the key to her, and then he walked her across the empty square. Standing in front of the door, Luke gave her a long, sweet kiss. Caroline took in everything. The cool of the evening. The feel of his muscular chest beneath her fingertips. The taste of him. She committed it all to memory. She would live on this the rest of her life.

"We have much to talk about," he said.

Wanting to put him off, she said, "I will be busy at Evie's tomorrow."

"I won't be there. Alex has asked me to go with him to look at some new horses he wishes to buy. They're near his estate. We'll go down to Fairfield early tomorrow morning and look at the stock, testing it. We'll come back late Sunday. We can see each other Monday night at the Wilsons' ball." He kissed her. "I'm expecting you to save the supper dance for me."

She hadn't replied to the invitation she'd received but nodded as if in agreement. If everything worked out as she planned, she would be gone by Monday night.

And never see Luke again.

# CHAPTER TWENTY-FIVE

C AROLINE WENT TO the stables behind the Merrick townhome, wanting to visit Davy and Tippet. She'd done so several times over the past few weeks and had seen how happy both the boy and dog were. The first person she saw was Brimley, the head groom, and she decided to ask him about Davy.

"Has Davy been fitting in well?"

The older man smiled broadly. "He has, my lady. I've never met a soul more eager to learn. He's a natural with the horses, that boy is. They seem to perk up when Davy comes around. I'll rue the day when you take him away. We'll all miss young Davy."

That made her rethink bringing the boy with her when she left London. He already had a job here he loved. Caroline had no idea what she would have him do out in the country. It might be best to leave him where he was and not force another change upon him. She excused herself and found Davy grooming a horse inside a stall. Tippet sat in the corner.

"Good morning, my lady. Isn't it a fine day?"

"Spring in London is very nice," she agreed. "How are you liking your work for the marquess?"

His eyes lit up. "I love horses. I can't imagine doing anything else. I'm so grateful you took me away from the sea. I never liked it. My stomach stayed queasy on every voyage."

She knew then that she couldn't bring this boy with her, much as she'd wanted to.

"You know I've opened a bookstore. Have you thought about working there in the future?"

He shook his head as he ran the brush along the horse. "I'd rather stay here, my lady, with the horses. I'm sorry if that disappoints you."

"It doesn't. It's important to find something you love and you've done so." She paused. "I'm leaving London for a bit to live in the country. Would you mind if Tippet stays with you? I wouldn't trust him to anyone's care but yours. In fact, he should be yours. You're the one who's cared for him since we've been in England."

Joy filled Davy's face. "Truly? He can be mine? You don't mind?"

"Not a bit. A dog needs a boy." She smiled. "And a boy needs a dog."

"Thank you, my lady. Tippet and me'll be friends for life, I'm sure of it."

"That's good to know. I will try to stop by and see you the next time I'm in London."

Davy grinned. "I'd like that." He paused from the brushing and said, "You've been right good to me, my lady. Teaching me to read and getting me a place here with the horses. May . . . I hug you?"

"Of course."

The boy came to her and Caroline wrapped her arms about him. She would miss Davy and Tippet but they had a new life and purpose, thanks to Evan's generosity.

"Goodbye," she said and went to find Brimley again.

"Mr. Brimley, I'd thought Davy might one day work for me in my bookstore but he seems happy where he is. Are you sure the marquess has room for him?"

"He does, my lady. Why, I can see Davy one day becoming head groom himself."

That assured Caroline that she was making the right decision.

"I'm glad to hear that. I will leave him and Tippet to your care then. I suppose live horses are more interesting to a boy than musty, old books."

She left and returned to her room, where the maid had already come and gone. She saw no need to take any of the ball gowns that Madame Toufours had made up for her. Instead, Caroline packed several day dresses, along with undergarments and a few night rails. She went downstairs and asked if Kent would have the small trunk in her chamber delivered to Evie's.

"It's some books that I want to have there in my office," she told the butler.

She'd never been deceitful in her life but her lies were stacking up.

Next, Caroline took a cab to Mr. Higgins' office. She knew the solicitor worked a half-day on Saturdays and wanted to catch him this morning. His surprise was obvious as she came through the door.

"Lady Caroline, what are you doing here? Have you changed your mind about the sale of your father's townhouse?"

"No, but I do have need of you regarding another matter, Mr. Higgins."

"I am at your service. Please, have a seat."

She perched on the edge of a chair. "I'm looking to leave London indefinitely. Mr. Stinch will manage my stores in my absence. I'd like to be by the sea. Do you know of anyone who might have a cottage for sale?"

"Not for sale, but my wife's aunt has one for let. It's in Dover."

"I'll take it."

Shock filled him. "But I haven't even told you about it," he protested.

"You would not have mentioned it to me if it were unsuitable. I trust that you would recommend it?"

"I would. It's in pristine condition and a short walk to the beach."

"Then I'd like you to handle the details for me. Could I take charge of it come Monday?"

"Monday? That's only two days from now. Is there a reason you're rushing to let it?"

Caroline gave him a long look. "I'll be frank with you, Mr. Higgins. I returned from America to learn my father was dead. I recently discovered he was murdered under dubious circumstances. That has affected me more than I would have thought, along with the gossip associated with it. He left me destitute and I have to earn a living for myself. The *ton* is not a forgiving group and I fear Evie's success might be tainted by my presence.

"Thus, I would like to retreat from society for now and lick my wounds. I long for peace and solitude. I've hired capable workers and an excellent manager and feel I can allow them to run Evie's for me. For now, at least."

"I understand, my lady." His eyes looked at her in sympathy. "I will take the mail coach down to Dover and make the arrangements for you. I'll deliver the key to Lord Merrick's."

She didn't want that. "Could you bring it to the bookstore instead on Monday morning?"

"If that's what you prefer."

"I do. You've gone above and beyond, Mr. Higgins. I can't thank you enough." She handed over the key to her father's townhouse. "Expect a generous bonus once the sale goes through."

Caroline left his office and returned to her waiting cab, directing the driver to take her to Mayfair. Once at Evie's she walked through, noting the number of customers and that the new shipment of Catherine's books had been placed on the shelves. She ventured to the tearoom and saw it was already doing brisk business at only half-past ten, even though it wasn't scheduled to open until eleven. Mrs. Withers must have taken the initiative to open early. Returning to her office, she placed the references she'd written yesterday in a bottom drawer of her desk. She doubted her employees would need them now.

Caroline left her office and found Walton hard at work ringing up customers' purchases. She saw Stinch and motioned him over.

"I see Mr. Walton is back at work today."

"He was most helpful during yesterday's opening, my lady. I know you'd said you had no more need of his services but I'm grateful he showed up yesterday—and again today. I don't know what we would have done without an extra pair of hands."

"You think he's needed on the floor?"

"For now. If business levels off, then we could use him for a few hours a day."

"I want to hire Mr. Walton as my bookkeeper. That wouldn't occupy all of his time and leave him available for when you needed him in the store."

Stinch studied her. "I thought you'd planned to keep the ledgers, Lady Caroline."

"I think it best for Evie's if I take a step back." She took a deep breath. "I learned how Father was murdered."

He winced. "I am sorry. I didn't think it my place to tell you. I'd hoped it would never come up since he was already dead and buried."

"It did—through gossip, the *ton's* favorite pastime. I feel Evie's has a better chance if I remove myself from the day-to-day affairs. You have proven to be an excellent manager. Mr. Walton would be an asset regarding the bookkeeping and could even make the bank deposits. I plan to go away for a while."

He frowned. "Where would you go?"

"I'm thinking the country. I need time to myself. I trust Evie's will be in good hands."

Determination filled Stinch's face. "I will not let you down, my lady."

She thanked him and asked that he send Mr. Walton to see her when things slowed a bit. Caroline returned to her office and a quarter-hour later, Mr. Walton appeared in the doorway.

"You asked to see me, my lady?"

"Yes, Mr. Walton. Come in and have a seat, please."

After he was situated, she opened the ledger on her desk and asked him to study it a moment. He poured over it, nodding to himself.

"What would you do differently?" she asked.

"You've done a very good job recording purchases and all it took to get Evie's up and running. I do have a few suggestions, though."

Walton explained some of the changes he would make, including keeping separate records for the bookstore and tearoom instead of combining the two. He also discussed a new method of recording items and why he believed it to be more efficient.

Caroline told him what she would want to see in a monthly report and asked how he would prepare those. Once he finished his explanation, she'd made up her mind.

"Mr. Walton, I know we discussed how you were only to work here temporarily."

He blushed. "I hope you don't mind that I asserted myself at yesterday's opening. The clerks were swamped and I knew what to do."

"On the contrary, I appreciated the initiative you showed and everything we've discussed. I would like to offer you the job as Evie's bookkeeper."

His face lit up. "Truly?"

"It would be a permanent position but I don't think it would keep you busy all the time. I would also need you to decide with the others what purchases we should make regarding our stock and log those in as you've been doing. I'd also like to have you work on the floor a few hours when necessary. This could be your office and Mr. Stinch could step in and ask you to help out when needed. Would you be interested?"

"Indeed, I would. It's more than I could have dreamed of. But may I ask what your role will be?"

"Strictly as the owner. I will have no visible presence in the store.

Mr. Stinch will manage both establishments. I will be kept abreast financially by your reports."

She offered him what she believed was a fair salary and he accepted it.

"You may start Monday morning in both positions if that's agreeable."

"It is, my lady. Thank you for this opportunity. I will not disappoint you."

Walton left the office and Caroline knew Evie's would be in solid hands.

CAROLINE SPENT A quiet Sunday with Rachel. Evan had decided to go with Luke and Alex to the country and so it left the two of them together. After attending church, Rachel declared she wanted to do nothing more than play with Seth and nap when her baby did.

"The Season is only a week old and I'm already tired."

"You recently had a baby, Rachel," Caroline pointed out. "You are still recovering from that."

"True. Oh, I already miss Evan."

She felt the same about Luke, having lain awake last night, reliving his every touch.

"He will return late this evening."

"I know," her friend grumbled good-naturedly. "I still miss him, though. It was hard to fall asleep last night without having him beside me."

"Seth favors the marquess a great deal. Playing with him should soothe you."

"Come with me," Rachel urged.

They went up to the nursery, where both women took turns holding and rocking the baby. A powerful feeling swept through Caroline as she looked down at the infant, a yearning she'd never known. It occurred to her that what she and Luke had done was how babies were made. Even now, she could be carrying his child. Fervently, she wished it were so. She would create a world for the two of them, mother and child.

And once more, lie to Luke.

When did lying become second nature to her? She'd lied that she had no feelings for him when she was in love with him. Then she'd seduced him into making love to her, knowing she would never wed him. She'd already taken clothes from this very household and would leave it tomorrow, never to return, knowing her disappearance would hurt Rachel. She was leaving behind all the friends she'd made, not revealing where she went.

She was a coward.

Admitting that to herself didn't change her mind. She was sacrificing her love of a good man and wonderful friendships in order to save all of these people. The *ton* had judged her and found her lacking. Caroline would not see the people she cared about condemned—even ostracized—due to their friendships with her. She wouldn't allow Luke to marry her and suffer the ugliness that would follow. He would move on and find someone more suitable for him. Luke St. Clair was a good man—too good for her—and he would make another woman happy. Very happy.

Thankfully, she wouldn't be around to witness their happiness. If she were, it would break her.

# CHAPTER TWENTY-SIX

C AROLINE TOOK BREAKFAST in her room. Rachel had suggested it, saying neither she nor Evan would be down for breakfast. Evan had returned late last night and Rachel said they would be sleeping in. From the hungry look in Evan's eyes, Caroline believed sleeping was the last thing that would occur in the Merrick bed.

She wore her favorite day dress today, one of the new ones Madame Toufours had made up. It was a cornflower blue. Her trunk with some of her clothing was already at Evie's in her office. She would attend to any last details there and then leave for Dover and her new life.

As she arrived at the bookstore, she saw her solicitor climbing from a cab.

"Good day, Mr. Higgins."

"The same to you, Lady Caroline."

He withdrew a key from his pocket and passed it to her. She placed it inside her reticule as he gave her the address of the cottage that would become her new home.

"I checked the mail coach schedule for you. One leaves for Dover at noon today. If you can't make that one, another departs at half-past three. It's the last one of the day."

"Thank you, Mr. Higgins. I apologize for rushing you."

"I was happy to arrange everything for you, my lady. The deed will be transferred to Mr. Studley today and the funds deposited into your account."

"Take ten percent for yourself," she said.

His eyes widened. "That's far too generous."

"I insist. You have been a godsend these past few weeks. I couldn't have accomplished nearly as much without your speed and discretion."

She gave him the key to the London townhouse. "Give Mr. Studley my best. Will you also see that my three investors receive their compensation in full once Mr. Studley's funds are placed in my account?"

He tapped his temple. "I have it all here, my lady. Lords Mayfield, Merrick, and Alford. They will be taken care of."

"And Mr. Higgins, would you do me one last favor?"

"Yes, my lady." He waited expectantly.

"Tell no one where I am. As I mentioned, I'm in need of solitude. If any of my friends wish to contact me, tell them I will write to them soon."

A frown creased his brow but he nodded. "If that's your wish."

"It is. Thank you again, Mr. Higgins. You've been most helpful."

He departed and Caroline entered the store. It was already a little past ten and she saw four customers, which she thought was a good sign. She waved to Stinch and found Walton in the office, papers scattered across the desk.

"Good morning, Lady Caroline."

"The same to you, Mr. Walton. I hope you have everything you need."

"I do. I plan to spend a few hours each week browsing at other bookstores. It will help decide what needs to be ordered."

She thought of one thing Luke had mentioned to her and said, "You saw how well the Duchess of Everton's reading went."

"Indeed. I heard her say she would be willing to do so again in the future."

"Since it proved popular, you might want to contact other authors to see if they would be interested in doing the same type of event at Evie's."

"Excellent idea, my lady." Walton made a note on a piece of paper.

"I suppose that's all. Would you help bring my trunk outside? It's in the corner there."

The bookkeeper lifted the small trunk with ease and followed her through the store. She said goodbye to Stinch and then opened the door to allow Walton access to the sidewalk, where he rested the trunk.

"May I hail a hansom cab for you?"

"Please."

One came by almost immediately, the advantage of being located in Mayfair, and Walton waved the driver over, indicating the trunk.

"I suppose this is goodbye, Lady Caroline. I'll be sure to prepare your monthly report. Did you leave a forwarding address with Mr. Stinch?"

"No, but I'll write to you both once I'm settled."

She turned and saw the driver waiting. "Goodbye, Mr. Walton." She watched him return inside the bookstore and stepped toward the cab.

"Lady Caroline?"

A man hurried toward her, He looked vaguely familiar. As he approached, she recognized him as one of Netherby's clerks, the one who'd been rude to her.

"I'm here to give you a message from Mr. Netherby. He would like to see you at once."

"I'm afraid—"

"He knows he was wrong, my lady. My employer wishes to extend an olive branch to you."

Caroline knew Netherby had the ear of many of London's booksellers. She supposed it would be best to part with him on good terms before she left the city.

"I only have a few minutes to spare," she told the clerk. "I need to make the noon mail coach to Dover."

He smiled. "Oh, it won't take long." He handed her into the cab. "Let me tell the driver where we're headed. That is, if you don't mind sharing the cab with me."

She did, not liking this fellow one bit, but she refused to be petty. "Not at all."

The clerk spoke to the driver and joined her.

Trying to be polite, she asked, "Have you worked for Mr. Netherby for long?"

"Several years."

An awkward silence fell and Caroline looked out the window to avoid further conversation. She noticed after a few blocks they were headed in the wrong direction.

"You need to tell the driver he's missed his turn."

"Oh, we're not going to the bookstore. Mr. Netherby isn't there now. He's at home."

Frowning, she said, "I don't have time to go out of my way. I told you I am in a hurry."

"It will actually save you time. We're headed in the direction of where the mail coaches leave London."

"Very well." She wasn't pleased and continued to stare out the window, lost in thought.

When the cab came to a halt, she looked at her surroundings and didn't recognize the part of town they were in. It looked seedy to her and she couldn't understand why Netherby would want to live here. The clerk, who'd never given her his name, jumped down and paid the driver, then handed her down.

Worried, Caroline looked at the driver. "You are to wait," she instructed. "I won't be but a few minutes."

He averted his eyes and bobbed his head up and down, giving her mixed signals. Before she could question him further, the clerk took her elbow and steered her toward a building with a bright blue door. His touch seemed forward to her and she pulled away, walking up the steps beside him. Without knocking, he opened the door and ushered her inside.

The place was dark. No drapes had been pulled to let in the morning light. She looked to her left and saw an unusually large, rectangular table and wondered why it stood in the center of the open room. No other furniture was evident.

Suddenly, a short, stout man appeared, a long scar running from the corner of his eye down his cheek to the corner of his mouth. She recoiled at the sight of him.

"Netherby's waiting," he said brusquely and headed up the stairs.

The clerk gestured for her to follow the stranger. Unease filled her. The clerk started to take her elbow again and she gave him a look that stopped him in his tracks. Caroline turned and went up the staircase, the clerk trailing behind her. She caught up to the scarred man and paused as he opened a door.

"Go on in," he said.

She did as he asked and heard the door close behind her. Straight ahead, a man sat behind a desk. He was in his mid-thirties, with dark hair already graying at the temples and a cruel mouth.

"You're not Netherby," she said, wondering where the bookseller was.

"I actually am, Lady Caroline," he said affably.

Understanding dawned on her. "You're Netherby's son. The one who didn't follow him into the book trade."

"That's right. He said you were sharp. We have that in common. I didn't see the point in selling old, smelly books when I could make a lot more in other ways."

"I'm here to see your father," she said stubbornly, tamping down the anxiety running through her. "Since he's not here, I'll be on my way."

Turning, she went and opened the door. The scarred stranger blocked her way. He took two steps forward, forcing her back into the room. She wheeled and faced the younger Netherby, hearing the door close again behind her.

"I would like to leave now, Mr. Netherby. I have an engagement."

"I'm afraid you'll have to cancel that, Lady Caroline. Father has asked a favor of me. I'm always eager to have him in my debt."

"What kind of favor?" she asked warily.

"One involving you."

"Where am I?" she demanded.

"My gaming hell."

That explained the long table she'd seen. It must be something used in gambling.

"I demand to leave at once," she said again, "Tell your man to step aside."

Netherby stood and came around from behind the desk, stopping in front of her. "You're spirited. I'll give you that. I'm afraid to tell you that you won't be leaving here until tomorrow evening. You see, one of my side business—beyond gambling—is running a very special auction each month. Tomorrow night is the upcoming one.

"You'll be on the block, Lady Caroline."

Numbness filled her. She thought she must have misunderstood him.

"You see, Father sees you as a threat to his business. Already, your store has flocks of patrons. He's afraid if you remain in business, he'll be ruined." He smiled. "He'd rather see *you* ruined. You'll be sold to the highest bidder. A blond, virgin beauty from the *ton* will draw a high price. Perhaps the highest price I've ever received."

"You're joking. You think to *sell* me?"

His gaze bored into her. "I never joke when it comes to money."

Caroline flung herself at him, knocking them both to the ground.

She raked her nails across his face as he shouted. Suddenly, she was yanked up, her arms pinned to her sides. She screamed as loudly as she could but the arms tightened about her. She couldn't breathe and began kicking her heels at the shins of the man who held her.

Netherby dragged himself to his feet. He took a handkerchief and wiped the blood from his face and then nodded. The arms relaxed and she was free. She whirled and slapped the scarred man. He struck her quickly, knocking her to her knees. Caroline fought for a breath as pain spread across her cheek.

"I've told you to handle the merchandise with care, Coswell. No bidder wants damaged goods."

"Sorry, Mr. Netherby." The man latched on to her elbow and jerked her to her feet, keeping her in place.

"No more screaming, Lady Caroline. It doesn't do any good. No one will come to your aid here. It's a true hell for ladies such as yourself. Coswell will take you to a room where you'll stay until the auction."

She began trembling. "You truly peddle women?"

"You'd be surprised at the dark taste of some gentlemen of the *ton*. Only beatings and torture excite them sexually. My father assures me that you have no living blood relatives since your father was murdered. You have no fiancé. With your disappearance, your bookstore will quickly fail."

"Why would you do this? For money? I have money."

He shook his head. "Not as much as I can fetch for you. I'll make a fortune off you and Father will have one less competitor to worry about."

Netherby returned to his seat. "Take her to her room, Coswell. I'll see you tomorrow evening, Lady Caroline."

The brute holding on to her opened the door. She jerked her arm away and walked into the hall under her own power. As he stepped out and closed the door, she took off running, knowing it might be her only chance at escape. He quickly caught up to her. Once again, the strong arms encased her, pinning her arms to her side. Pressed against him, she felt the beginning of his erection and thought she might be ill.

Into her ear, he softly said, "If I have to, I'll tame you, my lady. Netherby doesn't want any wild ones. I'll tie you to a bed and have my way with you, over and over, until I break you. Unless you cooperate. Do you think you can do that?"

He licked her ear. Revulsion swept through her.

"I'll behave," she said quietly, knowing for now she was defeated.

He released his hold and marched past her.

Caroline had no choice but to meekly follow, not wanting to chance the punishment he threatened. They went to a door marked with a huge X and he removed the keyring hanging from a nail pounded into the wall. Unlocking the door, he gestured for her to enter.

She walked into the small room. A bed and chamber pot were the only things she saw.

"You'll get a meal tonight. None the day of the auction. Netherby likes you to be hungry."

With that, Coswell closed the door. She heard him lock it again and then his steps receded.

Caroline looked at the unmade bed and saw a large bug crawling in the sheets. Bile rose in her throat. She went to the window and pulled back the curtain, seeing bars across it. She pressed her back against the wall and slowly slid down until she touched the ground. Dropping her head against her knees, she wept.

# CHAPTER TWENTY-SEVEN

L UKE HAD WANTED to visit Caroline at the bookstore. Spending
two days away from her had seemed like an eternity. He vowed
never to do so again. At the same time, he wanted her to enjoy her
independence and not have him hovering about all the time. That very
independence was one of the things he loved most about her. He
forced himself to stay away from Evie's all of Monday.

His compromise was to head to the Merrick townhouse so he
could ride with her to tonight's ball. He planned to sign her programme as many times as she would allow him.

Kent greeted him and stepped aside so he could enter. Luke looked
around and spying no one asked, "Has Lady Caroline come downstairs
yet?"

"No, Lord Mayfield. She hasn't returned from the bookstore yet."

"What?" He glanced at the grandfather clock standing in the foyer.
"It's half-past eight. Are you sure she's not here?"

Uneasiness filled him. Before Kent could answer, Luke bounded up
the stairs. He had no clue which was her bedchamber, so he started
shouting her name. A door opened and Rachel and Evan stepped out,
dressed for tonight's ball.

"What are you doing, Luke?" his sister asked.

"Which is Caroline's bedchamber?"

"The third on the right."

Luke ran down the corridor and threw open the door, startling a maid who was turning back the bed.

"Have you seen Lady Caroline?" he demanded as he hurried inside the room.

The maid shook her head. "No, my lord. Not since early this morning. She's not back from the—"

"Then where the devil could she be?" he shouted.

The girl burst into tears.

By now, Rachel and Evan had arrived and his sister said, "Quit terrorizing my servants." To the maid she said, "You may go," and the girl rushed from the room.

"Didn't you miss her at dinner?" Luke asked.

"She mentioned to Kent that she might stay late tonight," Evan said.

"Surely, she wouldn't be at Evie's at this time of night."

Something made him go to the wardrobe and open it. To the left hung several gowns suitable for balls. To the right was a gap.

He turned. "Explain this."

Rachel joined him. "It looks as if some of her clothes are missing," she said, a tremor in her voice.

"She knows how I feel about her," Luke said.

"You told her you love her?" she asked.

"Not in so many words. I told her she was my entire world. That we would speak once I returned from my weekend in the country. Would that make her flee?" he asked, his anguish obvious.

Rachel lay a hand on his arm. "Women do need to hear the words, Luke. Are you . . . are you sure Caroline felt the same as you?"

"You don't make love to a woman three times in one night and—"

"You *ruined* her?" Rachel accused.

"There was no ruining to it. No compromising. She wanted to be with me." He took Rachel's shoulders. "It was the most incredible experience of my life."

"There has to be a reason she's gone," Evan pointed out.

"She wouldn't leave without telling me," Rachel insisted weakly.

Luke released his sister and raked his fingers through his hair. "It's got to be those damned rumors. She was upset before. About her father's death. She overheard he'd been murdered. She hadn't known that."

"Oh, that must have been awful for her," Rachel said.

"She also has this notion that the *ton* won't accept her because she owns and runs two businesses," he continued.

"Caroline mentioned the same to me," Evan said. "I tried to dissuade her of the notion."

"There was more to it, though," he said. "Something that she wasn't telling me. I was determined to get to the bottom of it when I saw her tonight."

Rachel snorted. "If anyone can clue you in as to what rumors are flying about, it would be the dreaded Three B's."

"Then I need to confront them," Luke said, determination filling him.

"You can't do it in front of a ballroom full of guests," Evan pointed out. "That only works with romantic declarations of love." He smiled at his wife. "You'll need to find a private spot to do so."

"Jeremy can help there," Rachel said. "He can ask Viscount Wilson. A viscount would never turn down a simple request from a duke needing privacy."

"Then let's go to the St. Clair townhouse," Luke said. "It's on our way."

They quickly went to the carriage and drove the short distance, finding Jeremy and Catherine emerging from the front door in their ballroom finery. Luke flung open the carriage door and hurried to his brother.

"Caroline's gone missing. I need your help. Ride with us."

On the way, he filled the pair in. Once they arrived and went through the receiving line, Jeremy told Viscount Wilson he had the need to attend to a brief bit of business and wished for a quiet place to do so. The viscount summoned a footman who led them to a small parlor off the ballroom.

"Everyone stay here," Luke said. "I'll retrieve the Three B's. I saw where they were lurking."

"I'll go with you," Jeremy said. "They may require some ducal persuasion."

The men approached the trio, surprise obvious on their faces, as Jeremy asked them to accompany him. They did so without any question. His brother shot him a look, one that said being a duke had its advantages. Once inside the room, Luke closed the door. No one invited the Three B's to sit.

Knowing he'd frightened Rachel's maid with his harsh tone, he did his best to remain calm and said, "You three seem to always know the current gossip bandied about. Tell me what's being said about Lady Caroline Andrews."

Immediately, Lady Bettina's eyes fell to the ground and Lady Betsy crossed her arms protectively in front of her as she stared off to the side. Only Lady Bethany, the obvious ringleader, stared up at him in defiance.

"Do you truly want to know, Lord Mayfield?" she asked.

"I do."

Lady Bethany sniffed. "First, her return to London and debut into society has dredged up the gossip of her father's murder. Everyone knew of the earl's gambling and whoring. What's now come to light is the possibility he was . . . a sodomite."

Luke held his tongue and merely nodded at the woman.

"There is a certain group within the *ton* that finds having Templeton's daughter at events unsavory. Especially now that she's gone and become the owner of that little teashop and bookstore." Her nose crinkled in disgust. "It's simply *wrong* for anyone in the *ton* to be involved in trade. And when it's a woman? She is not wanted at society events."

So far, he hadn't learned anything he didn't already know so he pressed her now. "What else, my lady? Surely, there's more."

She swallowed and said, "I would think that would be enough, Lord Mayfield."

Lady Bettina's head whipped up. She stared at her friend as Lady Betsy's jaw fell open.

"Tell him, Bethany," Lady Bettina urged.

"No."

"Then I will," Lady Bettina said. She looked at Luke, pain in her eyes. "A portion of the *ton*—a very small group—has been spreading rumors. The Duke of Everton danced with Lady Caroline at his ball and he dances with no one but his duchess. That's what started the gossip."

"I was hoping to help introduce Lady Caroline into society," Jeremy said. "I wanted the *ton* to see she was a family friend and had our support."

Lady Bettina nodded nervously. "Most did, Your Grace, but a few took that as an indication she was . . . under . . . your protection."

"What do you mean? Say it plainly, my lady," Luke demanded.

"That the duke and others—you and Lord Merrick—are sharing . . . her favors."

Rachel and Catherine gasped audibly. Rage poured through Luke. So this was what Caroline had hidden from him. That rumors flew declaring her the mistress of men in the St. Clair family. He couldn't imagine the humiliation and hurt she'd experienced.

He gazed steadily at Lady Bettina. "You know it's false, don't you? That my brother and brother-in-law are faithful to their wives."

"I do, Lord Mayfield. The love between them is genuine. I cannot ever see either man being unfaithful to his wife." She hesitated. "You do have a certain reputation, though, my lord."

"I've rid myself of my mistress. I haven't looked at another woman since the Season began. Except for Lady Caroline," he said. "I would never compromise her. I love her."

Lady Bettina nodded. "Then the best thing you could do would be to announce your engagement. It would put an end to the rumors."

"You really think so?" Lady Bethany asked. "I, for one, think the St. Clairs will be looked down upon for allowing Lord Mayfield to wed the little trollop."

It took everything in Luke's power not to strike the vile woman.

Lady Betsy finally found her voice. "You're wrong, Bethany. I find Lady Caroline very sweet. And I went to her bookstore on Saturday. I don't think the *ton* will judge her as harshly as you claim. I'm done with you."

"I am, too," Lady Bettina declared. "We've followed you around like lost puppies and where has it gotten us? You're an angry, vicious person, Bethany. Our friendship is over. Do not attempt to speak to either of us ever again or our cut direct will become public."

The two women linked arms and marched from the room, leaving their friend looking unsure for the first time.

Luke said to the remaining B, "If you ever say another word about Lady Caroline, you will live to regret it."

Lady Bethany had gone stark white, the gravity of her situation finally sinking in. "I understand," she whispered. "If you'll excuse me." She left the room.

"At least we know what upset Caroline so," Catherine said. "But where could she have gone?"

"I haven't a clue where her staff lives," Luke said. "If she's left London, she would have had to tell Mr. Stinch since he manages both the bookstore and tearoom. And possibly Higgins, her solicitor." He paused. "I plan to be at the bookstore before it opens tomorrow. I'll find out where she's gone—and bring her home. To us all."

CAROLINE REMAINED ON the floor, not trusting the bed. A woman, under Coswell's watchful eye, had brought her a meal last night of cold chicken and stale bread. She'd forced it down, wanting to keep up her strength. Still, she was hungry this morning—and knew she wouldn't be fed the rest of the day.

She'd been over every inch of the room, looking for a way out or something she could fashion into a weapon. It had proved fruitless. She still couldn't reconcile the thought of Leland Netherby hating her so much that he would have this done to her—to have her sold to a stranger who would do unimaginable things to her. Tears formed in her eyes again and she angrily wiped them away. They did no good. She had to think of a way to escape before tonight's auction.

The key sounded in the lock and she quickly rose to her feet. If it were only the woman, she would rush at her and knock her to the ground. Caroline fisted her hands, readying herself.

It was Coswell—but he wasn't alone. He had two women with him and he pushed them into the room then brandished a knife about. She held her breath and backed against the wall as he entered. He spun the one with dark hair around and Caroline saw the woman's hands bound in front of her. Coswell cut through the rope and pushed her aside. He freed the second woman, as well, younger than the first and dressed as a servant.

He glanced at Caroline, his eyes raking down her body. "Need any lessons taught, my lady?"

"No," she said firmly, looking him in the eye. She was deathly afraid of this man but would do anything to prove otherwise.

"Too bad," he said and then left the room, the lock turning once more.

She looked at the two women. "I am Lady Caroline Andrews," she said simply.

The older one was dressed in a similar fashion to her. "I am Belinda Barrow, bastard daughter to a viscount who decided to sell me in order to pay his gambling debts to Netherby."

Shock ran through Caroline. She wondered if her own father would have resorted to such measures had she not been in Boston.

"This is Emily," Belinda continued. "My maid."

The girl looked no older than fifteen. She began crying and Belinda wrapped her arms about the girl, trying to comfort the servant. Caroline could see the rope burns on both women's wrists.

"There, there, it's not so bad." Belinda's gaze met Caroline's and she could see the young woman didn't believe her own words.

"Who put you here?" Belinda asked.

"Netherby's father," she replied.

"Why? Who are you to him?"

"I am the owner of a new bookstore and tearoom in Mayfair. Netherby believed the competition too great for his own establishment and he wanted me eliminated."

"You actually own two businesses?" Belinda asked. "I've never heard of a woman of the *ton* doing so. From your dress and speech, it's obvious you are a lady."

"I won't own anything if we can't get out of here," she said. "Let's put our heads together and see if we can figure a way out of this."

Despite her brave front, Caroline believed their situation hopeless.

# CHAPTER TWENTY-EIGHT

L UKE ARRIVED AT Evie's Bookstore and Tearoom an hour before its ten o'clock opening, knowing that was the time the employees reported. Jeremy and Evan insisted upon accompanying him. They'd agreed if they learned something from Stinch, they might have to break up in order to cover more ground.

He pounded on the locked door and, through the glass, saw a clerk scurry his way. Without opening the door, the man said, "We're not open, sir."

"Get Mr. Stinch," Luke demanded, glaring at the clerk, who quickly retreated.

Less than a minute later, the manager arrived and opened the door. "Lord Mayfield. Lord Merrick. Your Grace. Please, come in."

The three men entered and Stinch closed and relocked the door.

Before Luke could speak, the former butler said, "I don't know where Lady Caroline is."

"But she's gone?" he asked.

"Yes, my lord."

"Tell me everything," he insisted.

Stinch glanced to the three clerks who seemed overly interested in the conversation. "Let's go back to her office," he suggested.

They went through the doors and as they arrived at Caroline's office, Luke saw Walton at the desk.

He stopped. "What are you doing in there?"

Walton shot to his feet. "I'm the new bookkeeper, my lord," he said nervously. "Lady Caroline offered me the job and use of this office."

"When?"

"On Saturday."

"Where did she go?"

Stinch answered. "We're not sure, my lord. Lady Caroline told me she'd learned of her father's murder. She hadn't known the circumstances of his death. She felt it best for Evie's if she stepped away from being seen here on a daily basis. She mentioned going to the country."

Walton added, "I'm to send her monthly reports regarding both establishments. She said she would send a forwarding address soon."

Despair filled Luke. Caroline had simply vanished—and he hadn't a clue where to search for her.

"I believe you could contact Mr. Higgins," Stinch said. "I saw him give her a key yesterday morning. He may have arranged for a place she could stay." He looked to Walton. "Did you hear her say anything to the driver when you took her trunk out to the cab?"

"No, but as I left, something odd happened."

"What?" Luke prompted, desperate for any helpful clue.

"I accompanied Lady Caroline to Leland Netherby's bookstore before Evie's opened. He invited her to come speak to him and was quite rude to her, insisting Evie's would fail and that he'd rally his fellow booksellers to ensure it did."

"What does that have to do with Lady Caroline's departure?" Jeremy asked impatiently.

"As she left yesterday, a clerk from Netherby's approached her. In fact, I saw him climb into the cab with her. I wondered if Netherby had a change of heart and wished to see her. It's all I can think of."

"And you don't know where she was going after that?" Evan asked.

Both Stinch and Walton shook their heads.

"Let's go to Netherby's Bookshop first," Luke said. "If we learn nothing there, we can visit Higgins and see what he can tell us. Thank you, gentlemen."

"Wait," Walton said. "Might I go with you? I could point out the clerk. He could possibly know where Lady Caroline went to after she left his employer's bookstore."

Luke agreed and they climbed into his carriage after he told his driver their destination.

"It is peculiar that Caroline would ride somewhere with a clerk from Netherby's," Evan noted.

"Hopefully, we'll have some answers soon," Jeremy said.

They arrived at the bookstore before its opening. Once more, Luke knocked until a clerk came and opened the door.

"We are open for business at ten o'clock," he said haughtily and started to close the door.

Luke placed his foot in the doorway, preventing it from closing. "We have business with Mr. Netherby." He pushed the door open and their group swept inside.

"Mr. Netherby hasn't arrived yet," the man told them.

"That's him!" Walton cried and pointed to his left.

Another clerk froze in place and then took off running, disappearing behind the stacks of books. Luke and the others pursued him, catching him as he exited through a door leading into the alley. Luke grabbed the man by the collar and slammed him against the brick wall.

"Where is she?"

"I don't know!" the clerk cried. "I don't even know who you're speaking of."

Walton stepped between Luke and the man. "You do, you little bastard. I saw you get into a carriage with Lady Caroline yesterday. Where is she?"

The clerk's eyes darted about and he sagged against the wall, seeing there was no means of escape.

"I only did as I was told," he said bitterly. "I would have lost my position otherwise."

"Told what?" Luke asked menacingly.

"Mr. Netherby—old Mr. Netherby—told me to take her to his son's place in St. James. Across from Mrs. Leach's on King Street."

Understanding rippled through Luke. "You mean The Blue Door. Ralph Netherby's gaming hell."

"That's the one," the clerk agreed nervously. "I was to leave her there. And I did. I don't know anything beyond that."

Luke slammed his fist into the man's face. "You left a lady in a gaming hell. Do you know what might happen to her there?"

He rained a series of blows until Evan pulled him off. "He can't talk if he's dead, Luke."

The clerk, his nose misshapen and his lip split turned his head and spit out blood and a tooth. "It's not my fault. Old Netherby wanted to be rid of her. Hardly anyone came into the shop Friday or Saturday. He said there wasn't room for the two of them and their bookstores in Mayfair. That one would have to go—and it wouldn't be him."

Jeremy stepped forward. "Go," he ordered and the clerk fled, running down the alley and turning the corner without a backward glance.

"Why did you let him go?" Luke shouted at his brother.

"Because we have a dire situation on our hands. Do you know anything about The Blue Door?" he asked.

"I've been there twice," Luke admitted. "It was nothing special. I thought the man running the hazard table was cheating the customers the second time I went, which is why I never returned. I wasn't interested in the women upstairs. God only knows what diseases they carry. It was safer to keep a mistress." He stopped. "Wait. You don't think Netherby would force Caroline to prostitute herself?"

"Worse," Jeremy said. "I've heard rumors of a secret auction that occurs every now and then. Where women are sold to the highest bidder. If Netherby truly wanted to eliminate Caroline, he could have asked his son to put her on the block."

"What?" Luke's anger exploded. He saw nothing but red. "I'll kill him!" he swore.

Both Evan and Walton grabbed him and pushed him against the wall.

"Calm down, Brother," Jeremy said. "If we're to get Caroline back, we have to be careful."

He struggled a moment and then stopped, knowing what Jeremy said was true. He slumped, the fight gone out of him, as he worried at what Caroline had already endured.

*And what might happen to her if they didn't find her in time.*

"We need to hire as many Bow Street Runners as possible," Luke concluded.

"We think alike, Brother. Let's go to Bow Street now."

Walton insisted on accompanying them. "I've known Lady Caroline since she was a child. If she's in danger, I want to help."

"Do you know how to use your fists?" Luke asked.

Walton cracked his knuckles. "Just watch me."

They decided to go to Number Four Bow Street first, where the magistrate's courthouse was located. The gang of men known as the Bow Street Runners operated from the space and acted as a detective force for London's citizens.

The moment they entered, Luke knew they'd come to the right place. The men in the halls all had the size and rough look that it would take to invade The Blue Door and claim Caroline. Jeremy asked to see the head magistrate and they were ushered in quickly. His brother deferred to him, allowing Luke to explain the situation.

"I've heard rumors of these types of auctions before but never specifically where they took place," the magistrate said, picking up a quill and dipping it in ink. As he wrote, he said, "I'm composing a list of five men to take with you. They'll round up anyone at The Blue

Door involved in this despicable situation. They'll bring in this bookseller, as well."

"I want his store shut down," Jeremy said with quiet authority. "It—and The Blue Door—are never to reopen."

"Of course, Your Grace," the magistrate said deferentially. He handed the list to Jeremy. "Give this to the clerk outside. He'll see these men are notified and ready at nine o'clock this evening. They'll invade the gaming hell at that time. We need to catch them in the act in order for charges to be brought."

"I'm going with them," Luke said, daring the magistrate to over-rule him.

"That is your prerogative, Lord Mayfield. I hope that you will find Lady Caroline without problem."

They gave the clerk the list and briefly explained the situation. He guaranteed the men would be waiting for them at the specified time tonight. He also suggest two other runners who would go to Leland Netherby's home and bring him in at the same time this evening.

Their group left the building and returned to the carriage. Luke felt adrift, helpless to do anything, wondering what Caroline was suffering.

Jeremy placed a hand on his shoulder. "Hold fast, Luke. We'll get her back."

"Not soon enough."

DESPERATION FILLED CAROLINE. They'd discovered no way out of the cramped room and the auction would begin soon. She decided to do whatever it took to get through that process and then look for a means to escape once she was taken from the gaming hell. As a lady of the *ton*, whoever bought her would underestimate her. Caroline would act meek as a lamb and then make her move when least expected. She'd learned from Josiah Long, back at Morton's Bookstore in Boston, that if a woman had a problem with a man, she was to knee him—or kick him—in the bollocks. Josiah swore it would incapacitate any man who bothered her. She'd never had to execute the move while in America but with her very life at stake, she was willing to do what was necessary to win her freedom.

And find her way back to Luke.

She regretted ever thinking she should leave him. She loved him and believed he loved her. The way he'd made love to her, both tender and fierce, spoke louder than any feelings he'd voiced. True, society might reject them but Luke was a St. Clair. They seemed to follow their own passions and not bend to society's conventions. Caroline believed in the two of them together.

She only hoped she would have the chance to tell Luke how much she loved him.

The same woman appeared with Coswell, bearing a tray with three cups.

"Drink up," he commanded as the woman gave each of them a cup.

Caroline took a sip of the unknown brew and thought it had an odd taste. She was unwilling to drink the rest, not knowing what it contained.

Suddenly, young Emily screamed shrilly, a last, desperate attempt to bring someone to their rescue. As every eye turned to the girl, Caroline tilted the cup and poured the liquid behind the bed. She quickly brought it to her lips and turned it upward as if she finished it off.

Coswell grabbed Emily by the throat and took the cup from her hands.

"Drink, bitch," he said, his voice low and deadly.

The maid did as instructed, tears leaking from the corners of her eyes. Belinda finished her cup, as well, and they returned them to the tray.

The women were left on their own again. Within minutes, both Belinda and Emily grew lethargic. Caroline supposed something such as laudanum had been placed in their drinks to make them more pliable. She would have to act the same when the others returned.

Within half an hour, Coswell and the woman were back, clothing hanging over both their arms. Coswell demanded they remove all their clothes. Caroline hid her horror and slowly began taking off her layers with the woman's help. Emily could barely move, though. Coswell took out his knife and cut her layers away. Caroline had to lower her eyes to hide her rage and humiliation as she continued removing what she wore.

The woman rouged their cheeks and lips. She also powdered Caroline's cheek, trying to hide the bruise from Coswell's blow.

The woman had them sit on the bed and she dressed the first of them in a chemise and then did the same with the other two. Then she placed stays on Caroline and laced them so tightly that she had trouble breathing. The stays were cut to reveal a large portion of her creamy flesh, forcing her bosom up until it almost spilled from the stays. She let her head loll, pretending the drink had affected her. The woman continued dressing them until each woman wore a tight, revealing dress, so unyielding that they could no longer sit and had to be leaned against the wall. Emily began sliding down it and Coswell caught her, throwing her over his shoulder. He grabbed Caroline's elbow and jerked her along as the woman brought Belinda.

They went down the long corridor and down a staircase, entering an anteroom. She could hear a voice and recognized it as Netherby's, the owner of this gaming hell.

"Tonight, we have three very different beauties for you to choose from. Remember, gentlemen, only gold is accepted, so bid accordingly."

Coswell propped her against the wall and pushed back a curtain.

She could see Netherby standing on what looked like a raised platform, a light shining brightly on him. Coswell joined him and slipped Emily from his shoulder, standing behind her and holding her at the waist so she wouldn't fall.

"This fresh-faced girl is but fifteen," she heard Netherby say. "What can I get for her?"

Voices began calling out sums, sickening Caroline. When the bidding slowed, Netherby declared a winner.

"You can claim your prize, Lord Sims, at the conclusion of the auction, when all payment is due."

Coswell lifted the maid over his shoulder again and brought her back, dumping her on the floor. By now, Emily didn't look conscious. Coswell grabbed Belinda and walked her out.

"This is a lord's daughter, though a bastard one. Only eighteen and a virgin, her nether curls as dark as her luxurious hair."

Caroline saw Netherby hoist Belinda's skirts up, revealing her as the audience cheered. It took everything she had not to show her disgust. She would get through this, whatever Netherby did, and hoped he and all of the men in that room burned in hell come Judgment Day.

New bids were called out. It took longer to sell Belinda but she was finally returned and placed on the ground next to Emily. Then Coswell grabbed Caroline's wrist and dragged her into the light. She let her head droop and her body sagged. Coswell latched on to her waist from behind to hold her up. He reeked of garlic.

"This, gentlemen, is our prize of the night. A caramel-haired beauty of the *ton* with everything your dark desires call out for."

She sensed anticipation rippling through the room and then a man called out a sum double what Belinda had gone for. A bidding war ensued between two men.

"I won't go a guinea higher unless I've seen her breasts," one of them called out.

Caroline couldn't believe his words. Already, more of her was on display than she'd thought possible. She bit her lip as Coswell's arm went about her waist, holding her to him. Then he yanked at her neckline, tearing the material, and her bosom was bared to the room. Shame filled her as the group whistled and stomped their feet.

Then it became worse. Coswell's hand squeezed her right breast hard and he called out, "Good and plump!"

The room roared in approval.

# CHAPTER TWENTY-NINE

T HE BOW STREET Runners had arrived, truncheons in hand, primed for a fight.

Luke addressed them. "You've been told of the auction going on inside The Blue Door. The woman I love is in there. Do whatever it takes to get her back."

"We will, Lord Mayfield," one of them said. "Step aside and let us do our job."

The five hardened men raced up the stairs, gripping their truncheons, and burst through the doors. Luke followed them, along with Jeremy, Evan, and Walton. Cigar smoke hung in the air and screams and shouts began as they disrupted the gaming. Scantily clad women began running and gentlemen of the *ton*, seeing what was happening, raced to reach the door and fade into the black night.

Luke didn't care about the gamers or whores. Reaching Caroline was all that mattered.

The men whipped and snapped their clubs, creating a path through the chaos. One runner grabbed a woman by the arm and shouted, "Where's the auction?"

"Upstairs. To the right."

Luke ran up the staircase and down the hall, ahead of the detectives, who sounding like a small army. Throwing open the last door he reached, a tiny waiting room was revealed. Two young women lay sprawled on the ground in revealing gowns, their cheeks and lips stained a dark red. An older woman started shrieking as the runners poured in behind him and ran through the anteroom into a larger one, where a raised stage stood.

Luke saw who stood on that stage.

*Caroline* . . .

A man held on to her, fondling her breast as laughter filled the room. Then Caroline's head snapped up and her foot slammed down on the man's. He cried out, releasing her. She whirled and viciously kicked him in the bollocks and he fell to the ground, gasping.

Luke followed the runners as they spread throughout the room. He ignored all the shouts and made it to Caroline. Quickly, he stripped off his coat and wrapped it around her, lifting her in his arms.

"Luke." She repeated his name several times as he carried her away, through the anteroom and back into the wide corridor.

"You're safe, love. It's over."

She stiffened in his arms. "Belinda! Emily! Where are they?" She began struggling. "I must help them!"

He saw Jeremy and Evan emerge, each of them with one of the unconscious women in their arms.

"See? They're unharmed," he reassured her. "We'll get all of you away from this place."

Tears cascaded down her cheeks. "I thought I would never see you again." She hiccupped loudly.

Luke lowered Caroline to her feet and wrapped his arms around her. He smoothed her hair and then cupped her bruised cheek. "You're going to see so much of me that you'll grow tired of me, Caroline. I love you, my darling. I plan to spend every minute of each day with you."

"You love me?" she sobbed. "I love you. I have for what seems like forever."

"So have I, my love." With that, he kissed her tenderly.

"Lord Mayfield? You need to leave," a voice said.

He looked up and saw one of the runners near him guiding the man who'd touched Caroline. The man was now handcuffed and being led away. Fury exploded within him and he released Caroline.

"No," she said, touching his arm. "Let them handle it, Luke. Please. I just want to go home."

He swept her into his arms again and carried her all the way to the carriage. Jeremy and Evan had already arrived and Walton was aiding them in getting the two women into the vehicle.

Another runner hurried up. "Were there just the three ladies?" he asked.

"Yes," Caroline replied. "We are all safe now."

"I'll need to interview you, my lady, and get as many details as I can so these villains can be charged," the detective said. "Can you manage speaking to me tomorrow morning? Along with the others?"

"Yes," she said firmly. "Come to the Marquess of Merrick's at ten o'clock. We'll all be available to answer your questions."

As the runner departed, pride filled Luke. "You are the bravest woman I know, Caroline Andrews. The most independent. The most loyal." He touched his lips to hers. "And the most kissable."

"Luke, get in the carriage," Jeremy admonished. "You can kiss Caroline all you want at home."

He broke the kiss and grinned. "Yes, Your Grace."

THE JUNE MORNING air had a touch of cool in it, thanks to the earlier shower. Caroline rode in a carriage with Rachel to the St. Clair chapel at Eversleigh in her wedding gown. She'd wanted to wear something Madame Toufours had already made up for her but the Frenchwoman insisted she create something new for Caroline. Sales for the modiste's products carried at Evie's had been brisk over the last six weeks and Madame said the gown would be her gift to Caroline, a way of saying thanks for including her goods at Evie's Bookstore and Tearoom. The white satin gown had an overdress of the palest blue and was trimmed with Brussels lace. She promised Madame that she would wear it at the first ball she and Luke attended once they returned from Dover. The cottage by the sea that she'd rented was to be their honeymoon destination after today's ceremony. They would stay for two weeks and then return the key to Higgins' relative before they came back to London for the rest of the Season. Once it ended, Luke would take her to Fairhaven, the country seat of the Earl of Mayfield.

She also wore her wedding gift from Luke, a pearl and diamond necklace and matching earrings. He given her several little presents in the weeks leading up to their wedding but the jewels were her favorite. He promised her many more over the years, teasing that for every child she gave him, she would have her pick of emeralds, rubies, or sapphires. It made her happy that he wanted a large family. She'd always wished for brothers and more sisters growing up. Knowing her fiancé was so good with children made her eager to begin. It had disappointed her when her courses came after they'd made love but he told her not to worry. It would happen in good time. In fact, they'd started working on their future family a week ago when they'd both arrived at Eversleigh. Rachel had caught her brother leaving Caroline's chamber one morning and they'd sworn her to secrecy.

They hadn't bothered hiding their affection in front of Luke's family, though. She thought they kissed even more than Jeremy and Catherine or Rachel and Evan did—which was quite a bit. Then Leah and Alex arrived and it was a toss-up which couple proved to be the most affectionate. Caroline felt blessed marrying into a family where such deep, abiding love was celebrated.

They reached the chapel and Rachel kissed her cheek. "I didn't know Luke could be as happy as he is. You have brought such joy into his life, my sweet friend."

"And you St. Clairs have welcomed me into your family and made me one of your own. I am the luckiest person in all of England."

"I'll see you inside."

The footman handed Rachel down and she entered the chapel to head to the front and serve as Caroline's attendant. Jeremy would stand with Luke.

She took a deep breath and nodded at the footman, who assisted her to the ground and then held open the door to the chapel. Caroline paused and looked over those in attendance. Besides the St. Clairs and their spouses, Amanda had come with her husband and Merrifield. Evie's had closed for the day so that all of the employees from the bookstore and tearoom could come down from London for the celebration. It included Emily, who sometimes worked taking orders in the tearoom when it got hectic, while the rest of her time was spent with Marie-Therese selling Madame Toufours' merchandise.

Last, she saw Belinda Barrow. They had grown close from the ordeal they had gone through together at The Blue Door, which had been boarded up. Netherby's Bookshop had also closed, with the elder Mr. Netherby now residing in a prison cell beside his son. Luke had helped Caroline buy the bookstore space and Madame Toufours was opening a second shop there, which Belinda would manage.

Her gaze went to the front of the altar and her heart began pounding with excitement as she caught sight of the man who held her heart. As she proceeded down the aisle, Luke strode toward her, meeting her halfway. He took her hands in his and smiled.

"I couldn't wait."

Then he kissed her, a sweet, lingering kiss that spoke of his love and the future they would share.

He finally broke it and told those gathered, "I couldn't wait for that, either."

Everyone chuckled as he escorted Caroline to the front and they spoke their vows. The words so often said by others seemed to have special meaning for them, knowing how close they'd come to being separated forever.

Her almost-husband slipped the wedding band onto her finger and then raised her hand to his lips, kissing it.

"I love you now. I'll love you forever," he said, his own addition to the vows touching her heart.

When the clergyman pronounced them man and wife and told Luke he could kiss his bride, the tenderness in his gaze made Caroline the happiest woman on earth.

He gathered her in his arms and kissed her deeply, taking her away to a place where it was only the two of them lost in one another.

Caroline didn't know how long they'd kissed but suddenly felt a tugging on her gown. Reluctantly, she pulled her lips from her new husband and glanced down to see an impatient-looking Delia St. Clair standing there.

"Uncle Luke, you need to stop kissing Aunt Caroline," Luke's niece demanded. "Mama said there's cake and I'm hungry."

Everyone burst out laughing as Luke lifted Delia and rested her on his hip. He kissed the tip of her nose and said, "Lead the way, Delia," before placing her on the ground.

The four-year-old happily skipped up the aisle, urging everyone to follow her.

"You heard Delia," Luke said. "Go on. My niece will see you back to Eversleigh. Caroline and I will follow."

As their guests stood and exited the chapel, Luke cupped her face and said, "I hope we'll have half a dozen girls with Delia's spirit. And half a dozen boys to try and keep their sisters in line."

With that, Luke kissed her again, making Caroline feel very married.

And very much in love.

# EPILOGUE

*Five years later . . .*

THE CARRIAGE ROLLED to a stop in front of Evie's Bookstore and Tearoom and Luke bounded out. His four-year-old son flung himself into his father's arms and Luke set the rowdy boy down on the sidewalk. He lifted his even more rambunctious two-year-old daughter from the coach and placed her beside her brother.

"Hold hands," he urged. "Always look out for one another."

Then he clasped Caroline's expanding waist and gently hoisted her to the ground. She would give birth in three months, when they were settled back at Fairhaven once the Season concluded. He'd always thought her beautiful but when she was with child, she became radiant.

"Have I told you I love you today?" he asked, brushing a soft kiss on her lips.

"Once when we awoke and a second time while we made love. Again when you offered me some jam at breakfast. Another time when we went to the nursery to retrieve those two scamps." She clucked her tongue. "I can't believe it's been almost an hour since I've heard the words. You're slipping, Lord Mayfield."

He lifted her hand and kissed her fingers. "I love you dearly, my precious countess." He heard a squeal and looked over his shoulder at their children who now tapped enthusiastically on the door, begging to be let in. "And I love this one," as he lightly touched her belly, "and those two, as well, though I think they're both putting gray in my hair."

Caroline laughed. "You're the one who riles them up so. They do love you. So do I."

Luke saw her love for him shining in her eyes and her smile. "Let's go save Stinch."

They entered Evie's and he looked around, seeing it was set up for the reading Catherine would do this morning. Her new book, *The Shy Spider*, was already a favorite in his household. Mr. Bellows was always kind enough to provide advanced copies of Catherine's books and Luke had read about Samuel Spider a good three dozen times already.

He nodded to Stinch, who'd married Mrs. Withers, and saw the children run through the archway into the tearoom. They were mad about Mrs. Baker's macaroons and would no doubt talk her into slipping them a few.

The bell tinkled and a wave of his relatives entered the bookstore. Rachel and Evan ushered in their three children and Leah and Alex their two. Jeremy herded in all five of his, followed by Catherine. He could just see her belly begin to round. She would give birth near Christmastime.

His brother came to stand next to him. "Did you banish your brood?"

"They're smart enough to go to beg Mrs. Baker for sweets."

"A capital idea. Children!" he called and all of them paid attention when the duke spoke. "I hear there are sweets for the asking if you're very nice to Mrs. Baker and Mrs. Stinch."

"Yea!" a chorus sounded and the small herd scrambled toward the tearoom, minus the baby Alex held in his arms.

As the brothers stood close, Luke turned away from the others and quietly said to Jeremy, "Are you ever going to tell Caroline that you were her benefactor? That you bought her father's townhouse so that she would have ample funds to open Evie's?"

For a moment, the cool façade of the Duke of Everton cracked. "How did you learn I was responsible? I've never told anyone."

Luke chuckled. "I didn't know for certain—until just now. I've always assumed it was you."

"Will you tell Caroline?" his brother asked.

"No. I know you did it so she would have a chance of succeeding. I think it best, though, if we keep this between us. Caroline need never find out." He placed a hand on Jeremy's shoulder. "Thank you, big brother. For everything you've done. I don't say it aloud often—but I love you."

Jeremy smiled. "I feel the same way, Luke."

By now, Rachel gathered the adults in a circle and Luke and Jeremy turned toward the others. Rachel asked how Caroline and Catherine were feeling. Both women had remarkably good health when carrying a child and Catherine said she was looking forward to today's reading.

"I invited you all here early so our children could claim the best spots," Caroline said.

An hour later, Evie's was filled to the brim with children and mothers and nursemaids. Luke stood to the side as Caroline introduced her sister-in-law and then joined him. Catherine began reading, every child enraptured by her voice.

He slipped an arm around his wife's waist, inhaling the floral perfume he loved so well. She'd done an outstanding job of keeping up with her businesses and working for several charities, as well as giving him his son and daughter and keeping Luke happy. Very happy. He thought back to his bachelor days, juggling mistresses and lovers and the empty feeling that had never seem to go away. It finally had, filled by the love of this enticing woman who was his wife. His lover. His partner. His best friend.

Luke leaned down and whispered into her ear. "Happy?"

Caroline nodded. "More than I ever imagined," she said softly.

"Do you know how much I look forward to all of the days ahead of us? The weeks? The years? The decades? All spent in love, with my countess by my side." He kissed her temple and she sighed.

"All it took was one embrace from my earl and I fell hopelessly in love," she replied.

"Would you like to go kiss for a few minutes while Catherine is reading? We could go to Walton's office. I see him standing next to Stinch. It would be a shame to waste such precious time."

Caroline's eyes twinkled with mischief. "You read my mind. Only this time, Luke, we better lock the door."

## THE END

# About the Author

Native Texan and former history teacher Alexa Aston lives with her husband in a Dallas suburb, where she eats her fair share of dark chocolate and plots out stories while she walks every morning. She enjoys reading, Netflix binge-watching, and attending sporting events when she's not watching *Survivor* or *The Crown*.

Alexa's Medieval and Regency historical romances bring to life dashing knights and loveable rogues and include the series *The Knights of Honor*, *The King's Cousins*, and *The St. Clairs*.

.

Made in the USA
Coppell, TX
20 December 2019